KT-571-143

CRITICAL ACCLAIM FOR LEIGH RUSSELL

'A million readers can't be wrong! Loyal fans of Geraldine Steel
will be thrilled with this latest compelling story from
Leigh Russell. New readers will discover a terrific crime
series to get their teeth into. Clear some time in your day,
sit back and enjoy a bloody good read'
– Howard Linskey

'*Class Murder* was just the type of gripping and gutsy police
thriller I have come to expect from the very accomplished
and devious mind of author Leigh Russell'
– Joanne Robertson, *My Chestnut Reading Tree*

'Russell at her very best and Steel crying out to
be turned into a TV series'
– The Mole, *Our Book Reviews Online*

'If you love a good action-packed crime novel,
full of complex characters and unexpected
twists this is one for you'
– Rachel Emms, *Chillers, Killers and Thrillers*

'I chased the pages in love with the narrative and style...
You have all you need within *Class Murder*
for the perfect crime story'
– Francesca Wright, *Cesca Lizzie Reads*

'This is an absorbing and compelling serial killer read
that explores the mind and motive of a killer,
and how the police work to track down that killer'
– Jo Worgan, *Brew & Books Review*

'An absolute delight'
– *The Literary Shed*

'I simply couldn't put it down'
– Shell Baker, *Chelle's Book Reviews*

'Highly engaging'
– Jacob Collins, *Hooked From Page One*

'This is a fantastic story that kept me gripped throughout'
– *A Crime Reader's Blog*

'A riveting story, pulling the reader in from page one'
– *So Many Books So Little Time*

'The thing I love about Leigh Russell's books is the fact that
there are so many aspects to the plot but they all slot together
like a perfectly formed jigsaw puzzle. The characters are
so well crafted, the settings are so vividly described and
the killer, well wow!'
– **Kate Noble,** *The Quiet Knitter*

'I'm completely annoyed with myself that I haven't
discovered the series sooner as I have totally been missing out'
– *Jen Lucas, Jen Med's Books Reviews*

'A masterclass in how to disrupt your protagonist's life
and seeing whether he/she sinks or swims'
– **Joy Kluver**

'An intricate, cleverly plotted police procedural
with a well-drawn cast of characters. A very enjoyable read'
– *Promoting Crime Fiction*

'Smoothly professional fare from the always-consistent Russell'
– *Crime Time*

'A great story with some interesting and unexpected
twists and turns. It ends with some scenes of high drama
and a clever and surprising outcome'
– *Fiction Is Stranger Than Fact*

'A fast-paced police procedural and a compelling read'
– *Mystery People*

'If you enjoy a well-written mystery with a well-constructed
and thought-out plot line then this is the book for you...'
– *Crime Book Club*

'Non-stop action, drama, suspense and intrigue
in each gripping page'
– *Kristen's Book Jungle*

'There is nothing like a good police procedural,
and this book was just that'
– **Lisa Hardy**, *Bookalicious*

'A great whodunit, some fabulous characters'
– **Anne Cater**, *Random Things Through My Letter Box*

'A definite page-turner, gripping to the end and full of pace'
– **Kim Nash**, *Kim the Bookworm*

'Russell cleverly creates a tale of murder, police investigation
and personal issues whilst trying to pursue the truth,
uphold the law and fling in some surprises to keep
the reader on their toes'
– **Lainy Swanson**, *Nudge Books*

'A most intriguing and well executed mystery and...
an engrossing read'
– **Sara Townsend**, *Shotsmag*

'A definite must read for crime thriller fans everywhere – 5 stars'
– **Eileen Thornton**, *New Books Mag*

'Russell's storytelling was strong enough to keep me
enticed right to the very end'
– **Lloyd Paige**

'A truly great author... enough mystery and drama
for the most ardent of mystery fans'
– *Bookaholic*

'All the things a mystery should be, intriguing,
enthralling, tense and utterly absorbing'
– *Best Crime Books*

'A whodunit of the highest order'
– *Crime Squad*

'A nail biting, murderous puzzle that will keep you
guessing until the very end'
– *Fresh Fiction*

'All the ingredients combine to make a tense,
clever police whodunnit'
– **Marcel Berlins, *The Times***

'A series that can rival other major crime writers out there...'
– *Best Books to Read*

'Sharp, intelligent and well plotted'
– *Crime Fiction Lover*

'Another corker of a book from Leigh Russell…
Russell's talent for writing top-quality crime
fiction just keeps on growing…'
– *Euro Crime*

'Taut and compelling, stylishly written
with a deeply human voice'
– **Peter James**

'A definite must read for crime thriller fans everywhere'
– *Newbooks Magazine*

'For lovers of crime fiction this is a brilliant,
not-to-be missed, novel'
– *Fiction Is Stranger Than Fact*

'An innovative and refreshing take
on the psychological thriller'
– *Books Plus Food*

'Russell's strength as a writer is her ability to portray
believable characters'
– *Crime Squad*

'A well-written, well-plotted crime novel with
fantastic pace and lots of intrigue'
– *Bookersatz*

'I could not put this book down'
– *Newbooks Magazine*

'An encounter that will take readers into the darkest
recesses of the human psyche'
– *Crime Time*

'Well written and chock full of surprises, this hard-hitting,
edge-of-the-seat instalment is yet another treat…
Geraldine Steel looks set to become a
household name. Highly recommended'
– *Euro Crime*

'Good, old-fashioned, heart-hammering police thriller…
a no-frills delivery of pure excitement'
– *SAGA Magazine*

'*Cut Short* is a stylish, top-of-the-line crime tale, a seamless
blending of psychological sophistication and gritty police
procedure. And you're just plain going to love
DI Geraldine Steel'
– **Jeffery Deaver**

'Russell paints a careful and intriguing portrait of a small
British community while developing a compassionate and
complex heroine who's sure to win fans'
– *Publishers Weekly*

'Simply awesome!'
– *Euro Crime*

'A sure-fire hit – a taut, slick, easy-to-read thriller'
– *Watford Observer*

'*Cut Short* is not a comfortable read, but it is a
compelling and important one. Highly recommended'
– *Mystery Women*

'A gritty and totally addictive novel'
– *New York Journal of Books*

Also by Leigh Russell

Geraldine Steel Mysteries
Cut Short
Road Closed
Dead End
Death Bed
Stop Dead
Fatal Act
Killer Plan
Murder Ring
Deadly Alibi
Class Murder

Ian Peterson Murder Investigations
Cold Sacrifice
Race to Death
Blood Axe

Lucy Hall Mysteries
Journey to Death
Girl in Danger
The Wrong Suspect

LEIGH RUSSELL

DEATH ROPE

A GERALDINE STEEL MYSTERY

NO EXIT PRESS

First published in 2018 by No Exit Press,
an imprint of Oldcastle Books Ltd,
PO Box 394, Harpenden,
Herts, AL5 1XJ, UK

noexit.co.uk
@noexitpress

© Leigh Russell 2018

The right of Leigh Russell to be identified as the author of this
work has been asserted in accordance with the
Copyright, Designs and Patents Act 1988.

All rights reserved. No part of this book may be reproduced, stored
in or introduced into a retrieval system, or transmitted, in any form
or by any means (electronic, mechanical, photocopying, recording or
otherwise) without the written permission of the publishers.

Any person who does any unauthorised act in relation to this publication
may be liable to criminal prosecution and civil claims for damages.

A CIP catalogue record for this book is available from the British Library.

This is a work of fiction. Names, characters, places, and incidents either
are the product of the author's imagination or are used fictitiously
and any resemblance to actual persons, living or dead, businesses,
companies, events or locales is entirely coincidental.

ISBN
978-1-84344-934-8 (Print)
978-1-84344-935-5 (Epub)
978-1-84344-936-2 (Kindle)
978-1-84344-937-9 (Pdf)

2 4 6 8 10 9 7 5 3 1
Typeset in 11.25pt Times New Roman
by Avocet Typeset, Somerton, Somerset, TA11 6RT

Printed and bound in Great Britain by Clays Ltd, Elcograf S.p.A.

To Michael, Joanna, Phillipa, Phil, Rian and Kezia

Acknowledgements

I would like to thank Dr Leonard Russell for his expert medical advice, and all my contacts in the Metropolitan Police for their invaluable assistance.

Producing a book is a team effort. I am fortunate to have the guidance of a brilliant editor, Keshini Naidoo. I am very grateful to Ion Mills, Claire Watts, Clare Quinlivan, Katherine Sunderland, Frances Teehan, Jem Cook and all the team at No Exit Press, who transform my words into books. I would also like to thank Anne Cater and her wonderful team for organising my blog tour. I am grateful for their support which has been invaluable.

My final thanks go to Michael, who is always with me.

Glossary of acronyms

DCI   – Detective Chief Inspector (senior officer on case)

DI   – Detective Inspector

DS   – Detective Sergeant

SOCO – scene of crime officer (collects forensic evidence at scene)

PM   – Post Mortem or Autopsy (examination of dead body to establish cause of death)

CCTV – Closed Circuit Television (security cameras)

VIIDO – Visual Images, Identification and Detections Office

MIT   – Murder Investigation Team

Preface

Reaching her in waves, the shrill sound seemed to come from somewhere inside her head. It was a few seconds before she realised she was listening to her own screams. For an instant she stood transfixed, a helpless spectator, before she ran outside, bawling for help. Thankfully the gardener was there, and he followed her back into the hall where her husband was hanging from the banister. As she fell silent, she could hear him grunting with the effort of supporting the body. His arms clasped around her husband's legs, he struggled to stop the rope from pulling taut. Above them, Mark's arms swung limply, and his head hung at an odd angle. She was aware of the gardener's mouth moving before she realised he was yelling at her to call an ambulance. Trying to nod, she couldn't move. Her eyes were glued to a ghoulish caricature of a familiar face, bloated tongue protruding between dry lips, tiny red dots of blood speckling the whites of bulging eyes. She stared, mesmerised, at a drop of saliva crawling down his chin, trying to work out whether it was still moving.

The gardener glared at her, and she realised he was still shouting at her to call for help. As if in a dream, she reached for her phone and dialled 999.

A voice on the line responded with unreal composure, assuring her that help was on its way.

'What does that mean?' she gabbled. 'When will they get here?'

'They're on their way.'

Time seemed to hang suspended, like the body.

They waited.

Looking down, she struggled to control an urge to salvage her shopping: tomatoes had rolled across the floor, along with other soft foods she had carefully packed on top of packets and tins. One tomato had already been trodden into the carpet. While she was dithering she heard a siren, followed by hammering at the door, and then her own voice, oddly calm, inviting uniformed men into the house.

Of course they were too late to save him. She had known that all along.

1

GERALDINE SMILED AT HER adopted sister. Despite her complaints about disturbed nights, Celia looked happier than Geraldine had seen her in a long time. Her month-old baby snuffled gently in his sleep as she rocked him gently in her arms.

'Would you like to hold him?' Celia asked.

Still smiling, Geraldine shook her head. 'It might wake him up. Anyway, I really should get going.'

'It's still early,' Celia protested. 'Even you can't pretend you've got to get back for work tonight. It's Sunday, for goodness sake. Why don't you stay overnight and go home tomorrow?'

As a detective sergeant working on murder investigations, Geraldine's job was no respecter of the time of day, but she wasn't on a case just then. All the same she shook her head. Even though there was no pressing reason for her to hurry away, she had a long journey ahead of her, and she was back on call in the morning.

'He's lovely,' she repeated for the hundredth time. Privately she thought that her tiny new nephew resembled a pink frog. 'Don't get up. We don't want to disturb him.'

Celia gave a sleepy smile. 'You'll come back soon?'

Geraldine was quick to reassure her sister that she would return as soon as she could. She made good time, and reached home in time for supper. She had been living in York for nearly three months and, after a miserable winter, she was starting to feel settled. She was even thinking of selling her flat in London and buying somewhere in York, putting a stamp of permanence on her move. The transformation in her feelings seemed to have taken place almost overnight. One evening she had gone to bed feeling displaced and lonely. The following morning she had woken up unaccountably at ease in her new home. Driving to work her spirits had lifted further on seeing a bank of daffodils, bright against the deep velvety green slope below the city wall. Already, early groups of oriental visitors were beginning to throng the pavements. She wasn't looking forward to an influx of summer tourists clogging up the bustling streets of a city that unexpectedly felt like home.

A few weeks had passed since then, and she was still undecided what to do. Celia would be disappointed if Geraldine decided to make her move to York permanent, but the idea of settling there seemed increasingly appealing with every passing week. She had to live somewhere, and York was as good a place as any. She liked it there. Besides, her oldest friend and colleague lived there. She wondered how Ian Peterson would react if he knew she was considering him in making a decision about where she wanted to spend the rest of her life.

Mid-morning on Monday, Geraldine was summoned to an interview room where a member of the public was waiting to lodge a complaint. As an experienced officer, Geraldine was used to fielding vexatious accusations. With a sigh she made her way along the corridor to the room where the irate woman was waiting for her. Stocky and square-jawed, with short grey hair, she sat with trousered knees pressed together and fleshy arms folded across her chest.

'What seems to be the problem, Ms Abbott?' Geraldine asked as she sat down.

The grey-haired woman's eyes glittered and her voice was unsteady. 'I want to talk to someone about my brother's murder.'

'Are you saying your brother's been murdered?'

'Yes, that's exactly what I'm saying.'

'And is this a murder case that's under investigation? What's your brother's name?'

The woman shook her head, and her ruddy face turned a deeper shade of red.

'No, no, no. You're not investigating it. No one's investigating anything. Look, my brother was found hanging from a banister nine days ago.' She leaned forward and lowered her voice. 'They said it was suicide, but that's simply not true.'

Geraldine frowned, and tried to look interested. She found it was usually best to let aggrieved members of the public have their say.

'Perhaps you'd better start at the beginning. What makes you suspect your brother's death wasn't suicide?'

'It's more than a suspicion. I know my brother – that is, I knew him. There's no way he would have taken his own life. He wasn't that sort of a person. He was – he was a robust man, Sergeant. He loved life.'

'Circumstances can have a devastating effect on people, even those we think we know well –'

'Please, don't dismiss this as the ramblings of a grieving woman. I knew my brother. He would never have killed himself. He was blessed with a cheerful disposition, and, before you say it, he didn't suffer from depression, and he didn't have money worries, or any problems with drink or drugs. There was nothing in his life that might have prompted him to end it. And hanging's not the kind of death that can happen by accident. No, he was murdered, I'm sure of it. I waited as long as I could before coming forward because I thought no one would believe he killed himself, but now she tells me they're burying him on Wednesday, so we don't have much time. I came here to plead with you to look into what happened, before it's too late.'

Geraldine did her best to pacify the distressed woman, wondering whether Amanda Abbott was simply trying to cause trouble for her brother's widow.

'Do you have any evidence that your brother was murdered?

At the moment, all you've given me is supposition.'

Amanda shrugged her square shoulders. 'I wasn't there, but I know – I knew my brother. Why would he have suddenly done away with himself?'

Geraldine was faintly intrigued. Amanda didn't strike her as the kind of woman who might be given to hysterical delusions.

'So if he didn't commit suicide, and it wasn't an accident, what do you think happened?'

'My sister-in-law did it,' Amanda answered promptly. 'It's obvious. They never got on. And now she gets her hands on everything he worked for.'

'How long were they married?'

'Over thirty years.'

'That's a long time for a couple who don't get on to stay together,' Geraldine said quietly.

'And she finally had enough of him and killed him, only she made it look like suicide so she could get away with it. I'm convinced that's what happened. Nothing else makes sense.'

Geraldine almost dismissed what she was hearing as a family disagreement, but Amanda was so insistent that she agreed to look into Mark Abbott's death.

'Please, you have to find out what happened,' Amanda said. 'He was my brother and I'm not going to sit back and see her get away with it, not if I can help it. Will you keep me posted,' she enquired as she stood up, 'or can I come back to see how you're getting on?'

Geraldine promised she would do her best to find out whether there might have been anything unlawful about the death. Having seen Amanda off the premises, she went to speak to her detective chief inspector, Eileen. A large woman, about ten years older than Geraldine, she had dark hair greying at the temples, sharp features, and an air of solidity that was both reassuring and overbearing at the same time.

'It sounds like family politics,' Eileen said, when she had listened to Geraldine's account. 'The sister of the deceased is going out of her way to make trouble for his widow. Perhaps she was expecting to be mentioned in his will and is disappointed to have been left out of it?'

'That's what I thought. But there's one more thing. The deceased took out a fairly hefty life insurance policy with a two-year suicide exclusion clause.'

Eileen nodded. 'And you're telling me the two years ran out –'

'A week before his death. Of course, that doesn't mean he didn't kill himself. He might have waited so his wife would benefit from the policy,' she added, speaking more to herself than to her senior officer. 'But there's something about it that doesn't feel right.'

'If you want to make a few discreet enquiries, that's up to you. I can't see we've really got anything to investigate, but you can take a look if you like, as long as it doesn't distract you from your work here.' Eileen paused. 'If every widow was accused of murdering her husband when she inherited his estate, we'd have more suspects than police officers.'

2

SOMETIMES CHARLOTTE FORGOT ABOUT her new circumstances. After more than thirty years of marriage, she still woke up expecting to hear her husband snoring beside her. She was used to lying awake at night, listening with growing irritation as each sonorous inhalation was followed by a brief hiatus before the sigh of air released from his lungs. Now it was the silence that disturbed her sleep. Somewhere overhead a pipe rattled and wheezed, a faint echo of the noise she had endured every night for decades, ever since they had moved into their spacious property. She flung one arm out sideways, savouring the empty expanse of bed beside her, the sheets cool and unwrinkled. Tentatively she stretched her leg out as well, until she was occupying half of her husband's share of the mattress. It didn't matter. There was no one to kick her back on to her own side of the bed. There were no longer any sides. The whole bed was hers.

The funeral had been set in motion. In two days' time mourners would gather to mumble hymns, someone would recite a eulogy, and everyone would talk about what a devoted husband and father Mark had been to her and Eddy. The thought of it irritated her, but there was no point in exposing his occasional lapses now he had gone. No one would want to hear about her dead husband's philandering, least of all his son. She drew her arm and leg quickly back on to her own side of the bed and wrapped her arms around her body, wondering who would attend the ceremony. Her stepson, Eddy, would be there, of course, accompanied by his wife. Her own sister was

20

unable to travel all the way over from New Zealand with her family, but they had all sent their condolences.

A few of Mark's work colleagues would show up out of a sense of duty, as would the handful of friends she and Mark had kept in touch with over the years. She wasn't close to any of them, but they had all known one another for a long time and that counted for something. It was partly pride that had prompted her to contact them. She didn't want people thinking she had no friends now that Mark was gone, although the truth was that she had no real friends of her own. She never had. But the main reason she had invited as many people as she could, was that it would be easier to avoid her sister-in-law in a room full of people. Much as she hated the prospect of seeing her, she could hardly have kept the news about Mark's death from his only sister.

'I suppose Aunt Amanda will have to be there,' Eddy had said, voicing his mother's feelings.

'Don't worry,' Charlotte had told him. 'I'll deal with her.'

She had felt nowhere near as confident about speaking to her sister-in-law as she had pretended. An overbearing woman, Amanda had understandably been shocked on hearing the news of her brother's death.

'But I don't understand,' she had barked, as though it was impossible to believe that an overweight man in his sixties could possibly have died. And that was before she had learned about the circumstances surrounding his death.

Charlotte could almost feel her sister-in-law glowering at her down the phone line. She hesitated, but there was no easy way to answer the question. Her one-word reply had prompted a cry of outrage.

'Suicide?' Amanda had repeated, her voice rising in a horrified shriek. 'What do you mean, it was suicide? How could it be? Mark would never have killed himself. I don't believe it.'

Charlotte had drawn in a deep shuddering breath and tried to sound sympathetic. Of course it was terrible for Amanda to lose her brother in that way, and Charlotte was devastated to have to pass on such terrible news. But she couldn't help feeling the tragedy was far harder for her to cope with. Not only had she lost her husband of over three decades, but she had been the one to find him, suspended from the banister. For the rest of her life she would be haunted by the memory of his swollen face, his dead eyes glaring at her in wordless accusation.

She had gritted her teeth as Amanda proceeded with her enquiries. Doing her best to avoid focusing on the horrible memory, Charlotte had tried to describe what had happened in a detached way, as though she was talking about a scene in a film. Amanda had a right to know and besides, until she was satisfied she would never stop bombarding Charlotte with questions. Amanda had never been sensitive to other people's feelings. As accurately as she could, Charlotte described how she had found Mark hanging in the hall and had rushed outside, screaming for help, and how the startled gardener had dropped his rake, narrowly missing injuring himself. To his credit he hadn't hesitated to run all the way up the length of the garden to go inside with her. Although clearly shocked, he had taken control of the situation, yelling at her to call an ambulance while he righted the upturned chair, clambered on to it, and flung his arms around Mark's legs to support him. All the time he had continued shouting at her to summon help.

'Why didn't you call an ambulance straight away?'

For an instant the question had hung between them unanswered, then Charlotte began babbling about shock and the urgent need at the time to free Mark from the noose. She hadn't added that for a moment she had been unable to move. Instead of calling for help she had stood, rooted to the spot, staring at the two men entangled in their macabre one-sided embrace. After that, she could remember nothing more until the pounding at the front door had shattered the silence. Even then the gardener had been forced to shout at her to open the front door, or the police would have smashed their way in.

'But I don't understand,' her sister-in-law had repeated when Charlotte finished speaking. 'It doesn't even make sense. How could he have reached the upstairs banister? Not Mark. I can't believe it of him.' She had sounded close to tears.

The last thing Charlotte wanted to do was talk about what had happened, but she supposed she might as well get it over with or Amanda would never let it rest.

'We think he went upstairs and tied the rope around the banister up there and then threw the end of the rope over, so he could reach it from the hall. Then he must have gone downstairs, climbed up on a chair, and...'

Her voice had tailed off. Surely Amanda wouldn't want her to continue.

'I see,' Amanda had replied curtly, too upset to continue.

'So I'm sorry,' Charlotte had resumed after an awkward pause, 'but –'

'I don't understand,' Amanda interrupted her. 'What could have driven him to do it? Mark wasn't the sort of man to take his own life. Something must have happened to make him do it, if it really was suicide, which I doubt.'

Charlotte hadn't replied to what sounded like a veiled accusation. Whatever vile conclusion Amanda chose to draw was of no consequence. She hadn't been there, and Charlotte had. The police were convinced that Mark had taken his own life, and nothing Amanda could say was going to change their minds. It was over, and Mark was gone.

3

GERALDINE HADN'T WORN HER long black jacket since her birth mother's cremation. It was hard to believe nearly a year had passed since then. Giving the jacket a shake, she pulled it on over black trousers and a grey shirt, an appropriate outfit to wear to a stranger's funeral. Fulford Cemetery was not far from where she worked, and easy enough to find, but all the same she was nearly late. The car park was three-quarters empty as she parked her car and hurried into the prayer hall. Although the front rows were only half full, she slipped into a seat near the back of the hall. She had barely sat down when the funeral cortège arrived and everyone shuffled to their feet. As the coffin was brought in, Amanda caught sight of Geraldine and her expression tautened with recognition. Other than that, no one seemed to notice the stranger in the back row.

It was a dreary service, even for a funeral, with a dull and generic eulogy. Geraldine was reminded of her birth mother's funeral, where no one had spoken apart from the celebrant who had never met the dead woman or her family, and had taken no trouble to find out anything about her. The ceremony seemed to drag on interminably, but at last it drew to a close and the congregation filed outside to gather in clusters in the chilly spring sunshine. Observing the mourners, Geraldine could see nothing to arouse suspicion. The widow's grief was evident but restrained. At her side a man, presumably her son, stood stiff and dignified. A young woman was holding his arm, a solemn expression on her face. Her hair was as black as Geraldine's but hung down to her shoulders, while Geraldine's was short.

A few people hovered near them, looking slightly awkward. It wasn't clear whether they belonged to their group or not.

The dead man's sister stood a few feet away from the widow and her party. After a brief hesitation, Geraldine joined her.

'That's his family,' Amanda said, nodding her head in the direction of the group. 'That's his widow, Charlotte, with my nephew, Eddy, and his wife, Luciana.'

If Geraldine hadn't heard Amanda accuse her sister-in-law of having murdered the dead man, she might have been startled by the hostility in her voice. But there was nothing Geraldine could do to question any of them, or to look into the circumstances of this death, and nothing about the funeral that prompted her curiosity. Amanda had been so insistent; Geraldine had allowed her own judgement to be overruled and had consequently wasted her time attending the service.

She was uncomfortably aware that she had only been tempted to investigate the death because it offered her an opportunity to assume some responsibility for her work. Having been recently demoted from detective inspector to the rank of sergeant, she was struggling to contain her frustration at waiting for tasks to be allocated to her when she had been accustomed to running her own team. Still, in attending the funeral, at least Geraldine had done her best to satisfy Amanda that her accusation had been taken seriously. With luck that would pacify her for a while, hopefully until she recovered from the shock of her brother's suicide – if he really had taken his own life.

Geraldine was about to return to her car when a portly man accosted her.

'Are you a relative?' he enquired.

About to reply that she had worked with the deceased, Geraldine hesitated. 'I used to be a neighbour,' she muttered vaguely. 'I kept in touch.'

It was as well she had been circumspect, because she learned that her interlocutor had been working with Mark Abbott until his death.

'It came as a shock, I can tell you,' he added, lowering his voice. 'I still can't believe it. Did you know him well?'

Geraldine shook her head and mumbled something appropriate.

'He was the last person I'd expect to go and do anything like that,' the man went on. 'Not that there is anything quite like that, is there? But I mean, Mark of all people. You knew him, didn't you?'

Geraldine mumbled quietly.

He glanced around, probably to check close family weren't within hearing. 'I thought it was a wind-up when I first heard the news. I mean, it would have been in pretty poor taste if it had been, but I simply couldn't believe it. He just wasn't that kind of person, was he?'

'No, he wasn't,' Geraldine agreed. 'Still, you never know.'

'True,' he nodded. 'You think you know someone and then –' he shrugged. 'What gets me is that we were out the night before it happened, and he was right as rain then. Well,' he hesitated, 'that is to say, he seemed all right. He told me he was planning a holiday, and we arranged a game of tennis for the weekend. We used to knock up once in a while, you know. Nothing too serious. Not like when I was younger and could move around the court.' He smiled ruefully. 'But it's hardly what you expect a chap to be talking about the night before he tops himself, is it? Oh well, you never can tell.'

He wandered off. Geraldine watched him go and talk to the widow and her son, before she turned to make her way back to the car park. Before she had left the forecourt, Amanda came over and barred her way.

'I'll be coming to see you again,' she announced. 'I'm not letting this go.' She leaned forward conspiratorially and went on, without lowering her foghorn of a voice. 'They think I'm going to give up, but I know what happened and I'm not going to stop until you find out who did it.'

'Oh for goodness sake,' Charlotte interrupted her sister-in-law, stepping forward and hissing at her in a furious whisper. 'Can't you ever shut up? This is his funeral.' She burst into tears and her son and daughter-in-law bustled her away, throwing angry glances at Amanda as they moved away.

'Oh yes, they'd like nothing better than to shut me up,' Amanda told Geraldine. 'Her and her crocodile tears.' She turned to glare at Geraldine. 'I'll see you tomorrow.'

'I'm not likely to have anything new to tell you tomorrow,' Geraldine said.

With a grunt, Amanda strode away. Nothing in the mourners' demeanour had borne out the accusation that had been levelled against them. But now a second person had cast doubt on the idea that Mark Abbott had killed himself, and the dead man's colleague from work was hardly likely to be harbouring a personal grudge against the widow. Aware that the dead man's sister might be acting maliciously, Geraldine had to acknowledge that the funeral had raised a further question over Mark Abbott's death. However hard she tried to ignore her unease about his suicide, she couldn't shake off the suspicion that something was wrong.

Returning to the police station, she shelved her curiosity about the alleged suicide, and settled down to work. It had taken her a few months to learn her way around York and get to know her colleagues at the police station in Fulford Road, but now her new place of work had become familiar, and she had struck up a friendship with a couple of her colleagues. Ted Allsop was a stocky man nearing retirement who had befriended Geraldine right from her first day at Fulford Road. She soon realised that he was equally sociable with everyone, but that only made her warm to his broad smile all the more. Another colleague who looked set to become a friend was a raven-haired woman called Ariadne, who had a Greek mother and an English father. She was about the same age as Geraldine and also single. Apart from that they had very little in common, but it was enough. If Geraldine could make just one real friend at work, she would be satisfied. Besides the relationships she was hoping to forge, her old friend, Ian Peterson, worked in York. His presence hopefully meant she was going to feel less lonely. Conscious that she could never return to London, she tried to focus on the positive aspects of her new life.

4

ALTHOUGH HE WANTED TO disagree with her, Eddy nodded at
his wife. He could never bring himself to argue with anything
she said. Her long thin face was animated under her straggly
black fringe, her cheeks flushed with exasperation, but she
spoke kindly.

'I'm sorry about your father, really I am. I know what it's
like to lose your parents.'

Eddy dropped his gaze. Luciana rarely spoke about her
parents who had died when she was in her teens. He had never
even seen photographs of them. All he knew was that her
mother had been an Italian who had married a Yorkshireman.

'It's not a competition,' he muttered, and was immediately
ashamed of his callous response.

'I know, but the point is, you aren't responsible for your
stepmother. That's all I'm saying. I don't want to sound
uncaring, but in the end she has to deal with her situation
herself, and she has to sort out her own life. You can't do it for
her. It's not fair of her to expect so much of you. It's not as if
she's even your real mother.'

'She's been my mother for thirty years.'

'And what about you? You lost your mother, and now you've
lost your father, but she isn't thinking about you, is she? She
only ever thinks about herself.'

'You never liked my stepmother.'

'That's not true, and you know it. She was the one who
resented me.'

'You could have made more of an effort.'

29

Luciana scowled. 'Yes, yes, I know. We could all be better people than we are. Listen, I know it's a cliché, but the truth is she hated me from the first time she met me. And I don't think she likes you much either.'

'She doesn't hate you.'

'Well, she didn't exactly welcome me into the family, so if I don't feel inclined to rush to support her now, it's hardly my fault. Don't blame me, is all I'm saying. She brought it on herself.'

Eddy shook his head. He hated feeling torn like this. In a way, Luciana was right. His stepmother *had* been distant with her right from the start. All the same, with his stepmother so recently widowed, he couldn't help feeling disappointed by Luciana's reaction. Apart from anything else, it would have helped him if his wife had been willing to shoulder some of the burden, but she had made it clear that she wasn't prepared to spend any more time with her mother-in-law than she had to. And Luciana didn't know the half of how his stepmother had been behaving, expecting him to help her in all sorts of ways, without any thanks or acknowledgement.

Organising the funeral had proved far more time-consuming than it should have been because his stepmother had kept changing her mind. It wasn't as if he didn't have a job to hold down, but she had expected him to do everything, and he would be the first to admit that he was hardly the most organised of people. His boss had been very understanding, but it wasn't really fair, considering that his stepmother didn't even work. He didn't mind being involved. He owed that much to his father, at least. But his stepmother had insisted on him accompanying her wherever she went. He had been pushed into making decisions, most of which she had overturned. She was an infuriating woman. He had even offered to lend her some cash until the probate was settled, when she knew he was hard up. It would have been reassuring to know she was going to give him his share, once she had her hands on the considerable estate his father had left. But so far she hadn't offered to pass any of it on to him. All he knew was that his father seemed to have left everything to her. Still, he wished she got on better with his wife. It would have made his life easier.

He spoke cautiously, wary of upsetting Luciana. 'I just think we should spend more time with her, at least until she comes to terms with what's happened.'

Luciana sighed. 'You're right, but be careful, Eddy. With some people, the more you give them, the more they demand. If you keep going round there every day, she'll come to expect it. She's one of those people who have an overblown sense of entitlement. I don't want you to get yourself into a situation where she relies on you to do everything for her.'

'I've only been going there to help her with the funeral, and then with sorting out the house.'

Luciana snorted, as though to say he couldn't sort out his own affairs, let alone his mother's.

'I get that you're trying to help her, but you can't carry on like this. It's unrealistic.'

He nodded. 'I know. But we ought to keep an eye on her.'

'She's not a child.'

'No, but she's on her own.'

They bickered for a while, finally arriving at an uneasy compromise. Eddy would visit his stepmother once a week, and he or Luciana would phone her every day for the first month. After that, they would review the situation.

'With any luck, she'll meet someone else, and then she won't be on her own any more, and we can stop worrying about her,' Eddy said. 'She's only fifty-six, young enough to start a new life with someone else. Lots of people do. It might be the best thing for her, after what's happened. She might meet a nice widower, or someone who's divorced.' He frowned. 'As long as she meets someone who doesn't spend all her money, and who hasn't got any children. My dad's left her a fortune. Once she's gone it should all come to me, every penny of it. He was my father. He wouldn't want his money going to some stranger.'

It was a sore point with him that the entire estate had been left to his stepmother. As a man in his early thirties, with a wife and a mortgage, Eddy was the one who needed money, not his stepmother. If her mortgage hadn't already been paid off, it would be now. Unlike Eddy, she didn't need money. If his father had only thought to mention his son in his will, Eddy could have sorted out his debts and Luciana would have been none the wiser. All he needed was one large windfall to free him of his problems. It wasn't an unrealistic expectation. Meanwhile, he was slowly getting himself in deeper and deeper. So while he mourned for his father, his grief was soured by resentment. His father could so easily have saved him.

Luciana shrugged. 'Let's not get ahead of ourselves. Your mother probably won't meet anyone. And in any case, she might decide to spend it all. You can't rely on anyone but yourself. But at least you're in with a chance of inheriting something,' she added bitterly.

No doubt she was recalling her own circumstances, and her vain attempt to claim compensation after a fire had killed her parents.

Eddy didn't answer.

5

GERALDINE HESITATED OVER WHETHER to pursue her suspicions concerning Mark Abbott's death. She was going to have to proceed discreetly, if at all, because there was no obvious crime to investigate. All the same, Eileen had told her she was free to look into the incident in her own time. Keen to take some initiative in her work, Geraldine was excited at the prospect of following a lead of her own. If it turned out, as seemed likely, that the verdict of suicide was correct, it could do no harm if Geraldine had gone around asking a few questions. Nothing but her professional pride would suffer, and since she was acting on her own, no one else need even know about it. Although she was fairly busy during the day processing reports of local crimes, the task was mundane compared to her work on murder investigations in London, and didn't occupy her mind in the evenings. She missed the challenge of a more serious investigation. So that evening she drove out to Charlotte Abbott's house in Clifton, reminding herself that this was not an official enquiry but a hunch she was following briefly. She drew up outside a well-maintained detached brick house. The front garden had been paved over, the only sign of life a couple of pots of wilting flowers that hung from brackets on either side of the front door.

The widow responded to the bell straight away. She looked surprised to see Geraldine on the doorstep, and glanced around as though she had been expecting to see someone else.

'Yes? Can I help you?' She listened with a puzzled frown as Geraldine introduced herself. 'What's this about?'

The door wasn't open wide enough to allow Geraldine to enter. There was a smell of fresh paint and a faint sound of scraping, but she couldn't see what was happening inside.

'Can I come in, Mrs Abbott?'

'What is it you want?'

Gently Geraldine explained that she had a few questions to ask about Mark.

The widow shook her head. 'Mark? You mean, my husband, Mark?'

'Yes.'

'But –' her face twisted in a bitter grimace, 'surely they've told you? Mark's dead.'

Evidently she hadn't noticed Geraldine at the funeral.

'I know. That's why I'm here, to ask you about him. It's just routine,' Geraldine added quickly.

'Oh well, I suppose you'd better come in.'

While they were speaking, Charlotte's stepson appeared in the hallway behind her.

'Who is it?' he asked.

'It's just someone from the police come to tie up a few loose ends,' Charlotte replied. 'Why don't you go home? I'll deal with this. Watch out for the wet paint,' she added, standing aside to let Geraldine to enter.

Eddy was standing in the hall, a wide brush in his hand, and a pot of paint on the floor beside him. The lower half of the banisters had been given a fresh coat of paint, some of which had dripped on to the carpet.

'You go on home,' Charlotte repeated.

'This won't take long,' Geraldine said. 'I just want to ask you a few questions.'

'I'll be back tomorrow evening, mum,' Eddy said, wiping his brush on a rag. 'I'll soon get this job finished.'

'Thank you,' she replied. She turned to Geraldine. 'I couldn't bear to look at it, knowing…'

Since Mark's death was not being investigated as suspicious, there was nothing Geraldine could do to stop his widow painting her hall. All the same, fresh paint could cover up telltale evidence. It might now be impossible to establish who else had been present when Mark had died. If Amanda's accusation was correct, there could be a sinister reason for Charlotte wanting her hall redecorated.

After some half-hearted protest Eddy left, with assurances that he would speak to his stepmother first thing in the morning.

'If you're sure you'll be OK, mum,' he said, glancing anxiously at Geraldine.

'Yes, of course. Stop fussing, will you, and get going.'

Having dismissed her stepson in a fairly peremptory manner, Charlotte led the way into a neat front room. Geraldine refused an offer of tea, and expressed her condolences, conscious that she had to proceed carefully. What Mark's former colleague had told her at the funeral seemed to support Amanda's accusation, but Geraldine had no hard evidence to substantiate the suggestion that Mark had been murdered. Not only was she unable to question the widow as though this was a regular interview, but she couldn't risk any complaint being raised about her visit, which hadn't been specifically sanctioned by a superior officer. Still unused to working as a sergeant, Geraldine knew she risked getting herself in trouble for allowing her pursuit of the truth to outweigh any other consideration, but once the suspicion of murder had been raised, she couldn't ignore it. Her life had been dedicated to seeking justice for the voiceless dead. She wasn't ready to stop.

'What is it you wanted to know?' Charlotte asked.

'Tell me about your husband.'

'What do you mean?'

Feeling as though she was fishing around in the dark, Geraldine almost gave up.

'What kind of a man was he?'

'He was – a man. Ordinary. A man, like anyone else. I don't know what you want me to say.'

'Did he suffer from depression?'

'Oh I see. No, there was nothing like that. He was quite even tempered, cheerful most of the time.'

Geraldine rephrased her question. 'Were you surprised by what happened?'

'You mean was I surprised to find he was dead? Well, yes, of course. It was a shock, a dreadful shock, to find him like that...' Her voice tailed off and she dabbed her nose with a tiny white hanky.

'Yes, it must have been terrible for you. But were you surprised by *how* he died?'

'If you're asking me whether I was expecting him to kill himself, no, of course I wasn't. If I'd had the slightest idea he might have had anything like that on his mind, I would have insisted he got help.' Charlotte spoke quite clearly, but although her voice was steady, her hands were trembling. 'Yes, of course I was surprised. More than surprised. I still can't believe it. But it's happened and we just have to accept it, don't we? I mean, there's no turning the clock back. If only I'd known...'

She insisted that she could think of no reason why her husband might have decided to kill himself. Geraldine understood that Charlotte might not want to admit that her husband had been suicidal, even if she had known about it, but she thought the widow seemed genuinely shocked by what had happened. Before Geraldine could attempt to probe further, Charlotte burst into tears. After a moment she pulled herself together, and Geraldine sounded her out gently about her husband's life insurance, but she didn't seem to know much about it.

'I've asked my son to speak to the lawyers about the will and everything,' Charlotte said. 'I'm not very good with money and that sort of thing. Mark used to deal with everything like that.' She looked up at Geraldine and burst out, 'Why did he do it? He had so much to live for. What reason could he have had for...?'

'That's what we're trying to find out. Charlotte, are you sure you can't think of any reason why Mark might have wanted to kill himself?'

'Nothing I know about. But he did it,' she added miserably, 'so I suppose there must have been a reason.' She looked directly at Geraldine, her eyes puffy and bloodshot from crying. 'It's driving me crazy, not knowing what was going on in his life. I keep asking myself, was it something I did? I thought we were jogging along OK. I didn't know there was any problem. How could I not have known how unhappy he was? If I'd known, if he'd talked to me, whatever it was, we could have worked it out. But not like this. Not this... please find out what happened. I need to know. Please...' she broke down in tears, sobbing incoherently.

Relieved that Charlotte didn't appear to resent her visit, Geraldine left after promising to let the grieving widow know if she discovered anything more about her husband's death. What Charlotte had told her seemed to bear out what Mark's colleague had said at the funeral. A man was unlikely to be planning a holiday, or arranging a tennis match, the night before he was intending to kill himself. Either something unexpected had come up on the day of his death, or he was mentally ill, or his death had not been a suicide at all. Although it wasn't Geraldine's place to enquire into the circumstances of Mark's death, she resolved to continue looking into it for just a little longer. She was committed to ensuring the guilty were brought to trial. That the outcome of such proceedings wasn't always fair was out of her control. She couldn't be judge and jury as well as a law enforcer. But her passion for justice had governed her life for so long, she couldn't walk away from a possibly suspicious death. Because if her suspicions were right, not only had Mark Abbott been murdered but his killer looked set to escape justice.

6

SHE USED TO COMPLAIN when he left her alone in the house. She especially hated it when he went out on jobs at night. She never knew who might be outside, watching the house in the darkness. He scoffed at her fears.

'What are you talking about, you daft cow? There's no one out there. Who'd be interested in you, anyway?'

Ironically, now that she was never alone in the house, she was more frightened than ever. Since he had brought the beast back with him, she had been living in constant fear. The animal had taken against her right from the start, growling and baring its yellow fangs at her whenever she entered the room. Every time she shrieked at him to keep the monster away from her he laughed, pretending to be amused by her terror, but she knew he was scared too. She could see his fear in the way he narrowed his eyes and pressed his lips together until they virtually disappeared.

She begged him to put the dog out in the garden, but he refused. When she tried to insist, he explained that he could get in serious trouble if any of the neighbours spotted a Pit bull crossed with a Rottweiler on the premises. He might even be reported to the police for keeping an illegal dangerous breed, in which case the dog would be taken away from him and he would be fined. So the animal, he said, would remain where it was, chained up in a kennel in the living room. Only rarely had she dared to contradict him, but for once she was too frightened to avoid a confrontation.

'You can't keep a large dog like that cooped up indoors,' she protested. 'It needs daily exercise. Besides, the whole house stinks. It's filthy. We'll all get sick. And people are going to notice the smell.'

'What are you talking about? What people? No one comes here.'

But he looked anxious, and she knew the presence of the dog in the house worried him. The next day he came home with a large cosh, and wound a length of barbed wire carefully around it. Her guts began churning, and she retreated, crying with fear. Ignoring her whimpering, he turned away from her and ran up to the dog. As the animal raised its head, he swiped at it with the stick, hitting the side of its head with a thud. The creature cowered back in its kennel, casting a baleful glare at her. As though any of this was her fault.

'What are you doing?' she cried out.

'Get out of the way!' he yelled at her.

The dog growled, crouching down in its kennel. As it leapt, snapping its jaws, the kennel jolted and jerked forwards. Restrained by its chains, the beast couldn't reach him. He whacked it again and it drew back. Dashing round behind the kennel, he bent down and began to push. The tendons in his neck bulged as he forced the kennel across the carpet towards the door.

'What the fuck are you doing?'

'I told you to get out of the way!'

Sobbing, she ran into the bedroom, slamming the door behind her, determined not to come out until the dog had gone. She had no idea what he was planning to do, and she didn't want to know. Through the door she heard his voice raised, and a lot of banging. Lying on the bed, she rolled herself a spliff. It wasn't enough, so she swallowed a couple of pills and then pulled a pillow over her head and lay there trembling. Hours seemed to pass before she heard the bedroom door open and felt the bed jolt as he flopped down beside her.

'I've done it,' he said.

She tossed her pillow aside.

'What you done?' Even to her own ears, her speech sounded slurred. 'What have you done?' she repeated, enunciating her words carefully.

He waved his forearm in front of her face. 'Look what that bleeding animal did to me!'

With horrible fascination, she watched a steady stream of blood trickling down as far as his elbow and then dripping on to the sheet.

'How'd you do that?'

But she didn't need to ask. She could see the gashes where vicious teeth had torn at his flesh.

'What have you done with it?' she whispered, hardly daring to hope. 'Is it dead?'

'Dead? No. But the kennel got smashed.' He laughed suddenly. 'It fell all the way down the stairs. You should've seen it. It's a miracle the bloody dog survived,' he went on, serious again. 'Bloody animal did this to me while I was chaining it to the wall. It would never have got me, if it hadn't caught me off guard. But I was lucky. If I wasn't so quick, it would've killed me.'

'And then it would have come for me,' she whispered. 'You got to get rid of it. Please. Get rid of it before it kills us.'

He told her how he had pushed the kennel, with the dog inside it, all the way across the hall to the cellar door. When it reached the top of the stairs, he hadn't been able to stop it toppling forwards and falling down into the cellar.

'I thought the dog was dead, but it was just stunned. That's how it got me.' He held up his injured arm again. 'It went batshit crazy. If I'd had a shooter I would've put a bullet in its head. Look what it did to me!' He held his arm up right in front of her face so the blood dripped on to her T-shirt.

She shuddered and drew back, pressing herself against the wall. 'Where is it now?'

He told her the dog was chained up in the cellar.

'Don't look so scared,' he said. 'It can't get out. That chain's unbreakable.'

But she knew the filthy brute was there, lurking in the darkness. She told him exactly what she thought about that, alternately pleading with him to get rid of it, and losing her temper with him over it. But nothing she said made any impression on him. When she threatened to leave if he didn't throw the beast out, he laughed at her.

'Go on then,' he taunted her. 'Bugger off. You're easy to replace. I can get another tart just like that.' He snapped his fingers in her face. 'That dog's a one-off, specially bred to be aggressive. I spent a fucking fortune on it, but it'll be worth it. You'll see.' He leaned forward and growled at her, making her squeal with alarm.

'Don't do that! Fuck off!'

He laughed again.

Weeks later she still hadn't forgiven him for refusing to get rid of the dog, but there was no point in arguing with him. If she aggravated him, he would raise his fist against her. He was no better than the dog, really. They were both vicious animals.

7

THE NEXT MORNING, GERALDINE reread the reports on Mark Abbott's death. Apart from his sister's unsubstantiated accusations, and a random comment made by one of his colleagues, there was nothing to suggest he had been murdered. Even his widow seemed resigned to the fact that he had taken his own life and just wanted to know why he had done it. The man was dead and buried and there, it seemed, the matter would rest. So when Amanda returned to the police station, Geraldine determined to put an end to her demands. But if anything, Amanda appeared even more het up than she had been on her first visit to the police station. Nostrils flaring, she launched into a tirade before Geraldine had even sat down.

'I can't believe it's nearly a week since I was here,' she began.

'Four days,' Geraldine corrected her quietly.

'And you've not got back to me yet,' Amanda continued, ignoring the interruption. 'Why not? This is my brother we're talking about. I have a right to know what's going on. I demand to know what's being done. I won't be fobbed off with excuses any longer.'

'The reason I haven't contacted you yet is because there's nothing to tell you. Rest assured I'll be in touch with you as soon as I discover anything new,' Geraldine replied with an air of finality.

This interview had gone on for long enough.

'Oh no,' Amanda said. 'You're not going to dismiss me out of hand like that. I want to know what you've been doing.'

Geraldine reminded herself that the woman scowling at

her across the table was grieving for her brother. Behind her outward show of anger, she was holding back tears that glistened in her eyes. As a single woman, Amanda's relationship with her brother might have been the only close bond she had with another human being. Shocked and distressed, she must be missing him. But that didn't alter the fact that Geraldine had nothing to tell her. As far as she knew, Mark had committed suicide.

'Nonsense,' Amanda insisted. In spite of her loud voice and fierce frown, she sounded plaintive.

'He left a suicide note.'

'It was forged.'

'There's no proof of that, is there? It's just a wild allegation.'

Amanda glared at her. 'How can anyone prove whether it's genuine or not when it was typed? But I'm telling you, it's a forgery.'

'What makes you so sure?'

'Because I knew my brother. He would never have killed himself. I know he wouldn't. You have to believe me.'

Geraldine could only reassure her visitor that she would look into the case again, and eventually Amanda left, threatening to return in a few days if Geraldine hadn't been in touch with her.

Ariadne's dark eyes sparkled with amusement when Geraldine voiced her suspicions.

'Don't tell me you're one of those officers who cry murder every time someone dies? If you had your way, we wouldn't be able to move for investigations. We'd all be drowning in paperwork. But seriously, Geraldine, you're not in London now.'

'And no one gets murdered in York?'

'You know that's not what I meant. Of course people get murdered here. Why else would we be here? I just meant it doesn't happen as often as in London. And in any case, this guy committed suicide, didn't he, so it's got nothing to do with us. That was the conclusion of the pathologist and the investigating team, so I can't see your problem. And if there's any doubt, it'll come out at the inquest.'

'You know very well that by the time there's an inquest, it will be too late to carry out any kind of investigation. And who's going to find out about a casual remark made by a colleague after so long?'

'What are you talking about? What casual remark?'

Geraldine explained that Mark had spent the last evening of his life talking about his holiday plans and arranging a tennis match.

'Well, maybe he didn't feel like ending it all then,' Ariadne replied. 'But clearly he changed his mind by the following day. In any case, people planning to commit suicide often do carry on as usual until they actually kill themselves, otherwise other people would stop them doing it. Honestly, I wouldn't waste your time on this. No one else is.'

Geraldine nodded, but she determined to do a little more ferreting around before she let the matter drop. Explaining to Ariadne that she had only followed it up to satisfy Amanda, she couldn't lie to herself. As an inspector she had been able to pursue her hunches, and colleagues had gradually come to respect her instincts. Now she felt as though she was starting all over again, no longer confident she could even trust herself. But some inner passion drove her on. It could have been a need to prove herself. Whatever her motivation, she decided to proceed with her private investigation, irregular though it was. It was Friday evening, and several of her colleagues were going for a drink at the end of the day. Ariadne invited Geraldine to join them, suggesting they go out for supper together afterwards. Although she was gratified by the friendly overture, Geraldine made her excuses, and set off home to give her attention to a dead man.

Her first task was to read all the reports of the incident. Returning home from the shops, Charlotte had discovered her husband's body hanging in the hall. With the help of the gardener she had tried to release her husband from the noose, but she had been too upset to be much use and he had struggled to both support the body and cut it down by himself. It wasn't until the police reached the scene that the body had been successfully lowered to the floor. That much was uncontentious. The doctor judged Mark had been dead for at least an hour by the time his wife had come home and found him which meant he must have hung himself as soon as she had driven away. That seemed to confirm that he had committed suicide, waiting only for his wife to leave the house before taking action.

The scene itself had been subjected to forensic examination. No sign of a struggle had been found, nor any evidence that anyone else had been in the house at the time of the hanging. CCTV footage from the local supermarket confirmed that Charlotte had been out shopping for at least an hour, coinciding with the time that her husband was at home dying. The dead man had been suspended from a brand new rope, which he was presumed to have purchased expressly for the purpose of killing himself. So far the purchase of the rope had not been traced, but that meant nothing. Anyone could buy a length of rope from a hardware store or garden centre, anonymously, for cash.

Not only was there a lack of evidence to suggest anyone else had been present at the hanging, but the final piece of evidence that had put an end to the enquiry was that the victim had left a suicide note which appeared to wrap up the case. When she tried to track it down and look at it for herself, Geraldine learned that it had been returned to his widow.

8

THIS TIME, THE WIDOW looked anxious to see her, rather than surprised.

'Have you found out anything?' she asked straight away. Her face was blotchy and she looked as though she hadn't slept for a while.

'Can I come in?'

Charlotte's stepson was sitting in the front room. He looked sullen rather than upset.

'I'd like you to leave my mother alone,' he said. 'She's been through a lot.'

'Be quiet, Eddy,' Charlotte interrupted. 'I want to hear what she's found out.'

'There's nothing to find out. Someone's persuaded my stepmother that my father didn't kill himself. It's understandable, but she has to stop grasping at straws. It'll be better for all of us in the long run if we face up to the truth and come to terms with it.'

'We don't know the truth,' Charlotte said.

'Of course we do. Anything else is just prolonging the agony. We have to accept what happened, and do our best to deal with it. In private,' he added, scowling at Geraldine.

'I'm sorry to intrude,' she said, 'and I'm afraid I haven't brought you any news. But I'd like to talk to you if I may.'

Charlotte's eyes narrowed. 'I've been going over and over what you said, and I think you could be right. There's more to it than they say.' She stared intently at Geraldine. 'You don't believe Mark killed himself, do you? It's just that –' she hesitated, struggling to explain herself. 'I'm not sure I really believe it. Mark always looked after himself.'

Eddy growled incomprehensibly.

Geraldine sighed. It would be cruel to lead the poor woman on. 'Honestly, I've no idea. I wasn't involved in the initial investigation. I assure you this is just a routine enquiry, in preparation for the inquest.'

That was a lie, but she couldn't think what else to say to explain her interest in the death without raising false expectations. It was terrible to think that it would be easier for the widow to cope with the thought that her husband had been murdered than that he had committed suicide, but anything must be preferable to believing someone you loved had taken their own life.

'I'm so sorry,' she muttered. 'The last thing I want to do is cause you any more distress.'

'Leave us alone then,' Eddy said.

Privately Geraldine thought Charlotte's son was right. It was time to stop. She could no longer remember exactly what had brought her there to intrude on the family's grief. On the strength of a vague hunch, based on a couple of unsubstantiated comments, she was opening up wounds that were better left alone. She was about to stand up, when Eddy spoke again.

'Look,' he said, relenting. 'I know you're just doing your job and you want to help us. But there's nothing you or anyone else can do. It is what it is. The inquest is going to be difficult enough as it is. But the harsh reality is that my father, for whatever reason we don't know, decided to do what he did. He even left a note.'

Geraldine nodded. Having concluded that she would back off, she couldn't ignore the opening that Eddy had inadvertently given her. Cautiously she reiterated her condolences, and her regret at having to raise the issue at all.

'But it would be helpful if I could have a look at the note your father wrote.'

Charlotte left the room and returned a few moments later, clutching an envelope. Belatedly, Geraldine slipped it into an evidence bag. It was frustrating trying to piece together an incident after the event. She was accustomed to attending the scene of a death promptly, able to examine all the evidence first-hand. Studying other people's reports was a clumsy way of approaching a potential crime scene. She already knew the suicide note had not been examined by a forensic handwriting officer. Clearly the investigating team hadn't thought it worthwhile, since the note had been typed on Mark's laptop at home and printed out on the printer in his office. Apart from the scrawl which served as a signature there were no other distinguishing features to the note which was worded quite simply and clearly, merely stating that he was ending his life. He gave no reason.

After promising to return the note as soon as she could, instead of going home she went back into the police station.

'Working late?' the duty sergeant greeted her.

She smiled, pleased to see Ted on the desk. 'Just a few odds and ends to tidy up.'

'And they can't wait until morning?'

'Well yes, they could, but I was passing and thought I'd just pop in and finish off.'

For an instant, Geraldine wasn't sure whether his curiosity was intrusive, but she decided he was just being friendly. It must be her own concern that she was pursuing this death too far that was making her uneasy. With a quick smile at him, she hurried into the open-plan office and over to her desk. A couple of other officers were working late, but no one else took any notice of her as she sat down and opened up her iPad to study the report into the suicide note again. The envelope and its contents had already been examined. It was frustrating, but the only fingerprints discernible on the paper belonged to Charlotte herself. Other than that, there were a few smudges that appeared to have been made by at least one person wearing gloves. She double checked to confirm that the dead man had not been wearing gloves, although that wasn't significant because he had printed out the note a week before his death. At any rate, the absence of his prints or even of his DNA on the paper was deemed to be inconclusive by the team who had conducted the initial investigation.

'You'd think he would have breathed on it, at least,' Geraldine muttered to herself.

One of her colleagues was passing her desk. 'What's that?'

'Oh, nothing. Just talking to myself.'

He laughed. 'You know what they say about people who talk to themselves?'

Geraldine smiled. 'They have no friends,' she thought. Aloud she replied, 'It's the first sign of madness?'

Her colleague grinned and returned to his own desk. Geraldine looked down. She hadn't intended to voice her thoughts aloud. It was too late to do anything more about the note that night, so she printed out as many copies of the dead man's signature as she could trace on official documents, and slipped the samples into an evidence bag along with the suicide note. Over the weekend, she would try to see what, if anything, might be discovered from further examination of the note. With that, she packed up her bag and went home. It had been an inconclusive lead. Wherever she turned, the report into Mark's suicide seemed to raise more questions than it answered.

9

ALTHOUGH GERALDINE WAS CLOSE to her sister, Celia, she felt hemmed in whenever she visited her. However long she stayed, Celia never wanted her to leave. It was tough for both of them, but Geraldine could never fill the void left in Celia's life by their mother's death. One day they would discuss the impact of their mother's death on both of them, but not yet. It was tricky, as Celia was their mother's natural daughter, and Geraldine had been adopted. Only as an adult had Geraldine finally met her birth mother and learned that she had an identical twin. She hadn't yet mentioned her birth sister to Celia. Geraldine told herself that she was avoiding the subject out of consideration for Celia's feelings, but in reality she knew she was keen to escape an emotional confrontation with her adopted sister. The longer she procrastinated, the trickier it became to bring up the subject.

Visiting her birth twin posed a different kind of challenge. Geraldine had arranged to spend that weekend in London. Arriving around midday on Saturday, she would take her twin sister out for an early lunch. It wasn't a meeting she was looking forward to with any pleasure. She was never quite sure what kind of greeting she would receive. As a recovering heroin addict, Helena needed more support than Geraldine was able to offer her from a distance, but she did as much as she could. To her relief, one of her former colleagues, Sam, had agreed to keep an eye on Helena, which meant she hopefully wasn't feeling completely abandoned. But whatever Geraldine did, Helena always seemed ready to give her a hard time.

'I'd rather face a difficult witness any day,' Geraldine complained to Sam. 'I can keep my temper with just about anyone else, but Helena always manages to get under my skin.'

Sam laughed. 'That's sisters for you. Everyone thinks my sister's lovely but –' she made a sound somewhere between a groan and a snort.

'I don't think that's it. I mean, I'm not like that with Celia, and I grew up with her,' Geraldine protested, citing her adopted sister as evidence that their inability to get on had nothing to do with Helena being her sister.

Sam was forced to concede. 'Well, she is a difficult character, but just look what she's been through.'

'I know, and I'm not blaming her. I just wish she'd cut me a bit of slack.'

'It must be tough,' Sam sympathised. 'I do wonder why she's like that, when you're so generous to her. I don't know if I would have your patience.'

Geraldine sighed. 'There but for the grace of God and all that. Besides, I promised my dying mother I'd look after Helena. I do little enough for her really.'

Their relationship was fraught with unspoken recriminations. Sometimes Geraldine wanted to yell at Helena. It wasn't Geraldine's fault she had done nothing to support her sister before their mother's death. Only in a letter from their dying mother had Geraldine learned of Helena's existence. Since then, she had done her best to help her sister but, far from being grateful, if anything Helena seemed to resent Geraldine's assistance. On this occasion Geraldine's reservations turned out to be well founded.

'It's all right for you,' Helena whined as they sat down to lunch. 'You've got a job and a home –'

'You've got a home.'

Reluctant to argue with her sister, Geraldine refrained from retaliating to Helena's barbed comments by pointing out that it was only thanks to her that Helena had been able to stay in her flat at all.

'You're looking well,' she said instead, in an attempt to change the subject.

She knew her twin well enough to understand that Helena wanted to make out she was hard done by, in an attempt to wheedle more money out of her. It was galling as Geraldine already paid Helena's rent and felt she was good enough to her, but she was desperate to keep her twin happy and stable, to prevent her running back to her former associates. Giving up heroin was hard enough. Being forced to turn her back on everyone she had ever known must have made it even more difficult.

'Has Sam been to see you?' she asked brightly.

Helena merely grunted. Geraldine knew her former colleague had visited her twin several times. Unwilling to admit she wasn't totally alone, nevertheless Helena could hardly deny it. She must realise that Geraldine would hear about it from Sam.

'Is there anything you need?' Geraldine asked finally, as they finished their lunch.

Helena promptly reeled off a list of things she needed for her flat. Listening, Geraldine felt an unexpected wave of pity for her twin. Apart from the rent, her demands were pathetically modest. Geraldine nodded. It was an unspoken agreement between them that Geraldine would buy things for her twin, but she flatly refused to hand her any cash.

'You still don't trust me, do you?' Helena grumbled. 'After all this time. What the fuck do I have to do to get you to see I'm a reformed character? I'm never touching that shit again, not for no money.'

Despite Helena's complaints, Geraldine was hugely relieved to see that her twin had put on weight, making the resemblance between them more pronounced than before. When they had first met, at their mother's funeral, Helena had been skeletal.

Now her cheeks had filled out and the bones and tendons in her hands were no longer so pronounced. Her teeth remained stained and broken, and her skin was as blemished as before, but it was obvious now that they had been born identical. As usual, Geraldine felt an overwhelming feeling of regret at the estrangement that persisted between them, despite her efforts to draw closer to Helena. She wasn't sure what more she could do to help her sister. It seemed that whatever she did would never be enough. For all that Helena whinged about her having moved to York, Geraldine suspected they would have fallen out by now had she lived in London. It was sad, but some relationships only worked at a distance.

'I'll come and see you again as soon as I can. And in the meantime, if there's anything you need, you can call me, or speak to Sam.'

'Yeah. Whatever.' Pulling on her jacket, Helena didn't even look up.

After lunch, Geraldine had arranged to meet a forensic handwriting analyst for a drink. She had worked with Sandra Bentley before and had been impressed with her acumen. It was an added benefit of her trip to London that she could consult a handwriting expert in her own time without anyone in York knowing about it.

'This is off the record, right?' Sandra asked her when they had exchanged greetings.

Geraldine looked at Sandra's broad fleshy face and hesitated. 'Yes and no,' she hedged.

Sandra arched her neatly pencilled eyebrows.

'I'm following something up in my own time,' Geraldine explained. 'So there's no need for any formal record of our discussion.' She paused.

'So, off the record then?'

Geraldine shrugged and returned Sandra's smile. 'I suppose it is.'

'So, what have you got for me? I hope it's a good sample.'

Geraldine took the suicide note out of the evidence bag, together with another sample of Mark Abbott's signature.

'I need to know if this is a forgery,' she said, pointing to the suicide note.

Sandra's eyebrows rose again when she saw what Geraldine had brought for her to examine. 'Is this all you have?'

'I'm afraid so.'

'The problem is, it's very difficult to say much with any certainty, given such a small sample. You've given me nothing much to compare with, and a signature can easily be forged. These aren't even written on similar paper, and the ink isn't the same either.' She held up the suicide note. 'This was written with a cheap biro.' She indicated another signature. 'The nib used here was thicker.'

'Does that make a difference?'

'Yes.' Sandra stared closely at the various samples, first with her eyes and then through a microscope.

'If you had to write a report stating whether or not you thought this was a forgery, what would you say?' Geraldine pressed her.

'The pressure of the strokes is considerable in the alleged suicide note,' Sandra said, 'but that's probably not significant if they were written at different times. And if this is a genuine suicide note, the writer might well have been stressed at the time of writing, which would also affect the way he signed his name. The slant of the strokes looks similar, the base of the letters are aligned more or less the same, and the size of the letters is almost identical which means we can measure the spacing between the letters.' She took out a ruler and using the microscope made some detailed measurements. 'The height relationship between the letters is more or less the same, and the connectors and loops are almost identical. No one replicates their own signature every time they write it.'

'What does that mean in layman's terms?' Geraldine asked impatiently.

'Forgers tend to write shakily, with slight tremors and blots, rather like elderly people. This signature,' Sandra pointed to the suicide note, 'looks quite steady and confident, suggesting it wasn't forged. Of course the writer might have practised until he or she could reproduce the signature closely enough without any wobbles.'

'So do you think it's a forgery, or not?'

Sandra shook her head. 'Honestly, it's impossible to say. This is far too small a sample, and if it is a forgery, it's too skilled to detect. It could be genuine, or it could be a decent copy of the original signature.'

'Is that all you can say?'

'I'm sorry but a signature really is a very small sample to base any useful conclusions on. The signatures look similar, but whether or not they were written by the same hand is impossible to say. Honestly, I'd be guessing. And my guess is as good as yours.'

'You must be able to deduce something from all this?'

Sandra gave a reluctant smile. 'I wish I could be more helpful. It's a pity the note was typed, but who handwrites these days? The fact that the suicide note is typed suggests a certain degree of self-control, as though the decision to kill himself wasn't a sudden whim but something that was carefully worked out in advance. Does that fit in with what you know?'

'Absolutely. The suicide had been carefully planned, and the note was printed out a week before he died.'

Sandra nodded. 'Yes, that fits the impression the note gives. It's quite factual and detached, isn't it? Almost businesslike. But everything's printed out these days, and it's becoming impossible to establish any individual's handwriting with certainty. There just aren't sufficient samples for comparison, even where notes are handwritten. If this was an official enquiry and you were asking me to write a detailed report, citing the statistical likelihood of it being a forgery which might be of some use as corroborating evidence, what I could tell you would really boil down to informed speculation. If I'm honest, by itself my opinion really isn't much use to you.'

'If you had to give a view, would you be inclined to say it's genuine or not? What are the chances?'

'It really isn't possible to be conclusive with such a small sample. I'm sorry.'

Geraldine thanked her and packed her samples away carefully through force of habit, even though they were of no use to her. The suicide note might be authentic, but if it was a fake, the killer was clever enough to know that the forgery would be impossible to detect.

10

IT WAS HARD TO believe that two weeks had passed since her husband's suicide. She still expected to see the hump of his body in bed, and found it difficult to fall asleep without hearing him snoring beside her. Although she used to find the noise irritating, the unfamiliar silence disturbed her. In spite of her shock, somehow the funeral had kept her going. With so much to do, she had barely had time to stop and think. Her stepson had done his best to assist her in making the arrangements, and the funeral director had been very helpful. Now everything was in the hands of the lawyers, and there was nothing for her to do but wait for them to sort out the probate. Her solicitor had assured her that it was a straightforward case, Mark having left everything to her in his will. Even so it seemed that his affairs were going to take a while to settle. Eddy had offered to lend her some cash in the meantime, but Charlotte knew he didn't have much money and whatever he could afford to lend her would be insignificant.

Now that several days had passed since they had buried her husband, the reality of her situation was beginning to sink in. She tried not to think about what had happened. Dwelling on it only upset her. She couldn't talk to Eddy, who had his own grief to deal with. The truth was, Mark's death hadn't made it easy for either of them. When she thought about him now, her overriding emotion was not sadness, but anger. She knew she ought not to blame her husband, but if he had been unhappy, he had also been dreadfully selfish.

'I don't understand. How could it happen? How did things

end up like this?' she asked her doctor. It was a relief to be able to admit her feelings freely. 'I'm so angry with him. And when I'm not feeling angry, I can't stop crying. Why did this have to happen? What have I done? What have I done?'

The GP prescribed her some pills to get her through the next couple of weeks but she resisted taking them, even though Eddy advised her to follow the doctor's advice. The pills came with a list of alarming potential side effects. Eddy assured her the pharmaceutical companies issued similar warnings for every medicine on the market, to cover themselves against any possible complaint.

'It says you shouldn't drive if they make you feel sleepy,' Charlotte objected. 'That doesn't sound very safe. They can't be good for you. How am I supposed to do anything if these pills are going to knock me out?'

She turned down her son's offer to drive her to Sainsbury's. It was kind of him, but now she was on her own, she had to get used to managing without help from other people. Besides, if he took her shopping, she would end up paying for his purchases as well as her own. During the day she managed to occupy herself, cleaning the house and watching a lot of television. Nights were the worst. Her guilt and loneliness grew so sharp it was like a physical pain in her chest. Meanwhile the police had concluded their investigation and were satisfied that Mark had committed suicide. As far as they were concerned, that was the end of the matter. But Charlotte knew that she was responsible for what had happened. She should have stopped it.

Determined to pull herself together, on Sunday evening she went to the supermarket and tried to pretend, for a short time at least, that her life had returned to normal. It was easier when she was out of the house where everything reminded her of Mark. The traffic was relatively light. She wasn't unhappy that she had to drive around the car park looking for a space, or that it took her a while to make her way along the busy aisles. She was in no hurry to return to her empty house. It felt strange, shopping for one. For the first time in her adult life she didn't have to take anyone else's preferences into consideration. The freedom was baffling. It had taken her a while to adjust to shopping only for herself and Mark when Eddy had left home. Now a couple of times she had to return items to the shelves because, without thinking, she had picked up things for Mark. Returning the toothpaste he liked, she walked slowly along the shelves of hair products and selected a new shampoo and conditioner. Pausing by the dyes she studied the different shades, wondering which might suit her if she decided to change her hair. She didn't mind the wasted time. Eddy had just finished decorating the hall, but she still experienced a strange cold feeling on stepping through the front door. It was her front door now. The whole house was hers. She should have been pleased. Instead she was beginning to hate the house because, wherever she went, Mark's presence seemed to linger, malevolent and accusing. She spent a long time making very few purchases but eventually she had to go home.

As she drove, she noticed a black van following her from the supermarket all the way along Wigginton Road, past the hospital, and out to Clifton where it turned behind her into her own side street. When she reached her house the black van drove straight past. It must have been guilt that was making her paranoid, but she felt uneasy. Dismissing her anxiety as foolish, she unpacked her shopping and put the kettle on. She would feel better after a cup of tea and something to eat. She felt unexpectedly tired after going to the supermarket, even though she had only bought a small proportion of her usual trolley load. Taking her cup of tea into the front room she sat down, glanced out of the window and paused, tea in hand. A black van was parked across the road. She couldn't be sure, but she thought she recognised it as the one that had followed her home earlier. She leaped up and closed the curtains. Her hands were shaking as she picked up her cup again. Sinking back into an armchair, she put her tea down, covered her face with her hands, and began to cry. Without Mark the world seemed hostile.

She had hardly slept for weeks and her head was aching. Not feeling hungry, she went upstairs. Buying a new bed was one of the first things she was going to do as soon as she got her hands on the money Mark had left. After what had happened, it sickened her to think she was sleeping in the bed she had shared with him for over thirty years. As she was cleaning her teeth, she saw that her eyes were swollen from crying. Anyone seeing her would think she had been crying from grief for her dead husband, but her feelings were more complex than that. More than anything, her fury and disappointment were becoming hard to control. Somehow she had to get a grip on herself. Returning to the bedroom, she peered outside through a gap in the curtains and drew back in alarm. The black van was still parked across the road. She was almost certain it was the van she had seen following her home from the supermarket. Hurriedly she closed the curtains. A new emotion had taken over from her anger: fear.

11

GERALDINE WOULD HAVE LIKED to take a train to Kent to visit her adopted sister, but there wasn't time to see Helena in London and then go and visit Celia as well, all in one day; so having seen Celia and her new baby the previous weekend she had, somewhat reluctantly, given Helena priority this time. It wouldn't have been her preferred choice, but she felt it was her duty to take care of her twin, who was clearly incapable of looking after herself. Having taken Helena out for lunch and met up with Sandra, she would have liked to meet her friend, Sam, for a drink but Sam was busy so Geraldine set off back to York. It had been an unsatisfactory day from start to finish and she was feeling thoroughly fed up.

Anticipating a quiet evening alone, she was pleased to receive a text from Ian naming a gastro pub in the city centre near the Jorvik Museum, and suggesting a time to meet that evening, if she was free. Not only was she always happy to spend time with Ian, but he was the only friend she had in York who knew about Helena's problems. Having a recovering addict for a twin sister wasn't something she wanted to share with all her new colleagues. She had known Ian for years and found him easy to talk to, and more importantly, she trusted him to be discreet. Looking forward to telling him how Helena was getting on and discussing what he thought she should do to support her twin, she accepted his invitation at once. She would just have time to return to her flat and shower and change before going to meet him. In an instant her dejection vanished. Somehow Ian affected her in a way that no one else

61

did, probably because they had known one another for such a long time and she was able to relax in his company.

Arriving in York, she took a taxi from the station to her flat to save time, and got ready as quickly as she could. She didn't want to be late for Ian. She tried to suppress her excitement, telling herself this was merely two colleagues going out for a bite to eat, and not a date. She might as well have been going out to see Ariadne for all the romance the evening promised. But she applied her make-up with extra care, and dithered stupidly over what to wear, as though it mattered, changing her clothes twice, before returning to her original choice. She checked her outfit in her long mirror one last time: smart black trousers with a black and white shirt that fitted her snugly enough to show off her slim build, but wasn't so tight that she would be uncomfortable if she ate a heavy meal. With a nervous fluttering in her stomach, she set off. It was a long time since she had felt this excited about going out with a man. Ambiguity about Ian's intentions only increased her nerves.

Entering the restaurant, Geraldine was surprised to see a small crowd of familiar faces. Ariadne was there, as were Naomi and Eileen and several other colleagues, all bunched together at the bar. A few more were sitting at a long table in the dining area. Thinking this was coincidence, she felt a tremor of disappointment that her evening alone with Ian was ruined. It was unlucky, but unless they wanted to appear unsociable – and probably set off unwelcome rumours – they would have to join the group.

Catching her eye, Ariadne came forward to greet her, beaming a welcome. 'I wasn't sure if you'd be here this evening. It was supposed to be a surprise, but of course he got wind of it –'

'He did?' Geraldine asked, catching sight of Ian talking to Naomi at the bar. She shook her head, perplexed. 'Who told him?'

'Oh, you know Ted. I think he knew about it before most of us did.'

Understanding what was happening, Geraldine forced a weak smile. Ian hadn't been inviting her out for an intimate evening; he had been passing on the details of Ted's retirement do. If she hadn't been so preoccupied with her concerns over Helena, and her suspicions about Mark's alleged suicide, she would have realised what was going on.

Naomi came over and joined them. 'I didn't realise you were so friendly with Ted,' she said, as though Geraldine was some kind of gatecrasher. 'I mean, you haven't been with us very long.'

Geraldine forced herself to smile. 'I thought everyone was friends with Ted.'

'It's only an informal get together,' Ariadne said. 'The official farewell party's not until next Friday. It was supposed to be just for a few friends but, like you say, everyone's friends with Ted. I'm going to miss him.'

Geraldine nodded. 'Me too. This is a nice idea.'

It had been a long day and all at once she felt tired. The gathering was not at all how she had envisaged spending her evening, but she could hardly leave. Stifling a sigh, she made the best of it and listened to a few colleagues discussing their holiday plans.

'I'm thinking of Norway,' Ariadne said, 'but it might be too cold.'

'It can be lovely there,' someone else replied. 'You can be lucky with the weather.'

'The weather these days is unreliable everywhere,' someone else said. 'You have to be lucky wherever you go.'

Thinking about her ruined evening, Geraldine murmured in agreement. She could have been at home, rereading the reports on Mark's death. Ian joined them, and offered to buy a round.

'Come on,' he said to Geraldine, 'you can make yourself

useful and help me carry the glasses.' Taking her gently by the elbow he steered her towards the bar.

'You're looking down in the dumps,' he said quietly when they were out of hearing of their colleagues. 'Is it Helena?'

She shook her head. 'Well, yes, a bit, I suppose. It's everything, really.'

Glancing up at his concerned blue eyes, she wished they were alone and could talk properly, but they were surrounded by colleagues, any one of whom might interrupt them at any moment. As they were ferrying drinks to the others, Ted arrived and went through the motions of feigning surprise at seeing so many of his colleagues gathered to greet him.

'I'll have to retire more often if it means you're all buying me a drink,' he laughed.

If her expectations hadn't been disappointed, Geraldine would have enjoyed the evening. As it was, she left as early as she could and was glad to get home and go to bed, too tired even to work.

12

'WHAT DO YOU MEAN, someone was following you?' Eddy demanded, frowning.

Charlotte was surprised to see how lined her stepson's forehead was. He seemed to have aged twenty years in a couple of weeks. His hair was greying at the temples, and pouches under his eyes gave him a worried look. He repeated his question. Feeling slightly embarrassed, she explained about the van she had noticed following her home from the supermarket. Far from sharing his stepmother's concern, Eddy scoffed at her.

'That's ridiculous. You're imagining things.'

'I know. That's what I thought at first.'

'At first? What do you mean? How long has this been going on?'

Charlotte explained that she had seen the van parked opposite her house.

'Did it follow you here?'

'No. I checked.'

'How can you be sure it was the same van?'

'Well, I think it was. It was a black van anyway.'

'A black van? Did you get the registration number?'

'Well, no. But it looked like the same van...'

Eddy was clearly irritated, but he spoke gently. 'Mum, there are vans everywhere, black vans, white vans. It doesn't mean they're interested in you.'

Charlotte bristled at his patronising tone. He sounded just like his father.

'I'm not an idiot,' she snapped. 'I know there are a lot of vans around. But I'm telling you, there's one that's following me, and you should take it seriously.'

'I think you're being paranoid, suspecting it was the same one. Why don't you talk to the doctor?'

Charlotte sighed. She might be in a vulnerable state of mind, but she knew what she had seen. There was nothing the doctor could do about that.

'You think I'm imagining it, don't you?'

As she spoke, Luciana came in and joined them.

'Who's imagining what?' she asked as she sat down.

'Mum's having a bad time of it,' Eddy replied. 'I mean, she's been coping really well, but she's having a bit of a reaction. It's understandable.' He gave Charlotte a sympathetic smile. 'You know, if there's anything we can do, you've only got to ask.'

She nodded gratefully, but they could no more protect her from her fears than they could restore Mark to life.

'She thinks she's being followed,' Eddy added.

Luciana looked startled. 'What do you mean, followed?'

With a sigh, Charlotte recounted her story. She expected Luciana to dismiss the account as fanciful, exactly as Eddy had done, but to her surprise Luciana leaned forward in her chair and questioned her earnestly.

'Are you sure it was the same van?'

'Well, no, I can't be sure, but it looked like the same one.'

'See,' Eddy cried. 'I told you, she's imagining it. Listen, mum, you're bound to be in a state. It's hardly surprising after –' he broke off and drew in a sharp breath. 'You just need to give yourself time to get used to it,' he added lamely.

He gazed anxiously at Charlotte, while Luciana questioned her further about what she had seen, asking for details Charlotte was unable to supply.

'If you spot that van outside your house again, you must go to the police,' Luciana concluded at last.

'You don't think I'm imagining it then?'

'Well, if you want my opinion, I think you're just nervous about living on your own,' Luciana answered. 'It's understandable. But you'll get used to it. And in the meantime, the police will be able to reassure you that you're quite safe.'

Eddy remonstrated with his wife, accusing her of winding his stepmother up.

'You'll only make a fool of yourself if you go to the police about this. I mean, what are you going to say? That you've seen a black van?' He gave a short laugh. 'Mum, don't you think you've got enough on your plate right now without getting the police involved?'

'I'm not getting them involved –'

'Once they start poking around, who knows what they might turn up?'

Charlotte was startled by her son's aggression. 'Eddy, is there something you're not telling me?'

But he protested that he was only thinking of her. 'This isn't about me. The police can be a real pain and I just don't think you need that in your life right now.'

Luciana protested that he was wrong to dismiss his stepmother's concerns so readily, but when Eddy asked who on earth might be following her, she had no answer. Listening to them, Charlotte had to admit her fears sounded silly. Who on earth would want to follow her home from the supermarket? She was hardly a celebrity. Right now she didn't even have much money, only a house and an inheritance due when the lawyers got their act together. Why would anyone be interested in her? Sitting chatting with Eddy and Luciana, Charlotte could acknowledge that she was being foolish. But once she was alone again, everything felt different.

She would have preferred to sleep at Eddy's house that night but they hadn't invited her to stay, and she didn't like to ask. In any case, there would be the next night to get through on her own, and the one after that. The fact was, she needed something to take her mind off her husband's suicide. It was a terrible experience for anyone to undergo and, although she knew she would never fully recover, she had to find a way of getting her own life back on track. In addition to prescribing her pills which she wasn't taking, the doctor had suggested bereavement counselling might help her, adding that there were therapists experienced in supporting people in her situation. She found it depressing yet selfishly reassuring to know that she wasn't the only woman whose partner had taken his own life.

'I expect you're right,' she admitted. 'I'm just all over the place at the moment. Forget I said anything. And don't worry, I'll go back to the doctor. You just concentrate on looking after yourself, and Luciana.'

'Are you sure you're all right?' Eddy asked.

He looked so worried that Charlotte was almost overwhelmed with guilt. Eddy had just lost his father in the most horrible circumstances imaginable and now, instead of comforting him, Charlotte was causing him to suffer further distress. Not only had she been the most terrible of wives, she was a dreadful stepmother, focusing only on herself and not giving a thought to how her stepson must be feeling. With an effort, she forced herself to smile as she reassured him that she was going to be fine. There was no point in upsetting him any further. Whatever was happening to her, she would have to deal with it by herself. She was alone now, for better or worse.

Leaving Eddy's, she drove out to the shopping centre in Monks Cross, more to delay returning to her empty house than because she really wanted anything. She spent a while wandering around the stores, and bought herself some shoes she didn't need. It was late and the place was nearly deserted by the time she left the shops. Crossing the car park, she heard footsteps close by. Glancing over her shoulder she saw a tall man striding towards her. With a tremor of fear, she walked faster. The man's pace quickened, closing the gap between them. It was hard to believe he would attack her in a public car park, but it had begun to rain and there was no one around to help her. She began to trot.

'Stop!' a deep voice called out.

She broke into a run. Looking back, she saw the man was sprinting after her. There was no way she could outrun him but she kept going, her breath coming in short painful gasps.

'Wait!' he called out.

As she turned her head, she saw him raise his hand. It was difficult to see clearly while they were both moving, but it looked as though he was holding a gun. It took a conscious effort to force her legs to keep moving. Ahead of her she could see her car, but she didn't think she would be able to reach it before the man caught up with her. Whimpering from the effort, she kept going. Her heart was pounding and her chest hurt from struggling to breathe.

13

GERALDINE FROWNED. THE SCRAP of handwriting in Mark's suicide note being too small to yield any information, Geraldine's next task had been to investigate the rope from which Mark had been suspended. By contrast to the report on the suicide note, the forensic report on that was very detailed. The rope had been brand new, a traditional flexible three strand Manila rope marketed for decorative use in gardens, but easily strong enough to hold a man's weight. Geraldine checked through Mark's credit card statements for the past year, but there were no purchases from any garden centre or DIY store that might have included payment for a length of rope. If she had been able to prove Mark had bought the rope himself that might have been suggestive, although not conclusive. The fact that she found no trace of any relevant transaction proved nothing. Had he been planning to hang himself, he could easily have paid cash for the rope.

Remembering that Charlotte had summoned help when she had discovered her husband's body, Geraldine had called at the widow's house once more, and asked for her gardener's phone number. On the doorstep, Charlotte replied that Mark used to deal with him. She had no idea where to find his contact details.

'Can you remember what your husband called him?'

'His name's Will. That's all I know about him. I've no idea where he lives or what his other name is.' She started to close the door.

Geraldine stepped forward and asked to see Mark's mobile

phone. Not sure whether she still had it, Charlotte left Geraldine waiting impatiently outside while she went to look for it. At last the front door reopened and Charlotte appeared, clutching a smartphone.

'I don't know his passcode,' she said. 'He never told me what it was. But here's the phone, if it's any use to you.'

She thrust the phone at Geraldine and slammed the door before Geraldine had a chance to thank her. She wanted the number of someone called Will, or possibly 'gardener'. She was soon back at the police station and within a few minutes one of the technical officers had unlocked the phone and given her a mobile number listed under the name Will. After thanking the technician, she returned to her desk and checked for any calls or messages between Mark and his gardener. There was a text from Mark which had been sent a week before his death, saying: 'Same time next week?' and a response from Will that had been received an hour later: 'OK'. That was all.

Geraldine called the number.

'Is that Will?'

'Yeah, this is Will. But – is that Mark's wife calling?'

There was a pause after Geraldine announced herself. She was afraid Will was going to hang up, but instead he asked her what she wanted.

'I'd like to come and speak to you about Mark. Are you able to give me a moment?'

'What do you want to know?'

When Geraldine asked to meet him, he told her he was very busy. 'I've got a big job just started,' he added apologetically.

'This won't take long,' she assured him. 'I need to speak to you about the incident you witnessed recently.'

'You mean the hanging?'

'Yes.'

'You can ask me anything you like.'

Aware that people's faces sometimes revealed more than their words, Geraldine didn't want to question him over the phone. When he refused to meet her, she hinted that he would have to come and speak to her at the police station if he wouldn't tell her where she could find him. People usually capitulated when threatened with the prospect of having to visit the police station but he repeated that he didn't have time, and she hesitated to insist in case he became uncooperative.

'I know this can't be easy for you,' she said gently, 'but I want to ask you about Mark Abbott.'

'I barely knew the guy. I just did some digging for him. He liked to fiddle about in his garden, but digging over is physical. So he called me in to do the heavy work. That's all it was.'

'How long have you been working for him?'

'I've been there a few times. I don't keep count. It's just –' he hesitated, 'just casual like. I only make a few bob here and there.' He paused. 'It's more of a favour, really, because I don't get much more than money for a few beers out of it. Nothing to write home about.'

Geraldine understood that he didn't want to admit his undeclared earnings. Quickly she reassured him that her questions had nothing to do with him or his income.

'Did you know Mrs Abbott?'

'You said it was Mark you wanted to ask about,' he growled, becoming surly. 'I don't know his wife and I didn't know him. There's nothing more to say. All I do is dig over his garden and see to the weeds and that. I just happened to be there when his wife found him. I don't know what you want me to say. What was I supposed to do? I just tried to help the poor woman.'

'We're investigating the possibility that he was murdered.'

'Oh. Well, I'm sorry to hear that. But I didn't know him and I can't help you. I thought he topped himself.'

'We're looking into the possibility that he was murdered and his death was set up to look like suicide. It's tricky to investigate now, as the scene of the crime has been cleaned up. His widow had the hallway redecorated as soon as her husband was buried. But you were there when he was cut down, weren't you?'

Will didn't answer straight away. She did her best to reassure him that she only wanted to find out what he could tell her about the discovery of Mark's body hanging in the hall.

'I don't know what you want me to say.'

'Can you describe what you saw?'

'She came running out into the garden, flapping about, and screeching at me to get him down…' He paused and cleared his throat. 'He was just hanging there, dead. It wasn't… it didn't seem real. It was horrible.'

'How did you know he was dead?'

'His face was all – swollen and dark. I was holding him up, just to support him, you know, although I knew he was a goner, and I tried to get the rope off his neck, but it was way too tight. I couldn't get my fingers inside it. Anyway, I tried, but there was no way I could get him down on my own and she was screaming and yabbering at me and I was yelling at her to get an ambulance and then your lot turned up and that was it. They asked me a few questions and said I was free to go. They never said anything about having to answer more questions,' he added, surly again.

However hard she tried, Geraldine couldn't prise any more information out of him.

'I told you all I know,' he insisted.

Geraldine reread the report that had been filed at the time Mark's death had been logged. It bore out what little Will had told her. There was nothing more to be gained from questioning him or Charlotte again about Mark's death. She had spoken to everyone who might have been able to shed light on the suicide, without learning anything new.

73

14

THE MAN RAISED HIS hand and Charlotte ducked instinctively, nearly losing her footing. As she regained her balance, he drew level with her.

'You dropped this back there in the shop,' he said, holding out her phone. 'Didn't you hear me calling you?'

As he was speaking, a woman trundled past with a loaded trolley, a small child at her heels. A car drew into a parking space nearby and two more people walked by. Stammering her thanks, Charlotte muttered an apology.

'I didn't hear you,' she lied, embarrassed to admit that she had been running away from a stranger in a busy car park in broad daylight because she was afraid. 'That's very kind of you.'

The man gave her a curious frown and turned away. He must have seen her glaring at him over her shoulder and been baffled by her response. She didn't care about that. She just wanted to get away from there. Thoroughly unnerved, she checked her rear view mirror repeatedly on her way home. There was no sign of the black van she had noticed the previous day, but when she reached her house she spotted a man standing motionless on the pavement opposite her house. Just the sight of him sent a cold thrill down her back. His face was almost completely concealed by a hood that shielded him from the light rain that had begun to fall, and he had wound his scarf around his mouth and chin. There was nothing to suggest he was interested in her, but at the same time there was no obvious reason for him to be standing out there in the street, doing nothing. Convinced he was watching her, she didn't know what to do. Although she was reluctant to make a fool of herself by going to the police and making a fuss, the trouble was she had no way of knowing whether she might actually be in danger. It really did look as though someone had discovered she was on her own and was planning to rob her.

Trying to decide what to do was tricky, but she couldn't ignore her pursuer, if that was who he was. As a woman living on her own, her life could be in danger. The more she thought about what had happened, the more frightened she became. There was no denying she felt threatened, and it was the job of the police to protect people like her. It could do no harm to report her concerns to them; it might even save her life if someone really was after her. Instead of taking her shopping into the house, she set off for the police station in Fulford Road.

She struggled to hide her trembling as she approached the desk. The sergeant she spoke to was very sympathetic, and wanted to know how the police could help her.

'It's difficult,' she hedged, overcome by an unexpected reluctance to admit her reason for coming there. 'I want to speak to someone privately.' Her voice wavered as she spoke.

The sergeant appeared to neither notice her nerves nor be surprised by her request. He just asked her to take a seat and she waited nervously, until a very young-looking girl in uniform appeared and invited Charlotte to accompany her. She followed the young policewoman through a door with a glass panel, into a small room where three grey chairs stood around a low table. She hoped she wasn't going to have to report her concerns to the constable who looked little older than a teenager, but the girl assured her that someone would be with her imminently and then left her. After a few minutes the door opened and Charlotte recognised the tall black-haired sergeant who had questioned her about Mark's suicide.

The sergeant greeted her in a low voice that seemed to encourage confidence. Charlotte took a deep breath and launched into her account, and the detective listened intently.

'Can you think of anyone who might be stalking you?' she asked when Charlotte finished speaking.

Charlotte drew in a breath on hearing the word 'stalking'. It sounded terrifying.

'I don't think –' she began, and broke off in confusion.

She had come to the police station resolved to do everything she could to persuade the police that she was being followed. Now that the detective seemed to accept her claim without question, she began to backtrack.

'That is,' she resumed, 'I want police protection. I don't feel safe. I think my life may be in danger.'

The detective gave a sympathetic smile, as though to say she was taking the matter seriously.

'What makes you say that?'

Awkwardly, Charlotte described how she had been followed, several times, by an unidentified van.

'Are you sure it was following you?'

'I think so.'

'If you give me the registration number, we can look into this for you.'

When Charlotte admitted that she hadn't got the number the detective's expression didn't change, but Charlotte knew she had lost ground. Having agreed to make a note of the number if she saw the van again, she was shown out. The police sergeant had been very kind, and had made a show of making detailed notes on everything she said, but her account had sounded questionable even to her own ears. Sitting in the safe claustrophobic atmosphere of a police station, her fears seemed groundless. The sun was shining, and for the first time since she had seen Mark hanging in the hall, Charlotte began to feel that perhaps everything was going to settle down and she would manage to create some sort of new normality in her life.

Although the detective had seemed sympathetic, when she

returned home, Charlotte wondered whether she had been too hasty in asking her son to redecorate the hall. The police might suspect she had something to hide. Unable to walk into the house without remembering the sight of Mark hanging there, she had been pleased when Eddy had agreed to get on with the job straight away. Mark had never acted so quickly when she had asked him to do something for her. But it was done now, and there was nothing she could do to change that, and she had felt better about entering the house since the banister had been painted. It made no real difference, but somehow knowing the rope that had killed Mark hadn't touched the actual surface of the banister made the memory of it seem slightly less real. Gradually she thought she might go round the whole house, redecorating, until there was nothing left that her husband had touched. She had already put everything in the kitchen through the dishwasher, to remove any trace of him. The thought of eating off a fork that had traces of her dead husband's sweat or skin cells on it made her feel nauseous.

As well as asking Eddy to paint the hall, she had made a start on the rest of the house by removing any photographs of Mark, and taking down the picture he had put up in the living room. She had never liked that picture. There were quite a few changes she was going to make to the house, after a decent interval of mourning. But right now it was only a few weeks since Mark's death. She still found it hard to believe he was really gone, for good. She felt as though at any moment he might come in through the front door, yelling at her that he was home and demanding to know where his picture had gone. But that was never going to happen. What did happen from now on was going to be her decision and hers alone. There was no one to tell her what to do.

So far decorating the house to her own taste was the only idea she had come up with. It was early days and she wasn't yet ready to make sweeping changes, but with her husband gone she was a wealthy woman since she had inherited everything from Mark. He had originally included his son in his will but Charlotte had assured him she would make sure Eddy received his fair share, only it would be better coming from her.

'Don't you see,' she had argued, 'if you leave a generous settlement to Eddy there would be nothing left to bind him to me. I know he's not my real son but he's like a son to me, and what's more important, he's your son, and he'd be the only family I'd have left if anything happened to you. So it would be better if he thought his inheritance came from me if you weren't here. That way we're sure not to grow apart without you there keeping us together as a family. Of course I'd tell him you wanted him to have half of what you left.' She paused. 'You know I sometimes get the impression he only tolerates me because we both love you.'

As a result of that conversation, and a few more along the same lines, for the rest of her life she could afford to do whatever she wanted. Eddy's loss was her gain. She was looking forward to making the most of her newfound freedom, confident she had done nothing wrong in persuading Mark to leave everything to her. After all, Eddy was a waster. In fact, it could only benefit Eddy and Luciana that Charlotte had been left in control of all Mark's money. Her stepson and his sour-faced wife would have spent their share in no time, still ending up with nothing. And if Charlotte chose to spend what had originally been intended for Eddy, he would be no worse off.

15

FOR A MOMENT AMANDA lay, befuddled, wondering what had woken her. She was drifting off to sleep again when she heard a ring at her door. Turning over, she ignored it, but the bell rang again. Muttering to herself, she clambered out of bed and peered through the curtains. The front step was out of sight but she could see a black van parked on her drive.

'Who's there?'

The only answer was another ring on the bell.

'Who is it? What do you want? What are you doing here?'

'I've got a delivery for you,' a man's voice answered.

'What is it? I'm not expecting anything.'

The doorbell rang again.

'You know it's seven o'clock in the morning?' she called down. 'I told you, I haven't ordered anything.'

The man stepped back from the door and came into view. He wasn't looking up, and most of his face was concealed beneath a grey baseball cap.

'Are you Amanda Abbott?'

She glanced at her watch, tempted to go back to bed, but the man was waiting on her doorstep and, besides, she was curious to know what he had brought her.

'Yes. Hang on!' she replied. 'I'm on my way. Wait there.'

Quickly pulling on her dressing gown and slippers, she hurried down the stairs and opened the door. The man who had rung her bell looked vaguely familiar, but she couldn't remember where she had seen him before. Tall and weather beaten, he had the kind of face that gave little away. He could have been anything from thirty to forty. His dark eyes glittered enigmatically at her from beneath his baseball cap.

'You said you were delivering something?'

'That's right.'

He wasn't holding a parcel, and there was nothing on the doorstep.

'Well, what is it?'

He jerked his head in the direction of the van which looked old and battered.

'I haven't ordered anything,' Amanda said. 'Where did you say you're from?'

'From the garden centre. I'm delivering your tree.'

'My tree? What are you talking about? What tree? I haven't bought a tree. I don't want a tree. There must be some mistake.'

'There's no mistake, lady. Not if you're Amanda Abbott.'

'I am Amanda Abbott, and I'm telling you, I haven't bought a tree. You've got the wrong house.'

He shrugged. 'They told me your brother bought it for you, but it's taken them a few weeks to get hold of one.' He paused but she just shook her head, too taken aback to reply. 'Oh well, your brother must have wanted to surprise you.'

'He's done that all right,' she muttered, speaking more to herself than to the delivery man.

'I don't mind waiting a moment if you want to check with him?'

Amanda drew in a sharp breath. The man had no way of knowing that her brother was dead. Making a snap decision, she decided she couldn't turn away the last gift her brother had bought her.

'If my brother chose it for me, then you'd better bring it in, whatever it is. At least let me have a look at it,' she added, wondering what kind of tree it was. 'Is it a rose bush? He knows – he knew how much I love roses.'

'As it's a gift, you'll need to take a look and confirm you

want this tree before I fetch it down. You're not obliged to accept it, and I'm not going to get it out only to have to hoist it into the van again if you don't want it. It weighs a ton.'

Amanda hesitated. 'If my brother bought it for me, I can assure you I'm going to want it. Anyway, I can't come outside. I'm in my slippers.'

He shrugged. 'I've been very patient with you, lady, but I can't hang around here all day. If you want to come and have a look at it, fine. Otherwise I can take it back and you and your brother can sort it out with the garden centre. I'm just the delivery man. And I've got other calls to make.'

He turned and began to walk away from her.

'No, wait,' she cried out. 'I do want it. My brother bought it for me. Please bring it round the back. I'll go and open the gate.'

'I'm not getting it out until you've seen it. You might change your mind.'

'Oh, very well.'

Amanda placed a shoe in the corner of the door frame to prevent the door from closing behind her and followed the man over to his van. Luckily it was early and there was no one else around to see her outside in her dressing gown and slippers. Not that she would have cared. She was about to receive a gift from her dead brother. The thought made her feel quite emotional. Unaware of her feelings, the man glanced towards the street before opening the van door. Then he stepped back so she could walk across behind the van and look inside. To her surprise, it was empty.

'But – there's nothing there. I don't understand –'

While she was speaking, a hand was slapped across her mouth and she was hoisted up and shoved forwards on to the floor of the van. She landed on her hands and knees with a painful jolt. For a few seconds she was too stunned to react. As she scrambled to her feet, the door of the van slammed shut. With a thrill of terror she spun round just as the van jerked forwards throwing her down on to her knees again. She yelped aloud in pain and fear.

'What the hell are you doing?' she called out. 'What's going on? Who are you?'

She climbed to her feet again and began banging on the side of the van. 'Stop this van! Stop it at once! Help! Help! I've been taken against my will. Help! I've been kidnapped!'

There wasn't much point in shouting because no one was likely to hear her above the noise of the engine. She slumped down on to the floor and waited, leaning against the side of the van. It was hard to determine what was going on, or to fathom why anyone would want to kidnap a woman of her age and modest means. She was neither wealthy, nor young and attractive.

'What do you want with me?' she called out.

The only answer was the steady roar of the engine

16

GERALDINE KEPT QUIET ABOUT her visit to a forensic handwriting expert in London. It wasn't that she was in any way uneasy about it. Eileen had given her the go ahead to look into Mark Abbott's death in her own time, and that was exactly what she had done on her day off. All the same, it was no one else's business if she chose to spend her free time pursuing an enquiry on her own. So far she had discovered nothing to suggest that Mark Abbott's death had been anything other than suicide. Only his sister's insistence, and a random comment from one of his work colleagues, had raised a question over whether he might have been murdered. Soon Geraldine was going to pay a visit to Mark's sister to assure her that her suspicions were unfounded, but first she wanted to question the dead man's lawyer and his doctor. That way, she hoped she would be able to satisfy Amanda that the police had done everything possible to establish the truth surrounding her brother's death. And she wanted to satisfy herself.

She arranged to go and speak to the lawyer on Tuesday. Williams and Bensonfield were located close to the centre of York, too far away for her to walk there and back in her lunch hour. Parking as near to the office as she could, she trotted up the stairs to the front door where a buzzer let her in straight away.

'I have an appointment to see Mr Jeffrey,' she said, holding up her identity card.

The young blonde receptionist barely looked up as she directed Geraldine to the right door. With curly ginger hair and a boyish face, the solicitor looked like a schoolboy caught sitting at the headmaster's desk. Geraldine smiled at him. Even a man in his position seemed to assume a guilty air when speaking to a police officer.

'How can I help you?' he asked, motioning her to a chair.

When Geraldine explained the reason for her visit, the lawyer looked solemn. 'I suppose there's no reason to conceal the details of the will from you,' he replied cautiously. Rising to his feet, he drew a Manila folder from a filing cabinet and glanced through it, resuming his seat as he perused the document. 'The will was perfectly straightforward. In the event of his predeceasing his wife, the entire estate went to her.'

Geraldine nodded. 'Did he leave very much?'

'Well, there's the house, of course, which is now paid off, and savings of over two hundred thousand.' He hesitated. 'And there's a policy on his life.'

'Wouldn't any life insurance normally be void if he committed suicide?'

The lawyer's eyebrows rose slightly. 'Yes, you're quite right, that's often the case, but it wasn't in this instance. There was a two year exclusion clause which meant he would need to survive for two years after taking out the policy in order for her to benefit from it.'

Geraldine nodded. The solicitor had confirmed the details of the will.

'He took his life two years and one week after taking out the policy, to be exact. The insurance company are trying to kick up a fuss, but they'll have to pay out.'

Geraldine sat forward and studied the solicitor's expression closely. 'Does anything about that strike you as odd?'

'You mean because he waited long enough for his wife to benefit from the policy?' He shook his head. 'No, not really. It's thankfully uncommon, of course, but not unheard of. One week after the policy became due may be cutting it a bit fine, but it's all above board. The insurance company are contesting it, but they know they'll have to pay up.'

The lawyer had nothing more to tell her and she went back to work in a slightly more thoughtful frame of mind than she had been in that morning. It was the work of a few moments to establish that Mark Abbott's financial situation appeared to be comfortable, and had been so for a while. There was nothing to indicate any reason for him to be suffering stress, no sudden unexplained payments, no evidence of blackmail or any other pressure. His sister had accused his widow of killing him. Certainly his death left Charlotte a wealthy woman, which could possibly be a motive for murder. But there was no evidence to suggest she had a hand in his death.

That evening Geraldine paid a visit to the doctor, her final enquiry before going to see Mark's sister. She wasn't looking forward to facing the aggrieved woman, but it would be better to put an end to the matter once and for all. If she didn't, Amanda was bound to continue pestering the police about her brother's death. Geraldine was already regretting having become involved. As Eileen had pointed out, if every widow was accused of murder when she inherited her husband's estate, there would be a lot more cases to look into than there were detectives to investigate them.

'Ah yes, Mark Abbott,' the doctor said, swivelling his chair around to look at her. He had a surprisingly young face beneath his grey hair. 'A sad case. It always seems such an unnecessary waste of a life when that happens, doesn't it?'

When Geraldine asked whether the victim had given any indication that he might be feeling suicidal in the days and weeks preceding his death, the doctor shook his head.

'Not a glimmering,' he said. 'Not that that's necessarily significant,' he added quickly. 'Unless a patient chooses to share his or her feelings, there's no way of knowing what might be going through someone's mind.' He shrugged. 'We're doctors, not mind readers. But if you're asking me if he was suffering from depression or illness of any kind, mental or physical, I'd have to tell you he was in sound health.' He checked his screen. 'He was on Lipitor to control his cholesterol, but that's not uncommon in men of his age, and he'd been taking it for over four years without any reported side effects. Apart from that, he was a stone or so overweight, had a sprained wrist ten years ago, and a bout of flu a couple of years back, and that's it. An uninteresting medical history. There was nothing wrong with him at all. He was in sound health both physically and, to all appearances, mentally as well. There was no way this could have been predicted,' he concluded, slightly on the defensive.

'So why would he have killed himself?'

The doctor shrugged again. 'You're the detective,' he said, adding quietly, 'who knows why anyone does anything?'

17

AFTER A HEAVY RAINFALL during the night, what had threatened to be a grey day turned into a sunny morning. Since her retirement, one of Moira's pleasures in life was exploring the parks in the city. But when the weather was changeable, as it had been for the past few days, she and her husband walked around the block instead of going into town. Geoff insisted on taking what he called his 'daily constitutional' in the fresh air, unless it was actually raining, and Moira usually accompanied him. She was happy looking at her neighbours' gardens, some of which were every bit as attractive as the public spaces they frequented. Smiling at her own neat front garden, she followed Geoff down the path. The daffodils were still out, along with crocuses and snowdrops and other early flowers.

'It's certainly turning out to be a lovely day,' Geoff said.

Checking the next-door garden as they passed by, Moira spotted something brown lying on the doorstep. Peering more carefully she saw it was a solitary leather walking shoe. Her neighbour must have dropped it without noticing. Always keen to do a good deed, Moira told her husband to wait for her while she went next door to return the shoe to its owner. The shoe must have been outside overnight because it was soaking wet. Holding it by the laces, she rang the bell, a smile prepared in readiness. After waiting for a moment she rang again, but there was no answer. Geoff was calling to her to get a move on so she put the shoe down and went on her way. It was nothing to do with her, really, if her neighbour had left a shoe out overnight. More fool her if it got ruined. She should have been more careful.

Returning from the walk, Moira glanced next door and saw the shoe was still there. As well as the shoe, her neighbour's black and white cat was sitting on the doorstep, scratching at the door and mewing.

'Hasn't she got a cat flap?' Geoff asked, catching sight of the animal.

'I don't know, do I? I've never been inside her house.'

'Well, it doesn't look like she has,' he said. 'Anyway, that cat's probably too fat to fit through one.' He chuckled. 'Come on, love, let's get home before it starts raining.'

Moira glanced up at the gathering clouds and hesitated. 'We can't just leave that poor cat sitting there. Do you think she's gone away and forgotten about it?'

'Now, don't start with your speculation.'

'Geoff, we have to do something.'

'What are you talking about? Anyway, even if you're right, and she has gone away, I'm sure the cat can fend for itself.'

'It's not a wild cat, Geoff. You can see it's used to being well fed.'

Ignoring her husband's remonstrations, Moira went up the path and rang the bell again. Still there was no answer. She lifted the flap on the letter box and tried to peer inside, but she couldn't see anything.

'Hello,' she called through the letter box. 'Are you home? You left a shoe out here and your cat wants to come in. Hello?'

The only answer was Geoff summoning her. 'Come on, love, she's obviously gone out. Let's go in and put the kettle on.'

Stepping away from the front door she stared at the window, but the curtains were closed.

'You poor old thing,' she said to the cat.

The cat followed them all the way to their own front door where Moira shooed it away. 'No, Moggy,' she said, 'you can't come in. You don't live here. You go on home.'

Then she felt guilty because of course the cat couldn't go home while her neighbour was out.

'I hope she hasn't really gone away and forgotten about that poor animal,' she said later, after she had brewed a pot of tea.

'What animal?'

'You know, that cat next door.'

'You're not still on about that, are you?'

Moira shrugged. Geoff was right. It was nothing to do with them. That evening she went outside to put the kitchen refuse in the bin. In the near darkness she yelped and nearly dropped the rubbish bag in fright as something brushed against her leg.

'Good lord,' she said, half laughing with relief, 'you nearly gave me a heart attack. Isn't she back yet? What are we going to do with you? I told you, you're not coming in my house.' She sighed as the cat followed her to her door, arching its back and rubbing itself against her legs. 'Oh, come on then, I suppose a saucer of milk won't be missed. Only don't think you can make a habit of it.'

18

THE STENCH WAS GETTING worse. She knew when he'd been down in the cellar because the whole house reeked. There was no point in tackling him about it directly. When he was sober, his temper was erratic at the best of times. She had only to say something he didn't like and he would become violent. She knew the danger signs well: his cheeks would flush slightly while his eyes took on a fixed glare, and if she was close enough she might hear his breathing quicken. Sometimes she had time to notice his fists clench before he struck, but usually he moved too quickly for that. In the early days of their relationship she had suffered terribly, and often hadn't been able to go out of the house for weeks at a time. Even after she had learned how best to avoid provoking him it wasn't always possible, but she had suffered enough bruises, and more than a few cigarette burns, to know when it was time to get away.

One time he had knocked out one of her teeth, so she couldn't smile without revealing an unsightly gap. He had been gutted when he sobered up, but there wasn't much she could do about it. She forgave him, of course, like she always did. What else could she do? She had nowhere else to go, and precious little chance of earning her own money. With a missing tooth and thinning hair, her chance of picking up punters was slim. She sometimes wondered if that was why he had done it, although he swore blind he'd been too pissed to know what he was doing. It wasn't generally difficult to predict his mood changes as long as he was sober, but when he had been drinking he could fly into a rage without warning. Fortunately she was more nimble than him when he was pissed, or he would probably have killed her by now.

She chose her moment with care, and made sure she was out of reach of his fists before she spoke. He was sprawled in a chair, half asleep. With another chair between them, and the door to the hall open behind her, she cleared her throat and began.

'What are you going to do about that animal in the cellar?'

When he didn't answer, she suspected he was planning to leap up and launch himself at her. Doing her best to keep her voice steady, she repeated the question.

'I said, what are you going to do about that animal in the cellar?'

Instead of jumping to his feet, he leaned further back in his chair.

'Are you going to answer me, or what?' she persisted.

This time he opened his eyes, squinted up at her and grunted. Her legs trembled and she struggled to conceal her agitation.

'What are you talking about?'

'That animal you're keeping in the cellar. What are you going to do about it?'

'Nothing.'

'You can't just leave it down there.'

'Jesus Christ, woman, you're the one who wanted it moved out of the living room. Are you saying you want it brought back up here again? You go and fetch it then.'

'Listen, all I'm saying is it's a big dog. It needs food and exercise.'

He nodded. 'You can take it for a walk if you like. Any time. Be my guest.'

It was hopeless. He was determined to bat away her concerns. All the same, she made one last attempt.

'It's cruel, keeping that animal cooped up down there. And it's not just cruel, it stinks. You can't just leave it there to die! It's not healthy for us or the dog!'

She glared at him but he just laughed and closed his eyes again.

'You want to do something about it?' he said. 'I won't stop you. But you know that dog's waiting to bite your hand off as soon as you go down there.'

'There's no way I'm going anywhere near that monster.'

'Just shut the fuck up then, will you? I'm trying to get to sleep here.'

'You've got to do something about it.'

He didn't open his eyes. 'You spill the beans to anyone about my dog, and you'll be down there with him.'

She wanted to run over and slap him, but she knew him too well to risk upsetting him. Miserably she went into the kitchen to find something to eat. Chewing on a slice of bread, she heard him calling her. Listening closely, she could tell he wasn't drunk.

'Where are you, bitch? This beer's warm! Get in here now, and bring me a cold beer.'

She took him the last two bottles of beer from the fridge.

'Thanks. You're a babe.' He took a swig from one of the bottles. 'I'm starving! Get me something to eat. I need to go out soon.'

As she scurried back to the kitchen to make him a sandwich, she wondered if the dog in the cellar had starved to death yet. However frightened of it she was, she didn't like to think of the creature dying down there, all alone in stinking darkness. She knew how it felt to be alone, hungry and afraid. But she was too scared to complain any more, and she certainly wasn't willing to go down there and feed it herself. Like her, the wretched creature would just have to rely on its owner to take care of it.

19

ON HIS WAY HOME from work, Eddy looked in on his stepmother. He glanced around furtively as he walked up the path, although no one was around, and it wouldn't matter if he was spotted there anyway. He was entitled to visit his stepmother. Luciana didn't need to know that he had already been to see her several times that week. It was not her place to dictate when he could or couldn't see his recently widowed stepmother. Not that he particularly wanted to see his stepmother, although naturally he was concerned to see that she was coping on her own. But he had something very particular to ask her, and if she agreed to his proposal Luciana would benefit too, so he felt no compunction in keeping his visits a secret from his wife. He just wasn't quite sure how to broach the subject with his stepmother. It was awkward. He sat in the front room while she fussed around, fetching him a beer and a slab of cake. When he had finished, he smacked his lips and grinned.

'Thanks mum, that was great.'

He leaned back in his chair and waved away her offer of more cake.

'I couldn't, really. It was great, but I'm stuffed.'

There was a pause.

'So dad's left all this to you?' he asked at last, despairing of finding a subtle way of raising the topic.

His stepmother raised her eyebrows. 'All this? What do you mean?'

He shrugged. 'The house and – everything.'

'Of course he left everything to me. It was ours, and now it's mine. I'm his wife. His widow,' she corrected herself. 'Who else would it go to? But don't worry, the mortgage is paid off. I'll be all right.'

He smiled weakly. He hadn't actually been thinking of her. He hesitated, but now he had started he had to continue.

'He didn't leave anything to me?'

Without a word his stepmother stood up and left the room. He started up too late. Falling back on his chair, he waited anxiously, wondering whether he ought to go after her to check she was all right. She was probably upstairs crying over his selfish question. If he upset her, she might leave him out of her will too and then he really would end up with nothing. Sitting alone, he rehearsed what he might say to her if he went to find her. 'I didn't mean to upset you. We're both cut up about what happened, mum.'

While he was prevaricating, he heard her coming downstairs. To his relief, when she came back in the room she didn't look as though she had been crying. On the contrary, she was smiling as she sat down on a chair facing him.

'He *did* leave something for you,' she said. 'I was just waiting for the right moment to give it to you.'

His spirits gave a leap. For an instant he felt as though he couldn't breathe. If this was what he thought it was, all his troubles would be over. He listened impatiently, trying not to fidget, as she talked about how much his father had cared for him.

'He might not have said much about it while he was alive,' she went on. 'He wasn't a demonstrative man. But he was always proud of you. You know he thought the world of you?'

She paused, as though expecting Eddy to respond.

'I know,' he mumbled. 'Thank you. I thought the world of him too.'

He could barely breathe, almost choking on his anticipation, speculating about how much he was about to receive.

His stepmother held out her hand. 'This is for you,' she said, her smile broadening.

'What is it?' he asked.

Her smile hadn't faltered. She was holding out a small black box.

'Open it.'

After the build-up, his disappointment was acute. Aware that he was gaping, he closed his mouth. He shook his head, unable to speak. It was a very nice watch, doubtless worth a few quid, but it was hardly going to solve his problems.

'It's a watch,' he blurted out, unable to hide his anger.

'Your father wanted you to have it,' she sought to reassure him, misinterpreting his response. 'I bought it for him on our first anniversary, and he wore it every day since then. It's real gold plate,' she added. 'Oh, it wasn't fantastically expensive, but it's the sentimental value, isn't it? You know he wore it all the time.' She smiled.

He was speechless. He had been given a box containing a dead man's watch. In a fury of desperation he pressed on, hardly knowing what he was saying any more.

'Isn't there something else? No money? It's just –' he drew in a deep shuddering breath. 'We're not doing so well right now. We're struggling to make ends meet. You know how it is –'

'You both work, don't you?'

'Yes, I know, but things are – it's all so expensive, bills and –'

'I'm sorry, Eddy, but if you're living beyond your means, you'll have to learn to be more restrained. We didn't bring you up to be extravagant, and if Luciana's turning out to be profligate, you'll just have to rein her in.' She leaned forward, looking concerned. 'Would you like me to have a word with her? I don't like to see you worried like this.'

He felt like throwing the watch in her face. Struggling to suppress his rage, he put the box down. It rested precariously on the arm of his chair. Staring at the floor, he almost broke down and confessed that his debts were spiralling out of control. His stepmother knew nothing about his problems. Luciana was the only person who had discovered the truth but she believed he had stopped now. Once or twice he had almost told his father, but he had never even been tempted to confess to his stepmother, and he was certain Luciana wouldn't have revealed his secret to her.

'She does like to spend,' he mumbled, ashamed of himself for blaming his difficulties on his wife. 'Don't let on that I told you, please.'

'There's no need to look so embarrassed,' his stepmother said kindly. 'This isn't your fault. But you're going to have to talk to Luciana about it. If you're really struggling –'

'Yes?'

'You need to take control of her spending. Tell her it can't go on. Be firm, Eddy. It might not be easy but you're going to have to do it sooner or later, or she'll ruin you.'

Eddy sighed. This was not how he had planned the conversation would go. Miserably he picked up the small black box in which his hopes were buried.

20

ALTHOUGH SHE COULDN'T PUT her finger on what was bothering her, Geraldine couldn't shake off the feeling that something wasn't right about the circumstances surrounding Mark's death. However traumatised they were following a suicide, relatives usually accepted the reality of what had happened. Accusations might be raised about who was responsible for having allowed it to happen, and how it could have been prevented, but this time a question had been raised over whether or not Mark had actually taken his own life. His sister had been so passionate in her demands that the police investigate, it was surprising that nearly a week had passed and she still hadn't followed up her visit with so much as a phone call. She hadn't struck Geraldine as flaky. And now Mark's widow had turned up claiming she was being stalked by some unidentified person. If nothing else, it was all slightly odd.

'Perhaps there's a strain of insanity in the family?' Ariadne had suggested when Geraldine had raised her concerns to her colleague. 'Although it's hardly surprising that people might behave irrationally after a suicide in the family, especially when it was so unexpected. Anyway, he's dead and buried, isn't he? The coroner didn't find anything suspicious.'

By Thursday evening, when Geraldine still hadn't heard from Amanda, she decided to speak to her to establish whether she had been serious in her allegations against Charlotte. Expecting Amanda to climb down and admit that she had been overreacting in her shock at losing her brother, Geraldine phoned her but there was no answer. On her way home from work that evening, on impulse she took a detour to Amanda's house. At least she might be able to put an end to one irritating line of enquiry, and it wasn't as though she had anything else to do. She had just opened the gate, when a voice called out.

'You know she's not in?'

Geraldine looked around and saw a small grey-haired woman standing outside the neighbouring front door.

'I saw you there and wondered if you knew where she was?' the woman called out.

Geraldine approached and introduced herself, explaining in the vaguest terms possible that she was there to talk to Amanda about a recent incident in her family.

'Oh, you mean her brother? Yes, we heard something about that. What a terrible thing to happen.'

'I don't suppose you know when she'll be back?'

'I was about to ask *you* where she's gone, although that's a bit of a stupid question, isn't it, since you've come here looking for her.' The woman gave a little laugh. 'The thing is,' she went on, serious again, 'I need to know where she's gone, and what we're supposed to do with her cat.' She looked expectantly at Geraldine.

'I'm sorry, but I don't know where she is.'

'But what are we going to do with her cat? It's not our responsibility, but someone's got to feed it.'

'I'm not sure what you mean,' Geraldine said, with an uneasy feeling about what she was hearing.

'You'd better come in,' the woman said.

Turning, she led the way indoors and into a small cosily furnished living room, with comfortable armchairs and matching sofa, all upholstered in brown and dark orange fabric.

'It's been scratching at the furniture again,' a middle-aged man grumbled. He paused and raised his eyebrows when Geraldine entered the room. A large black and white cat was sitting on his lap, purring, while he stroked it gently. 'Hello, who's this? Have you come to take this animal off our hands?'

It didn't take long for Geraldine to establish that Amanda had gone away, leaving her cat unattended.

'I can't believe she was the type to abandon a poor animal,' Moira said. 'She always seemed such a sensible woman. And you can see the cat's been well looked after.'

'Too well,' Geoff added, patting the cat. 'We wondered if she'd been rushed to hospital, didn't we?'

'Yes, because there was the shoe she left outside.'

'What shoe?' Geraldine asked.

'It's out in the hall,' Moira answered. 'We didn't know what to do with it, did we, Geoff?'

Geraldine frowned. 'When did you last see your neighbour?'

'It was yesterday, wasn't it, Geoff?' She turned back to Geraldine. 'We wondered whether to say something, you know, report it to the police, and now here you are.'

'What's happened to her then?' Geoff asked.

Geraldine shook her head. 'Nothing as far as we know.'

He looked sceptical. 'How come you're here looking for her then?'

Geraldine did her best to reassure them that she had only turned up to give Amanda information about the circumstances surrounding her brother's death. She could tell the couple weren't convinced, but wasn't sure what else she could say to satisfy their curiosity. There wasn't much more she could do to prevent them spreading rumours about Amanda's disappearance, apart from telling them she hoped their neighbour would return home soon. In the meantime, she could only suggest that Amanda must be taking a holiday.

'But what about this poor creature?' Geoff asked, still stroking the purring cat.

'How could she have gone away and left it like that?' Moira asked indignantly.

'It can't stay here,' Geoff added. 'It's tearing our furniture to shreds.'

Geraldine sighed. 'I suggest you contact the RSPCA if your

neighbour doesn't return soon. They can advise you what to do.'

Despite her reassuring words, Geraldine was perturbed by Amanda's disappearance. And it wasn't only the cat she was worried about.

21

EDDY FIDDLED WITH THE small black box.

'Do you like it?' Charlotte asked anxiously.

He nodded wordlessly, hating himself. It wasn't long before she launched into a complaint about being on her own so much of the time.

'It's not as if dad was here all day,' he replied. 'You must be used to spending time by yourself.'

Not wanting to annoy his stepmother when he had come to ask a favour, he did his best to hide his irritation. He hadn't yet given up all hope of a handout.

'So are you pleased with the hall?' he asked, building gradually to his question.

'Pleased? How can I be pleased when that's where your father...' she broke off in tears.

Cursing under his breath, Eddy waited for her to calm down before continuing.

'I meant are you pleased with what I did, the decorating? Bloody hell, mum, I worked like a slave on that, because you wanted it done straight away. I nearly broke my back getting it done for you.'

Smiling through her tears, she patted his hand. This was more like it.

'It looks lovely,' she said.

'The thing is –' he hesitated. 'The paint came to a lot more than I originally estimated.'

She laughed. 'You sound like a real tradesman.'

'I was happy to do it for you, mum, you know that, but I

101

didn't think you'd want me to be out of pocket over it.'

'Out of pocket? What are you talking about?'

It was an awkward conversation, especially when his request for reimbursement led on to a suggestion that she advance him some of the inheritance he would come into on her death.

'For goodness sake, Eddy,' she remonstrated. 'We've only just buried your father and now you want to talk about what's going to happen when I die. I'm fifty-six! I intend to be around for a good many years yet.'

'And I hope you are,' he answered lamely.

But he did get some cash from her for the paint, which was something. By itself it wasn't much, but it could lead to something a whole lot better, because Eddy had a feeling this was going to be his night. His run of bad luck couldn't continue indefinitely. If he hadn't been convinced of that, he would never have stepped inside a bookies again. That was what Luciana failed to grasp. He wasn't about to throw good money away. He was no fool. It was insulting that she would think that of him. No, he was there to recoup his losses and make sure he ended up quids in, overall. It was just going to take time. He wasn't addicted to gambling, not in the true sense of the word, because that would mean he was incapable of stopping. In fact, he could walk away at any time. But there was no sense in quitting when he was losing. Once he bagged a sizeable win, he would walk out of the bookies, head held high, and never return.

Even his fantastically successful father had encountered setbacks in the course of his career.

'But I never gave up,' he had told Eddy. 'Whatever you do in life, stick with it. That's what gets you through in the end.'

Perseverance was going to solve all of Eddy's problems and make him every bit as successful as his father had been. Temporarily broke, he wasn't going to settle for being a failure. By refusing to give up until he was back on top, before long he would be able to offer Luciana the life he had promised her. It was no more than she deserved. Although she pretended not to care, he knew how hurt she still was by the way her own family had abandoned her after the death of her parents. He was going to right that wrong and give her a life more luxurious than she could ever have hoped to enjoy with her own family. Admittedly he was betting again, having solemnly promised her he was done with gambling, but he wasn't one of those idiots who would keep going regardless of circumstances. He wasn't there for the thrill of the game, he was there to win, and that made all the difference.

He had seen too many guys make a packet only to lose it all because they kept going long after any sensible person would have stopped. He had done that himself in the past. But having learned his lesson the hard way, he was wiser now, and ready to walk away with his pockets stuffed full of cash. But before he could finish with the bookies for good, he had to bag that win. Although it was proving elusive right now, he refused to be put off. The whole venture had always been a test of nerve. Not everyone understood that. Like most people, Luciana lacked the grit to keep going when things went against her. If only she wasn't so impatient, she would appreciate that he wasn't a fool frittering away his hard-earned cash. But she steadfastly refused to acknowledge the sense behind his strategy. In the end he had caved in to her demands, and promised to stop gambling.

For a while, he had kept his word. But the lure of winning was too powerful, even for someone as strong-willed as him. He knew Luciana would accuse him of being weak if she found out he had relapsed, but the reality was very different. He was a man of vision, and he knew that if he was tenacious enough, he was bound to win eventually. Given enough chances, he really couldn't lose, and this time he would be clever enough to leave at the right time, when he was ahead, not like the other losers he saw placing their bets with no hope of ever coming out on top. In any case, he had now lost so much he really no longer had any choice. He had to recoup his debt or Luciana might never forgive his deception.

He could imagine her endlessly haranguing him. 'We're ruined!' and 'How can I ever trust you again? It's not just that you're gambling again, but you lied to me.'

In a way she would be right, but it was her intransigence that had driven him to be so secretive. He would have been happy to share his plans and dreams with her if she had been open-minded. Donning the cap he wore at such times as a kind of rough disguise, he pushed the door open and slipped into a different world where no one judged him, and no one even cared whether he won or lost. Sometimes he exchanged a brief glance with someone else placing a bet, their eyes sliding rapidly away from one another with a faint smile of complicity. Occasionally, they might wish each other good luck but mostly they went about their affairs in silence, each engrossed in their own private rituals that would bring good fortune.

He felt both tension and a sense of liberation as he placed his bet, because this was the only place where he felt no guilt. The secret he was compelled to conceal was out in the open here, and no one condemned or criticised him, or even noticed what he was doing. In this place, gambling was not merely acceptable, it was the norm. He took a deep breath, considering the horses listed for the next race. When he was a teenager, long before he met Luciana, his father used to take him to the races at The Knavesmire. Closing his eyes, he tried to recall every detail of the experience: bookies shouting out the odds, horses stamping past, jockeys flying by, women in fancy frocks, their companions drinking and smoking and laughing, everyone joyous on their day out. He had never seen his father look so happy as when they were at the races together, just the two of them.

'This one's for you, dad,' he whispered as he placed his bet, adding as an afterthought, 'and I hope you rot in hell.'

If his father had left him even a quarter of his estate, Eddy's life would be so different now. It was no matter. He didn't need anyone else bailing him out. He would sort out his problems himself. With a sudden rush of confidence, he increased his bet. He was one of life's winners and soon everyone would know about it.

22

EVEN THOUGH IT WAS Friday Matt was in a foul mood, and Suzie was predictably bad-tempered that early in the morning. It was disappointing but hardly surprising that they were having a row.

'You're like a bear with a sore head,' she complained. 'I don't know what you've got to be grumpy about. You like your job. You like working there. You can have a laugh with your colleagues. What the hell have you got to be miserable about?'

'Are you joking?'

Her blue eyes blazed at him. Turning back to the road, his attention was caught by what looked like a body lying on the grass verge. He slammed on the brakes.

'What the hell are you doing?' Suzie cried out.

Without answering, he slowed down and pulled into the side of the road.

'What's going on? Why are we stopping? Matt, I'll be late.'

Ignoring her cries, he leapt out of the car. Running towards the bundle of clothes, his fears were confirmed as he saw that it was in fact a person lying motionless by the roadside. At the same time, he became aware of a faint whining noise.

'I think someone needs help over here!' he panted, slowing down to a walk and advancing cautiously, afraid of what he might find.

Reluctant to investigate further, he was tempted to turn round and call the emergency services from the car, but he kept going. If someone had collapsed at the side of the road, he might be able to help. The buzzing sound grew louder as he approached the bundle, and he detected a fetid smell. Reaching the prone figure he stooped over it, and a small cloud of flies rose from what he could now see was a woman lying on the ground. Cursing himself for having left his phone in the car, he shouted out to Suzie.

'Oh Jesus, call an ambulance! No, call the police. Call both!'

He heard Suzie shouting back at him from the car. 'What's going on, Matt?'

He knew he should feel for a pulse and check whether the woman was still breathing, but he couldn't bring himself to touch her. He crouched beside her, staring at the hump of her torso. The woman was lying on her side, her face half hidden from view. Mud was splattered over her legs and back, her feet were bare, and she appeared to be wearing a dressing gown. The side of her face that was visible looked crushed, her nose crooked as though it had been broken, and there was a clear indentation across the middle of her body. It didn't take a genius to see that she had been run over. He wondered what she had been doing, walking out there alone in her night clothes, with no shoes.

As he straightened up, he realised that Suzie was yelling at him.

'Have you called an ambulance?' he shouted back at her. It looked like a hit and run, which meant the police would need to be involved. 'You'd better call the police as well.'

Wanting to protect Suzie from seeing the dead woman, he called out to her to stay where she was, but it was too late. She was already out of the car and coming towards him. Catching sight of the body lying beside him, she screamed.

'Call an ambulance, will you?' he repeated.

'Is she all right, Matt? Is she –?'

He turned towards Suzie. 'I think she's dead.'

'Is she breathing? Has she got a pulse? Shouldn't we be giving her – I don't know. What is it we're supposed to do? Matt, do something! Resuscitate her!'

'Calm down and call 999. There's nothing else we can do. Tell them a woman's been run over. Do it, now!'

He could see Suzie shaking. 'I don't know if I'll get a signal out here,' she muttered, but a few seconds later he heard her talking rapidly.

'Please hurry,' she gabbled. 'The woman's dead. She's dead.'

Staring at the battered face beside him, Matt sighed. It didn't make any difference to the dead woman how long the ambulance took to arrive.

'Can we go now?' Suzie whispered. 'I mean, do we have to stay here?'

Seeing her shiver, Matt told her to go and wait for him in the car. When she remonstrated about leaving him there on his own, he insisted.

'Come back to the car with me, then,' she said.

He didn't want to stay where he was but, irrationally, he felt it would be disrespectful to abandon his post. There was no one else to watch over the dead woman.

'We can watch her from the car,' Suzie added. She was shivering. 'Come on, let's go. It's cold standing around here. It's not as if there's anything we can do for her.'

Matt's girlfriend needed his support; the dead woman wouldn't appreciate his presence. All the same, he shook his head and said that he would stay where he was until the police arrived.

'It just feels like the right thing to do,' he mumbled.

'Well, I'm going back to the car. I don't want to hang around a stiff. She could be diseased. Come with me, Matt. Please!' She hesitated when he shook his head. 'Oh, suit yourself. Although I don't know what you think might happen to her now. You said yourself she's been run over. It's not as if you knew her.'

'It won't be for long. The emergency services know we are here, don't they? You phoned them.'

With a shrug, Suzie went back to the car. Matt wondered whether she was right. The dead woman was a stranger to them. If he hadn't discovered her body, he wouldn't have been particularly interested in hearing about the victim of a hit and run. His own sense of shock was already fading and the whole incident was beginning to feel like nothing more than a serious inconvenience. He had no idea how long they would have to hang around there, waiting for the police and ambulance to arrive. A moment ago he had been afraid the sight of the battered face of the corpse would haunt him afterwards. It was strange how being there had made him feel involved with this woman. But the feeling had been transient. He had never even spoken to the woman during her lifetime. She meant nothing to him. He was shocked by how rapidly he had become disengaged.

'She's dead,' he whispered, trying to rekindle the fleeting sense of grief that had gripped him only a few moments earlier.

He straightened up, his thoughts already drifting away from the dead woman as he stretched his aching knees and rehearsed what he was going to say to his colleagues at work. Only a moment ago he had felt somehow responsible for watching over his find. Now he just wanted to leave this desolate place and get to work. He was gripped by a sudden sense of futility, as though he had glimpsed into an abyss. A human being's death ought to matter more than this.

23

IT WAS GENERALLY QUIET during the day, but at night she was sure she could hear the animal whining and whimpering. Occasionally she thought it let out a long low howl. Never a sound sleeper, her nights were now disturbed not only by bad dreams, but the thought of what was in the cellar, only a few feet below where she was lying in bed. When she asked him what he would do if the beast clawed its way up through the floorboards, he laughed at her and slapped her cheeks playfully, forcing her head back against the pillow.

'I told you, he's tied up, you stupid bitch. Nothing and no one can break that chain. There's no way it's getting out of there.' She tried to keep her head still as he gave her another slap. 'You think I want that fucking animal running amok around here? Bloody hell, you saw what it did to me. Imagine what it would do to you. Look!'

Wincing, he pulled back his grubby sleeve and held up his arm to display an ugly wound. The blood had dried and formed a large scab around which the skin looked pink and puffy. When she reached out and touched it gently with the tip of one finger, he drew back with a curse.

'Fuck off out of it, you stupid cow.'

'Does it hurt that bad?' she asked. 'It shouldn't still hurt, not after all this time. You need to get that seen to.'

'What are you talking about, you stupid bitch? Of course it bloody hurts.' He frowned, extending his neck to peer down at his arm. 'If that brute comes near me again, I'll kill it.'

'If it doesn't get you first,' she muttered.

'What did you say?'

'Nothing. I never said anything.'

She slid down under the covers in an attempt to hide her shaking, inhaling the bodily smells of sweat and flatulence, warm as hot sausages. Sometimes it excited him to see how much he frightened her, but at other times her fear provoked his anger, and she could never predict which way he was going to flip. It depended on how high he was, and why, and that was anybody's guess because he wasn't choosy. Anything that made him high would do. They had that in common at least, although there was very little else about him that she understood. Most of his actions baffled her, like why he was keeping that creature locked in the cellar.

'Why would you do it?'

She hadn't intended to ask the question out loud. Fortunately for her he was feeling lazy and just laughed at her. With a sigh he lay down beside her and began stroking her hair.

'I'm not going to let that hound down there hurt you,' he said kindly. 'But I've got to keep it for a while. You just have to trust me. I'll keep you safe.'

When he was nice to her it made her want to cry because she wanted him to be like this all the time.

'You need to get that arm seen to,' she repeated. 'If it gets infected, you might get sick. Really sick. If your blood gets poisoned it can kill you.'

His good humour vanished in an instant. 'How come you're suddenly the expert?' He grabbed her hair and yanked it until she yelped. 'What makes you such a big mouth? Are you a doctor all of a sudden?' He released her. 'You don't know jack shit.'

'I know your own blood can kill you if it turns to poison. I know it's true because it happened to a mate of mine.'

'You got no mates.'

'She had a bite, like that, only they thought hers was from a rat, and anyway she never went to no doctor and she ended up with septicaemia and it killed her stone dead. You want to get that seen to.'

'Don't talk shit. You said yourself that whore was bitten by a rat. What I got down in the cellar is more dangerous than a fucking rat.'

He laughed and slapped her face again, his good humour restored. She lay there in silence for a while but it wasn't long before she thought she heard the beast whining again.

'If you ask me, it's scared of the dark,' she said.

'Who's scared of the dark?'

'That animal. That's why it keeps howling at night.'

'Don't talk bollocks. You can't hear it through that floor. It's concrete. If it wasn't for the air vent, it wouldn't even be able to breathe down there.'

'I hope it suffocates.'

'For the last time, bitch, no one's getting rid of that animal. I'm more likely to get rid of you if you don't shut up.'

'What you keeping it for?'

He grunted and didn't bother to answer.

'Where did you get it from anyway?'

'What business is that of yours? What's with all the questions? How come you're so nosey all of a sudden, poking around in my business?'

'I just wondered, no reason, only I never saw a dog like that before.'

He half sat up and grinned. 'That's because it's a special. A one off. A rare breed. A rare crossbreed, I should say. Pit bull and Rottweiler.' He punched the air. 'There aren't many people can control a beast like that.'

She didn't point out that he hadn't done a very good job of controlling it himself, before he had managed to lock it in the cellar. She might not know much, but she knew she wasn't alone in being frightened of the giant dog.

24

HAVING DONE WHAT SHE could to discover the truth, Geraldine rang Amanda to say there was no evidence to support the allegation that her brother had been murdered. There was no answer, so Geraldine left a message. That evening she tried again, but there was still no reply.

'It's complicated,' she told Ariadne the following morning. 'And I'm not sure whether I should be doing anything.'

'Careful what you admit to,' Ariadne warned Geraldine in a stage whisper, 'there's an inspector listening.'

Geraldine looked around and saw Ian Peterson standing behind her.

'Don't mind me,' he laughed. 'So, what's Geraldine plotting now?'

Ariadne looked slightly surprised. Evidently she wasn't aware that Geraldine and Ian had worked together years before, when she had been an inspector and he had been newly promoted to sergeant.

'Geraldine's always up to something,' he added with a conspiratorial wink.

'Do you two know each other, then?'

'We used to work together, years ago,' Geraldine replied.

'I thought...' Ariadne broke off. 'Oh, nothing.'

'So you were saying?' Ian prompted Geraldine.

As he spoke, Naomi came over and joined them. She often seemed to turn up when Ian was around. Geraldine wasn't sure she wanted to share her concerns with so many of her colleagues, but there was no help for it. Briefly she explained Amanda's suspicions.

'He was found hanging, wasn't he?' Ian asked.

'Yes, that's the one. Anyway, I looked into it but I couldn't find anything to suggest he'd been murdered.'

'People don't always advertise it beforehand when they're planning to top themselves,' Naomi said. 'But I can't believe you took it seriously, just because his sister said he didn't kill himself.'

Geraldine told them Mark had been making holiday plans and arranging a game of tennis with a colleague the night before he died.

'There isn't always a rational explanation when someone takes their own life,' Naomi said firmly. She turned to Ian. 'Are you going to the pub this evening?'

That seemed to end the conversation and they all drifted back to their desks. Geraldine was ready for a break, when Ian came to find her. He looked tense as he told her the pathologist wanted to see them. Geraldine nodded, understanding Ian's reluctance to attend an autopsy.

'I'll go,' she replied, and he smiled his relief.

Always happy to seize an excuse to leave her desk, Geraldine set out for the mortuary mystified as to why Jonah wanted to see her when no murder had been reported. Avril smiled when she arrived. Geraldine wasn't sure it was actually a good thing that her face had so quickly become familiar to the anatomical pathology technician. Without stopping to chat, Geraldine put on a protective suit and went in to see Jonah who was standing beside the table, the corpse of a stout woman stretched out in front of him. Geraldine looked down at the body and drew in a sharp breath.

'Her name –' Jonah began.

'I know who she is,' Geraldine interrupted him. 'Amanda Abbott. What happened to her?'

Jonah's smile faded. 'This was called in as a hit and run.'

'She was run over? What a terrible coincidence. Her brother

committed suicide three weeks ago. And now this accident –'

'It wasn't an accident.'

'How do you know?'

'Because by the time this vehicle drove over her, she couldn't have run anywhere.'

'I'm not sure that I follow you,' Geraldine replied, although she had an uncomfortable feeling she knew exactly what he meant.

'She'd been dead for some hours by the time she was run over.'

'So this was a murder set up to look like an accident?'

'It's looking that way.'

Geraldine frowned. 'Her brother's death could have been a murder set up to look like suicide.' She stared down at the body of the woman who had been so forceful and full of life. 'How did she die?'

'She was strangled.' Jonah pointed to dark weals on the victim's neck.

'Could it have been an accident?'

'No chance.'

Geraldine nodded. She had expected that response. 'What else can you tell me?'

Jonah shrugged. 'We found a few traces of some material on her neck and they've gone off for examination.'

'How long has she been dead?'

'She was killed yesterday, probably late afternoon, maybe around five or six o'clock. It's difficult to be precise about the time of death because she was left outside overnight. The body was only brought in late this morning. It was spotted by a passing driver at the edge of the Tadcaster Road where it had been lying all night. I'll let you have a detailed report when I've finished my examination. But in the meantime I wanted to alert you to the fact that we're looking at a murder here.'

'Is there anything else to go on?'

He shook his head. 'Just some mud and other detritus on the back of her clothes, where she'd been dragged along the ground. That might be able to tell us something. I'll let you know if we discover anything. I know you've had your suspicions about her brother's death, so I thought you'd be particularly interested in this one.'

Geraldine thanked him. He was right. She most definitely was interested.

An apparently baseless accusation had turned into a double murder case. Despite her better nature, she couldn't help feeling excited. Not only had her instincts been proved right, but she had a complex case to work on.

Driving through heavy traffic along the Tadcaster Road towards Leeds, Geraldine looked out for a white forensic tent. It was a pity no one had noticed the body sooner. As she drove along she wondered whether it could conceivably be coincidence, Amanda's murder following so soon after Mark's apparent suicide. Amanda's death could have been a revenge killing, but it was more likely that she had threatened to expose her brother's killer. Alternatively, a killer could be targeting Mark and Amanda's family, for reasons so far unknown to the police.

She pulled up just before the cordon that closed off one lane of the busy road. The clouds had cleared, allowing the sun to warm the air. Treading carefully along the common approach path, she pulled on her protective suit and entered the tent. A small team of white-suited scene of crime officers were busy scrutinising the ground, collecting samples and taking photographs. They worked in silence, absorbed in their search. One of them glanced up and greeted Geraldine.

'Being exposed to the open air and the weather, everything's deteriorated since the victim was killed,' he said with a rueful shrug. 'And unfortunately there was a heavy shower last night, which doesn't help, although the ground had mostly dried out by the time we got here. And then to cap it all, the whole scene's been contaminated by the idiot who found her trampling all around the body.'

The scene of crime officer raised his eyebrows and whistled as Geraldine explained that the victim had been strangled, and run over after she was dead.

'So this was set up to look like a road accident?'

'Only whoever killed her didn't do a very good job of covering up the murder.'

'Yes, a bit clumsy, wasn't it? We all realised there was something not right about the scene.'

If this was the work of the same killer who had faked Mark's suicide, he had done a far better job first time around. Either Amanda had been despatched by a different hand, or the killer had been in a hurry with her, perhaps because he had attacked her in an exposed place.

'Was she killed here?' she asked.

'It's difficult to say for sure, with so many footprints. But there's no sign of a struggle where the body was found, or anywhere round about.'

Geraldine nodded. 'It's unlikely she would have been strangled at the side of the road, where anyone could have driven past while she was being attacked. Was she brought here from the fields? There was mud on her clothes.'

'Analysis of the soil on her clothes should be able to establish that.'

'Have you managed to find out anything about her killer?'

'We've got some partial footprints, quite distinct from those of the couple who found her. It's not much, but it's enough to establish that we're probably looking for a man, maybe with size ten feet. There's no evidence of another vehicle stopping here, or of anyone arriving on foot, so it appears she was brought here in the vehicle that ran over her.'

'After she was dead.'

'Yes. She was transported here in a van.'

He gave Geraldine details of the tyres, which were quite common.

LEIGH RUSSELL

'Not very helpful, I know,' he added. 'But there was quite a lot of debris on her clothes so we've sent various samples off for analysis.'

'What kind of debris?'

'Difficult to say really. There was mud, and bits of grit probably from the road here.'

'I'm not sure mud's going to tell us very much,' Geraldine said, frowning.

'You'd be surprised. They might find all sorts of traces, not just mud. They can identify minerals, microscopic traces of plant life, even animal waste, and – well, it's incredible what they can detect.'

Geraldine nodded. Her colleague was right. The evidence would not only confirm that Amanda had been dead when she had been brought to the roadside, it might help identify where she had been killed. Leaving him to his work, Geraldine went back outside. The scene of crime officers were examining every centimetre of the site, looking for potential evidence. She would only be in the way. Peeling off her protective outer clothing, she walked slowly back to her car. The body had been deposited beside a field in an open area, empty and bleak. Cars sped by, carrying anonymous drivers and passengers. Drawing level with the tent, traffic slowed down momentarily, the drivers' curiosity aroused by the crime scene. Without knowing it, they were right to be puzzled. The crime scene was baffling.

Back at the police station, Geraldine's colleagues shared her suspicions.

'It does make you question whether Mark's death was suicide, don't you think?' Naomi asked, as they waited for Eileen to arrive and begin the formal briefing.

Ian shrugged. 'That's what Geraldine's been saying all along. I told you she's usually right about these things. She has an uncanny instinct for the truth.'

Geraldine smiled, momentarily buoyed up by his comment. 'It was just a feeling I had,' she said, dismissing the compliment.

118

'It's dangerous to be influenced by an unsubstantiated hunch.'

Ian smiled at her. 'True, but still, your random hunches do have a way of turning out to be right.'

Although pleased by Ian's praise, Geraldine hoped she would be proved wrong in this case and they wouldn't be looking for a serial killer who might strike again at any moment.

25

'NOW HIS SISTER'S BEEN murdered,' Eileen said, 'we have to re-examine Mark's suicide. We'll keep an open mind on whether he was murdered or took his own life. But –' she broke off and shook her head.

Whispers of consternation rippled through the assembled team. No one wanted to be working on a double murder case.

'And if someone's killed twice, what's to say there won't be more victims?' Naomi said, wide-eyed.

'Let's not start any pesky nonsense like that,' Eileen barked. 'We'll have no talk of serial killers or mass murders here, please. So far we have one probable suicide and one murder.'

There was a general murmur of consent, but Geraldine wondered how many of her colleagues were still in any doubt over whether Mark had been murdered. Meanwhile, there were several perplexing aspects to the circumstances surrounding Amanda's death, and the subsequent dumping of her body on the Tadcaster Road. The fact that her feet were bare was puzzling. When a pair of women's slippers was found not far from where her body was lying, the discovery hardly helped. Muddy and ripped, they were the right size for her and appeared to have been torn off her feet when her body had been run over.

'But what was she doing out there in her nightie, dressing gown and slippers?' Eileen asked. 'It suggests she was killed at home, but there's no sign of any struggle in her house. And if she went out willingly, why didn't she put on her shoes?'

After the briefing, tasks were allocated, and Geraldine drove to Amanda's house where the forensic team were still out in force searching for any trace of the killer's identity. With the road outside the house reopened for access, a small group of local residents had gathered on the pavement, curious to know what had happened. Cynically, Geraldine wondered whether any of them had shown as much interest in Amanda while she had been alive.

'Don't you people have homes to go to?' a uniformed constable was grumbling at them with a good-natured grin.

'Can someone please tell us what's going on?' a young man asked.

'What's happened to the woman who lives here?' another voice chipped in.

As she approached the house, Geraldine saw a blonde reporter with red lipstick and a red jumper, waving a Dictaphone in front of the police officer. Glancing round, the blonde woman recognised Geraldine and dashed towards her, blocking her way.

'Is this another murder?' the blonde woman demanded, her voice shrill with excitement.

'I'm sorry. We don't have any information for you yet.'

Predictably, the reporter insisted that Geraldine tell her whatever the police knew. 'The public have a right to know,' she screeched. 'You can't stay silent on such an important matter.'

'Yes,' another woman chimed in, 'we have a right to know.'

'At the moment all we have is mere speculation,' Geraldine replied, concealing her irritation with a smile. 'As soon as we have any news worth reporting, we'll hold a press conference. If you don't want to wait along with everyone else, you can give your number to one of the constables. You know we work through the night, but I take it you'd be happy to be contacted at any time? Now if you'll excuse me, I have to get on and I'm sure you wouldn't want to obstruct us in our investigation.'

'Can you confirm this is a murder investigation?'

Without answering, Geraldine pushed her way past the

strident blonde woman. The uniformed constable moved aside to let her through, and stepped smartly back into position before anyone could follow her. As she hurried up the path to the front door, Geraldine could hear the reporter demanding answers to her questions. Hardly significant in the context of what had occurred, attention from the media was still unwelcome, and this was just the beginning. Until the case was closed it was only going to get worse. At best the intrusion was merely an irritating distraction, but there was a risk of it turning public opinion against the investigating police team and deterring potential witnesses from coming forward.

Ignoring the voices clamouring behind her, Geraldine hurriedly pulled on a white protective suit and plastic overshoes. Once she was inside, she stared around the hallway. Even with scene of crime officers photographing everything in sight, and checking and testing all the contents of the house including personal bric-a-brac, the police were no closer to wrapping the case up. In spite of scene of crime officers crawling all over the stairs and along the hall, the house looked tidy. Glancing around, Geraldine noticed a shoe matching the one that Moira had found on Amanda's doorstep. So Amanda hadn't been wearing them and lost one on her way out of the house. Geraldine frowned, wondering why one shoe would be inside the house and the other one outside, but such speculation could only get her so far. What they needed was more hard evidence. She changed her protective suit and overshoes before making her way out into the back garden where several white-suited scene of crime officers were busy examining the grass and shrubs, gathering samples, and taking photographs.

After watching for a moment, she called out to the nearest officer and asked him what, if anything, had been discovered. He paused in his close scrutiny of a patch of grass and straightened up.

'There's nothing here to suggest a struggle.'

'Have you found anything at all?'

The scene of crime officer shook his head. 'So far as we've been able to tell, no one else has been in the house or garden recently.'

Geraldine gazed around the garden, so lush and full of life, remembering the robust woman who had harangued her just a few days ago.

'I wonder why she was killed,' she said quietly. 'And what one of her shoes was doing outside the house.'

The scene of crime officer didn't answer. He seemed to understand that she was talking to herself. In any case, his job was to establish what had been done, not to speculate about why it had happened. Geraldine gazed in silence at the carefully tended garden, wondering who would take care of it now that Amanda was dead.

By the time Geraldine returned to the police station, everyone seemed to share the view that Mark's suicide had been faked. If it had been the other way round, with a murder followed by a suicide, the second death might have been a distressed reaction to the first, but it hardly seemed likely that a suicide would prompt a murder. With Amanda's murder calling into question whether Mark had really taken his own life, Eileen raised the possibility that a killer might be targeting the family. The procedure to exhume Mark's body had already been set in motion.

When both Ariadne and Naomi told her independently they had suspected all along that Mark's suicide had been faked, Geraldine smiled to herself, and held back from asking why they hadn't voiced their opinions earlier. Eileen was intimidating, and Naomi was clearly doing her best to impress the detective chief inspector. Geraldine wondered whether Ariadne might also be angling for promotion. Since her demotion Geraldine had no chance of advancing in her career and very little to lose by opposing her senior officer's views. Observing her colleagues, she appreciated for the first time how wonderfully liberating it was to have fallen off the career ladder. She had never regarded herself as a maverick officer, but the prospect of acting without fear of the consequences to her professional reputation was exhilarating.

'What are you grinning about?' Ian asked her, seeing her smiling to herself as she sat at her desk.

'Oh, nothing.'

'You're usually so earnest,' he persisted. 'Is it because the old battleaxe has come round to your way of thinking?'

Geraldine shrugged. 'Something like that.'

She looked away, deflated by his comment. Was that how he saw her, as serious and intense? It made her sound boring. Perhaps she was. With a dismissive sniff, she focused her attention on her screen, muttering about having work to do. While they waited for the results of DNA tests on all the traces of blood and skin that could be found in Amanda's house, Ian set to work coordinating a team to question all the neighbours of both victims. Geraldine barely had time to register that he had elected to work with Naomi before she settled down to investigate Mark and Amanda's family background. It was possible the reason for their deaths lay in their common past.

Neither Mark nor his sister had left York where they had grown up. On their father's death, their mother had continued to live in the family home with Amanda who had cared for her and kept the house when her mother had died. Both of the parents had died years ago of natural causes. The property had been left to Amanda, but there was nothing to suggest that Mark had disputed his mother's will. Established in a lucrative career, he had his own expensive property by then, and wasn't reliant on inheriting anything from his parents' estate. By contrast, Amanda's will was controversial. She hadn't named any of her brother's family, choosing instead to leave her entire estate to a cousin in Wales who ran a home for stray cats.

The only interesting discovery that day came from the team examining CCTV film from the area around Amanda's house that spotted a dark van driving in the vicinity two hours before the probable time of her death. The same vehicle was also identified driving along the Tadcaster Road the evening before her body was discovered. The times fitted. But the van couldn't be traced as it was using false licence plates. They might have found how Amanda's body had been transported to the roadside, but they were no closer to discovering the identity of her killer.

26

GERALDINE WONDERED WHETHER THEIR mother's house had been a source of friction between Amanda and her brother. The following morning she decided to pursue her investigation by looking into their relationship. Charlotte looked vaguely irritated when she came to the door. Although her eyes were no longer bloodshot, she seemed exhausted and dazed. Geraldine wondered if her doctor had prescribed her something to help her cope with the shock.

'I've told you people everything I know,' she said, speaking in a slightly slurred voice. 'Can't you go away and leave me in peace?'

Nevertheless, she led the way submissively enough into the living room.

'Amanda dead?' Charlotte repeated, staring blankly at Geraldine who had just given her the news. 'What do you mean, she's dead?'

Geraldine repeated her account of what had happened. Although Charlotte appeared to be listening, she didn't say anything.

'Did you hear what I said?' Geraldine asked after they had sat in silence for a few moments.

Charlotte continued staring blankly at her. 'My husband's dead,' she whispered at last. 'What am I going to do with myself now? I know he was older than me, and I knew he might die first, but not yet. I'm too young to be left on my own like this.'

Speaking very slowly, Geraldine repeated what she had said

about Amanda. 'Charlotte, can you think of anyone who might have wanted to kill her?'

The widow shook her head. 'They said it was suicide,' she mumbled. 'They said he killed himself.'

It took a while for Geraldine to get through to Charlotte that she hadn't come there to talk about her husband's death. Eventually Charlotte seemed to grasp that Amanda had been murdered, and Geraldine repeated her question.

'Can you think of anyone who might have wanted to kill her?'

Charlotte shook her head. 'What's going on?' she whispered. 'Why is everyone dying? What's happening?'

Geraldine shook her head. 'That's what we're trying to find out. Charlotte, can you think of anyone who might have wanted to kill your husband and sister-in-law?'

'I don't know, I don't know.'

'Charlotte, are you feeling all right?'

'Of course I'm not all right. My husband's dead.'

'Have you been to see your doctor? They might be able to help you.'

'Oh yes, the doctor. She gave me some pills, but they just make me feel tired.' She shrugged. 'How can pills help me when my husband's dead? They won't bring him back, will they?'

'How did you feel about your mother-in-law leaving her house to Amanda?' Geraldine asked, changing the subject abruptly.

Intending to catch Charlotte off guard, Geraldine was disappointed by her response.

'Amanda lived with her, so obviously she kept the house,' Charlotte replied, sniffing vigorously. 'We all knew Amanda would inherit just about everything. And before you ask, no, of course we weren't happy about it, but we didn't need the money and Amanda had nowhere else to go. If she hadn't kept the house, where would she have gone? What were we supposed to do with her? We weren't going to have her come and live here. In any case, we thought she'd leave everything to Eddy when she died anyway. I mean, we assumed... although knowing Amanda she's probably left everything to her cat. We never spoke to her about it. We weren't on bad terms or anything like that. I mean, there wasn't an argument, but it's not as if she ever gave us so much as the time of day when she was alive. She only ever thought about herself. Oh,' she broke off, embarrassed, 'I don't mean to speak ill of the dead. She wasn't a bad person, but she was difficult. She kept herself to herself, and that suited us. We weren't close, but I had nothing against her. She never did us any harm.'

Geraldine wondered whether Charlotte had any idea that Amanda had been to the police to accuse her of murdering her husband, but nothing would be gained from letting her know. It was a dreadful accusation to level against someone – unless it was true.

'So you were expecting Amanda to leave her house to Eddy?'

Charlotte hedged, sensing that she had said too much already. 'Well, it makes sense, doesn't it? I mean, she is family, after all, and it's not as if she's got anyone else.'

Geraldine pressed her to continue, but it was no use. Charlotte was careful to say nothing further against her sister-in-law. She didn't mention her previous allegation that she had been stalked, and Geraldine made no reference to it. Leaving, she went to speak to Eddy who lived about three miles away from his stepmother, in a small house on the other side of the city. Brushing her long black hair off her face with the back of her hand, Luciana scowled at her visitor as she opened the door. Without any make-up, her skin was pasty and she looked far less attractive than when Geraldine had seen her at the funeral. As she turned her head to the light, fine lines were visible on her forehead and around her eyes.

'Oh, it's you,' she said ungraciously. 'What do you want?'

Before Geraldine could answer, Eddy joined her in the doorway. 'Yes? Can we help you?'

Thin and wiry, he spoke softly, with a nasal quality to his voice that made it sound as though he was whining, and his hazel eyes narrowed when he saw Geraldine. Used to people's expressions altering when they saw her, especially when she came to call on them at home, she wasn't bothered by his air of faint hostility.

'I'd like to have another word with you,' she said. 'It won't take long.'

Eddy frowned. 'Do we have a choice?'

'Mark died over a month ago,' Luciana said. 'Do you really have to come here and rake it all up again? Can't you see how your questions upset Eddy? You've got no business coming here and pestering us like this.' She nodded at her husband. 'You go back inside, love. I'll deal with this.' She turned back to Geraldine. 'If you've got any more questions, you can ask me.'

'Actually, I'd like to have a word with both of you,' she said. 'This isn't about Mark, at least not directly.'

'What do you mean?' Luciana asked, putting one hand on her husband's arm.

Eddy seemed more shocked than his stepmother had been to hear of Amanda's death.

'You'd better come in then,' Luciana said.

Eddy remonstrated that Geraldine had no right to come barging into their home, disturbing their evening, but Luciana quietened him.

'She's only doing her job,' she said. 'We might as well find out what she wants and get it over with.'

Eddy confirmed that his aunt hadn't got on with his parents, and for that reason he hadn't known Amanda very well. Luciana said little while her husband talked, but sat watching him protectively.

'I don't know what you expect *me* to say,' she replied when

Geraldine asked her about Amanda. 'I hardly knew Eddy's aunt. I only met her a few times even though she didn't live far away. She seemed like a decent woman.'

'Was there a falling out?' Geraldine asked.

Eddy shrugged. 'My aunt and grandmother used to come to us every year on Christmas Day. But after my father remarried, they stopped coming. I don't think there was an argument or anything like that. They just stopped coming round. My father grumbled about it a bit, but my stepmother said there was nothing she could do if they didn't want to come round. There was no point in asking them over if they always refused, and it only caused rows between my mother and father.'

'Rows?'

'Yes, he wanted to keep asking them over and my stepmother said there was no point. She was right, because they never came anyway. Then my grandmother died and my stepmother said there wasn't any point in asking my aunt. I don't think my father was really that bothered any more.'

'Just because someone's family doesn't mean you have to get on with them,' Luciana interjected. 'That's not a crime, is it?'

27

'IT CAN'T BE COINCIDENCE, a brother and sister dying so soon after one another. There's something going on that we don't know about. But we'll find it.'

While they waited for the results of the exhumation of Mark's body, the team had assembled for a briefing. Geraldine almost felt sorry for the detective chief inspector. Eileen clearly wanted to stay in control of the investigation, but she was hardly likely to retain that responsibility if the case grew beyond the scope of the regional team. As they were talking, information arrived from the forensic laboratory. Microscopic fibres from the cord used to strangle Amanda came from a rope similar to the one used to hang Mark. It stretched credulity to suggest that this was another coincidence. Eileen was forced to abandon the theory that Mark's death had been suicide. The similarity between the rope used in both deaths seemed conclusive proof that the two were connected.

'So we're looking at a double murder,' Eileen said heavily. 'And to make matters worse, Mark's been buried for over a week. We've lost so much time and possible evidence.'

'Do you think both murders were planned all along in advance?' Geraldine asked. 'Or was Amanda killed because she knew, or discovered something, about the circumstances of her brother's death?'

There was a murmur around the room as colleagues responded to the question.

Eileen looked at Geraldine. 'You spoke to Amanda, didn't you? What do you think?'

'I'd say Mark's murder was thought out very carefully. We don't yet know how the killer managed it, but at the time only his sister suspected it was anything other than suicide. No one else even questioned whether he might have been murdered. It was a very slick job. To pull it off would have taken considerable planning. By contrast, Amanda's murder was clumsy and careless. The attempt to pass her death off as a hit and run was really amateurish. It didn't take the pathologist long to see through it, and the SOCOs suspected something wasn't right at the scene before the body had even been removed for examination. Any one of us could have worked out that all her injuries from the vehicle happened after she was dead, even apart from the markings on her neck where she'd been strangled.'

'Are you suggesting they weren't victims of the same killer?' Ian asked.

'Which would mean we've got two different killers using the same rope,' Ariadne pointed out. 'There has to be a connection, at least. Two killers working together if it wasn't the same killer.'

'It's possible two killers were working together,' Ian said.

'Or perhaps there's only one killer and he was in a hurry, and didn't have time to plan out the second murder properly,' Geraldine suggested.

Eileen frowned. '"Properly" is hardly a word I'd use to describe what happened.'

'Or maybe he wasn't planning to kill her just then, but the opportunity came up and he seized it,' Geraldine went on. 'My guess is that Mark was murdered in a meticulously planned attack that left nothing to suggest he had been killed. Amanda seems to have been alone in refusing to believe her brother had committed suicide.'

'Why was she sceptical?' Eileen asked.

Geraldine thought for a second. 'She was adamant that her brother wasn't the kind of man who would kill himself.'

'What does that mean?' Eileen pressed her.

Geraldine frowned with the effort to remember. 'She told me he loved life. He wasn't a weak man, and in any case he had no reason to want to end his life. He was in robust health and had never suffered from depression.'

'Do you want to check your notes? It's important to be exact,' Eileen said.

Geraldine shook her head. Slowly she went through a mental list of points covering what Amanda had told her. 'I don't need to check. I can remember everything she said. "I knew my brother. He would never have killed himself. He had a cheerful disposition. He didn't suffer from depression. He didn't have money worries, or a problem with drink or drugs. There was nothing in his life that might have made him want to end it. Hanging doesn't happen by accident." That's the gist of what she told me.'

Eileen had been checking her iPad while Geraldine was talking. She must have been impressed by Geraldine's accurate recall of what she had heard nearly a week earlier, because she smiled approvingly at her.

'It's a mercy Mark and Amanda's parents aren't alive,' Ariadne said softly.

Geraldine nodded in agreement. To lose even one child in so violent a manner would be unbearable. Two was unthinkable. Yet it had happened.

'What I don't understand is why she was wearing her slippers and what one of her shoes was doing outside the house,' Naomi said.

'What we need is not speculation, but more evidence to clarify what really happened to the two victims,' Eileen said.

'I think you're right; Amanda must have known something about Mark's murder and that's why she was killed,' Naomi told Geraldine when they met by chance in the canteen that afternoon.

They sat down at a table together to drink coffee and discuss the questions raised by Amanda's death. Geraldine couldn't understand why the killer had attempted to disguise the murder as a hit and run, when it must be obvious to any fool that the ruse would be exposed as soon as the body was examined.

'The killer's an idiot,' Naomi responded promptly. 'Good thing too. It'll make our job a whole lot easier.'

Geraldine put her mug down and shook her head. 'But that doesn't stack up with the first murder being so cleverly managed.'

'Maybe that was just luck?'

Geraldine shook her head again. No one concealed a murder by fluke. The police had too many sophisticated resources at their disposal for analysing the minutest shred of evidence. Mark had been killed by someone capable of plotting and executing a plan as clever as it was diabolical. Given that they were fairly certain both Mark and Amanda had been killed by the same person, using the same kind of rope, the only answer that made any sense was that Amanda had been killed in a hurry, meaning the killer hadn't been able to cover his tracks so skilfully. It seemed that Amanda had been killed in order to prevent her from convincing the police that Mark had been murdered. Ironically, not only had that scheme failed, but Amanda's murder had been the catalyst for opening an investigation into Mark's death which would hopefully result in a conviction. In killing Amanda to protect himself from discovery, the killer had sealed his own fate. But first they had to find him. And in the meantime, there might be other witnesses whose lives were at risk.

'We'll soon track him down,' Naomi said.

'We could be looking for a woman,' Geraldine pointed out.

'Either way, he or she can't stay hidden for long.'

Geraldine frowned. The killer didn't need to hide, because no one knew who had committed the murders. Right at that moment he or she could be walking the streets in broad daylight, planning another murder.

28

By Sunday Geraldine was exhausted but there was no time for her to have a lie in. She had too much to do, but she didn't mind that. Her days off were generally empty, unless she was going to see one of her sisters. She thought wistfully of her lazy mornings in North London, when she had been working for the Met. Occasionally she used to get up late and wander along Upper Street for coffee and breakfast in one of the smart cafés along the High Street in Islington. Today she had to settle for a home-brewed pot of coffee and some toast. She had decided not to go and see either Helena or Celia that weekend. For a while she had been bouncing from one to the other, depending on which sister she felt most guilty about not visiting.

Celia had a new baby, which gave her a claim on Geraldine's attention. Although they were only sisters by adoption, they had grown up together and developed a far closer relationship than Geraldine was ever likely to establish with the birth twin she had recently met. But balanced against Celia's situation was the fact that Helena was a recovering heroin addict who had recently come out of a private rehabilitation clinic, which Geraldine had paid for. It was difficult having to opt for one sister or the other, and she was never sure whether she had made the right choice. But today was different, because she had work to do.

Geraldine resolved to call them both that day, whatever else happened. Right now, her immediate concern was the investigation into the deaths of Mark and Amanda. Over breakfast she phoned Celia to apologise for not being able to see her that weekend, due to pressure of work. Helena's call could wait until later. She probably wasn't even awake yet.

'Don't worry, I know you're on a case,' Celia replied promptly. 'And I know you'd come and see us if you could.'

Somehow Celia being so understanding made Geraldine feel more guilty than before. Both of her sisters seemed to react to her in extreme ways, at opposite ends of the spectrum. Promising to call Celia for a proper chat as soon as she could, she hung up and leaned back in her chair, momentarily overcome by weariness. Life was never simple. If only Helena could be even half as reasonable as Celia, she and Geraldine might be able to build a relationship.

She spent most of the day sitting at her kitchen table with a pot of coffee, poring over her iPad. She had to stay on top of information flooding in as all the officers on the case logged their reports. If she failed to keep up to speed, the amount of new information could become impossible to absorb. Initially she focused her attention on Mark's wife and son. Close to the victim, they were the most likely suspects in the absence of any hard evidence. Charlotte had an obvious motive for killing Mark, since his death made her a wealthy woman. Eddy seemed an improbable suspect. Not only was he Mark's son, he was less likely to inherit any of his father's estate now that it had all gone to his stepmother. So although he had struck Geraldine as a shady character, he had no apparent motive for killing his father. In fact, it would have served Eddy's interests had his stepmother died before his father as the latter was more likely to bequeath his fortune to his son.

Of the two suspects so far, Charlotte also seemed more likely to have wanted to kill Amanda, considering her sister-in-law had accused her of murdering Mark. If Charlotte really was responsible for Mark's death, and Amanda had been outspoken in her presence, Charlotte might have wanted to silence her, especially if she learned that Amanda had reported her suspicions to the police. But without evidence, this kind of speculation led nowhere. In the end Geraldine gave up trying to work out the reason for the two murders, and focused on reading all the reports, hoping that a detail would strike her as significant, or a pattern would become apparent, as sometimes happened. But she was disappointed.

Before preparing her supper, she phoned Helena.

'There's someone here who wants to say hello,' her sister said.

Geraldine was surprised to hear the voice of her former sergeant, Sam.

'Geraldine!' Sam greeted her. 'How's it going up there in York?'

'We've got a new case.'

Before she could elaborate, Helena came back on the line.

'I've got to go,' Helena said. 'Sam and I are going out for supper.'

'That's nice.'

Helena hung up without even saying goodbye.

'Well, please don't wait to go out on my account,' Geraldine muttered. 'It was nice talking to you too.'

Geraldine had asked Sam to look in on Helena once in a while, and she and Helena seemed to have hit it off leaving Geraldine relieved, but also slightly envious of their friendship. The possibility that Helena was putting on an act in order to make her jealous seemed too petty to be true. All the same, she was bitterly disappointed about the way Helena treated her. It seemed that nothing Geraldine said or did satisfied her sister. She desperately wanted to bond with the only blood relative she had, but Helena seemed to have an agenda of her own, which involved blatantly taking as much from Geraldine as she could.

Reminding herself about the sad life Helena had led before they had met, she wondered whether she might be partly to blame for Helena's shortness with her. She could hardly have done more to help her twin, but she hadn't invited Helena to come and live with her, balking at such an unwelcome intrusion into her own life. They were effectively strangers who had known nothing of one another's existence until they were forty. They just happened to have been born together. Geraldine had been far more generous than many other people would have been in her situation, footing the bill for Helena's stay in a rehab clinic and now paying her rent. Perhaps Helena resented her because Geraldine was in a position to do that. In Helena's eyes, Geraldine must appear wealthy and successful. The reality was very different. But she was afraid that if she exposed her own needs, she might end up suffering worse humiliation. Appreciating Geraldine's neediness might encourage Helena to try and exploit her even more, and if she failed to wheedle more money out of Geraldine, she might use the knowledge of Geraldine's emotional vulnerability to punish her. Geraldine felt uncomfortable acknowledging that she didn't trust her sister, but it was the truth.

She wished she could be more like Sam, and make allowances for what Helena had suffered. But Sam could remain emotionally detached from it all. If Helena returned to her former habit Sam would be disappointed, but she could choose to walk away from the situation. Helena knew that if she reverted to her former lifestyle, Geraldine would be devastated. All Geraldine could do was try to conceal that she would do almost anything to try and protect her sister. She had already ruined her own career by helping Helena to escape from her drug dealer. Thinking about how Helena was taking advantage of her without any show of gratitude, she wondered miserably what more Helena could want from her.

Even a phone call from Ariadne asking if she wanted to go out for dinner failed to lift her spirits. She explained that she was too tired, and they agreed to go out the following evening. Geraldine should have been pleased. She wanted to start making friends in York, and she liked Ariadne, but as she leaned back and closed her eyes, she felt miserable. She tried to reassure herself that slowly she would establish a new life for herself in York, and Helena would settle down into her new life in London, and meanwhile they would track down whoever had killed Mark and Amanda, and everything would be all right. But she felt increasingly uneasy knowing that somewhere in the darkness outside a killer was hiding.

29

EDDY HAD BEEN GROWING increasingly desperate. After two more surreptitious trips to the bookies that week to lift himself back up out of trouble, he had only sunk deeper into debt. It was heartbreaking. But his run of rotten luck had to end soon. It defied all the odds that he would keep on losing. If he could just hold his nerve, it would all come right in the end. He had seen other guys fall apart in a losing streak and bottle it, but it was idiotic to stop when you were down on your luck. The time to throw in the towel was when you were ahead. All he needed was one massive hit and he'd be able to retire from the game. It had to happen. Sooner or later he was going to make a killing. So in the face of mounting debt, he remained sanguine. In fact, he had started increasing his bets, at higher odds. The greater the risk, the sooner he'd be able to cash in and call it a day.

He hadn't been able to get away from Luciana even for a moment on Saturday, but on Sunday she announced she was going out for a drink in the evening with her girlfriends from work. Eddy tried to look interested as Luciana told him about it, but all he could think was that she would be going out later and she would be gone for the whole evening. This was it. He could feel his luck was about to turn. As soon as she had left the house he hurriedly pulled on his old jacket and retrieved his baseball cap from the back of his wardrobe. It was a carefully selected disguise, enough to prevent his wife recognising him if she spotted him from a distance, but sufficiently trifling to explain away if he did happen to bump into her on the street. He had rehearsed possible conversations to himself.

'What on earth have you got on your head?' she might say.

'What? This old thing? I've had it for years. It looked like it was going to rain,' or perhaps, 'It's been so hot today it seemed a good idea to wear a hat,' or simply, 'I came across it and thought I might wear it. What do you think?'

So far he hadn't needed to resort to any excuse because he had only gone out when she wasn't around to notice his absence. And now he had a whole evening stretching ahead of him, and a good feeling about his chances. After stowing the stash of cash he'd withdrawn from the bank in readiness, he set off. Whistling, he walked down to the bus stop where he only had to wait a few minutes for his bus. Yes, for once everything was going his way and he was seeing the back of his nightmare run of bad luck. Sitting on the bus, he hunched his shoulders and pulled his cap right down over his eyes. It wasn't much of a disguise, but wearing it added to the thrill of his outings. He felt like a schoolboy playing truant. But if he left home feeling like a disobedient child, he was going to return as a conquering hero, hundreds of thousands of pounds better off.

It wasn't as though he was leaving anything to chance. If he kept going for long enough, it stood to reason that he had to have a lucky break sooner or later. It had taken him nearly two years to amass such a huge debt. Keeping their financial troubles concealed from his wife had taken some doing, but he had been clever enough to keep her more or less in the dark. Before she discovered any more about their financial straits, not only would he have repaid everything he had borrowed but they would be seriously wealthy. She was bound to understand then that he had done all this for her, to give her everything she wanted.

Entering the bookies he found the brightly lit shop half empty. Screens displayed hypocritical messages about gambling responsibly and setting a time limit and a cash limit, even warning that 'chasing your losses leads to bigger losses' interspersed with adverts for 'new' games and online 'bonuses'!

A young man entered, gabbling into his phone in a low voice. An old man sat hunched over a table, studying a newspaper. Everyone seemed to be ignoring a woman's voice calling out odds on horses from one of the screens on the walls. Another man standing in a corner looked round and dipped his head in a wordless nod, their eyes meeting in tacit camaraderie. Of course half a dozen or so fellow gamblers weren't going to affect the odds, but Eddy always felt there was less competition when there were very few other people there.

He had walked in thinking this was his night, but now he could feel his confidence seeping away. He took a deep breath, reminding himself that he was no ordinary gambler. Most of them were losers, but he had a strategy, and he had the willpower to walk away at the right time. He started out with a few little bets. After losing three or four times, he had a small win. It was insignificant compared to what he had lost so far, but although he wasn't a superstitious man, he had to accept that was a good sign. Holding his breath, he reached into his pocket and drew out the envelope stuffed with cash. This was his moment of glory, the bet that was going to solve all his financial difficulties in one stroke.

He physically staggered when he lost.

Stunned, he gazed around the betting shop, willing this to be a nightmare. The screens continued to display results, a couple of men Eddy hadn't seen before stood staring at them, while the man behind the counter didn't even look up. The whole shop was quiet and dull as though nothing had just happened. The old man at the table watched Eddy as he sat down on a stool. His legs were shaking. The disappointment was so huge he couldn't even comprehend it. Unless his fortune was reversed soon, he would be homeless. He was already behind on the rent. Luciana had no idea he had stopped paying it, but he simply didn't have the money. The bailiffs had already been round once, thankfully when she was out, but it was only a matter of time before they returned. He had given them his father's old watch and whatever else he could find that she might not miss, but he had been forced to hand over the television. When Luciana came home, he had to spin her a yarn about having taken it back to the shop to get it fixed. He couldn't go on like this. He had to get his hands on some money.

'You had a bad hit,' a low voice said, right by his ear.

Eddy spun round to see a stranger staring at him. The man's eyes glittered with unspoken interest as he smiled, displaying yellowing teeth.

'What's it to you?' Eddy muttered. 'Fuck off, will you, and mind your own business.'

The man shrugged, undeterred by Eddy's hostile response. There was something uncompromising in his expression. 'You're in the shit, mate. Maybe I can help you.'

He was standing very close to Eddy, almost pinning him against the wall.

'I told you to fuck off. What makes you think I need anyone's help?'

The man grinned. 'Let's go for a drink and talk.'

Eddy wasn't inclined to discuss his private affairs with a stranger, but he could certainly do with a drink. Without another word, he slipped down off the stool and followed his new acquaintance out of the betting shop. Aware that a desperate man risked getting himself into all sorts of trouble he was determined to be on his guard, but one drink couldn't do any harm, and it would help him to think clearly. As he followed the man along the street and across the road into the pub, he wondered whether he might persuade Luciana to emigrate. Perhaps they could go and live in Australia and start all over again, and she would never find out he had returned to his old habits. He sighed, knowing that was just pie in the sky. It would be impossible to persuade her to leave home without any preparation or discussion, and anyway he had no money to buy plane tickets. He could barely pay for his bus fare home.

And throughout all of his troubles his stepmother was sitting on a small fortune, refusing to share a penny of it with him, even though he must be entitled to inherit something from his father. If his father had been alive, Eddy could have gone to him and discussed his problems, man to man. His father would have understood. He used to enjoy a flutter on the horses. If it hadn't been for his father, Eddy might never have begun to gamble in the first place, so his father had a kind of moral responsibility for his difficulties. But his father was dead, and Eddy couldn't confide in his stepmother. He would have to find another way to relieve her of some of his father's money.

His new acquaintance put a pint down on the table. 'Cheers. Drink up. And then we can talk business.'

30

GERALDINE NEEDED TO FIND out more about Mark. When she
had found out all she could from official sources, instead of
questioning his family again she decided to speak to other
people who had known him. If she hurried, there was still time
to visit the law firm where he had worked before they closed
for the day. After parking near the station she walked along
Micklegate to the office where a well turned-out young woman
looked up from her computer screen and smiled at her as she
walked into the building.

'Can I help you?'

Briefly Geraldine introduced herself. As she was talking, the
man she had met at Mark's funeral walked past. He nodded at
her, with a quizzical expression.

'You were Mark's neighbour,' he said. 'We met at his funeral,
didn't we? This is a pleasant coincidence.'

'Rodney, this is Detective Sergeant Geraldine Steel,' the
receptionist interrupted him quickly.

The lawyer looked surprised, then nodded. 'But it *was* you I
saw at the funeral?'

'Yes. I was there.' She hesitated. 'I found what you told me
very interesting. I wonder if you have time to talk to me right
now?'

The lawyer glanced at his watch and then nodded. 'Would
you mind waiting for a moment? Please, take a seat.'

Hoping he wouldn't keep her waiting long, Geraldine sat
down. After a moment she stood up and went over to talk to the
receptionist. It was unlikely the girl would tell her anything she

didn't already know about Mark, but it wasn't in Geraldine's nature to overlook a potential source of information.

'You knew Mark Abbott, didn't you?'

The girl looked flustered. 'Yes, I knew him. He's dead, isn't he?' She lowered her voice and glanced around. 'What happened to him? They haven't told us anything. I mean, nothing at all. I know the senior partner went to the funeral, but they haven't given us any details about how Mark died. It was so sudden.'

'There isn't time for me to give you all the details right now,' Geraldine replied, deliberately implying she might share more information after she had finished speaking with the senior partner. She leaned forward. 'What was he like to work with?' She listened to the girl trot out platitudes, before asking whether Mark had any enemies.

'Apart from his wife, you mean?'

'What makes you say that?'

According to the receptionist, Mark's wife had called to ask if she could recommend a divorce lawyer.

'She wanted to see someone who wasn't associated with the firm. I don't think she wanted Mark to find out until she was ready.'

'When was this?'

'About a year ago, I guess. Anyway, I said I'd get back to her with a few names, but when I did, she said it wasn't necessary any more, so I suppose they sorted out their differences.' The girl shrugged. 'That's all I know.'

Geraldine thanked her and a moment later the senior partner emerged from his inner office.

'Please, come in.'

Leading her into a small white room, he sat behind a large wooden desk that dominated the space, and invited her to take a seat. Then he waited to hear what she had to say.

'How well did you know Mark Abbott?'

At the funeral, Mark's colleague had been forthcoming.

Now, seated at his lawyer's desk, he hesitated, aware of whom he was addressing. He gazed thoughtfully out of his high window, considering his answer, before he replied.

'We worked together for many years,' he hedged. 'We were colleagues. So I'd have to say I've known him for a long time, but as to whether I could say I knew him well, that's a different question. How well do we really know the people we work with, day after day? We couldn't even be said to have worked together. We each had our own office, and our own clients.'

Geraldine listened patiently, but this was going nowhere.

Gently, she tried to press him. 'You said at the funeral that he didn't strike you as the kind of man who would take his own life?'

He inclined his head. 'Yes, I recall saying something to that effect.'

'What did you mean by it?'

He shrugged and glanced out of the window again. 'Mark wasn't volatile. On the contrary, he was an even-tempered chap, at least here at work.'

'What about at home?'

'As far as I knew, he was happily married. But of course people can behave very differently in different circumstances, and things go on behind closed doors that outsiders would never imagine, as I'm sure you know very well in your line of work, Inspector.'

Geraldine didn't correct him. If she came across as higher up the hierarchy than she actually was, that was only to be expected, given that until recently she had been a detective inspector. She hoped the lawyer might be more inclined to confide in her if he thought she was more senior than she now was. But he was circumspect in his responses, and gave little away. She was fairly convinced he knew no more than he had already told her.

'Off the record, is there anything you could tell me that you're not prepared to say officially?' she asked at last. 'Anything that might possibly help me build a picture of Mark's character or circumstances?'

His response was assured. 'Nothing at all, Inspector. I'm sorry. I'd help you if I could.'

'Was he particularly friendly with anyone else here?' Geraldine asked as she thanked him and stood up.

He shook his head again. 'Not that I was aware of, but you're free to have a word with everyone here. If there's anything we can tell you that helps answer any queries you have over the circumstances of Mark's death, we'd all be more than happy to help. If you have a word with Nellie on reception, she'll tell you who's in today. We have a few part-timers,' he added, with a faint grimace.

Geraldine wondered if the part-time solicitors were women. Without being an out-and-out misogynist, the senior partner must be old enough to remember the days when the firm had been staffed by men working full-time. She had a suspicion he might hark back to those days with a feeling of nostalgia. But she didn't say anything. If her impression was correct, that was his problem. Old men like him weren't going to turn the clock back.

She spoke to several other solicitors working in Mark's firm and a similar picture emerged from them all, of a reasonable man who had been efficient and pleasant to work with. No one had anything to say that was anything other than bland and ultimately unhelpful, confirming only that Mark didn't sound like a man who had drunk excessively or suffered from mood swings or depression. He had never had any unexplained absences from work. In over twenty years, he had only taken one week off when he had gone down with flu a few years ago, in an illness that had already been mentioned by his doctor. Healthy in mind and body, he had given no indication that he might be considering suicide. Back in her car, Geraldine double checked her notes from her visit to Mark's doctor the previous week. Everyone told her Mark was physically healthy and mentally stable. Everything pointed to his having been murdered, but she was no closer to discovering who had killed him.

31

'WELL? HAVE YOU THOUGHT about what I said?' he asked, putting a glass down on the table in front of Eddy.

Eddy was pretty sure Abe wasn't his real name. He regretted having told the man his own name, but it was too late to change that now. He shifted uncomfortably on his chair and reached for his pint. The man calling himself Abe leaned right across the small wooden table until his face was very close to Eddy's.

'Well? What do you say?' he hissed.

His breath stank of stale cigarettes and grease. Eddy held his breath and looked away, refusing to meet Abe's stare. At last, feeling under pressure to say something, he spoke as breezily as he could.

'Cold in here, isn't it?'

Abe leaned back in his chair. 'Don't give me that crap,' he said. 'If you're not interested in my offer, it's no skin off my nose. There's plenty of blokes would jump at a chance to make some easy money.'

They sat for a moment without speaking. Eddy knew he ought to stand up and walk away. In fact, that was what he was going to do, just as soon as he finished his pint. There was obviously something dodgy about Abe's job, and Eddy was in enough trouble already without landing himself in more hot water. Meanwhile the silence was becoming oppressive.

'All you've got to do is drive a car,' Abe said. 'Surely you can manage that?'

'You haven't told me what it's all about yet.'

Abe grinned and tapped the side of his nose. 'You know

nothing, you say nothing. Like I said, it's easy money, and that's all you need to know. So, are you in or not? I need an answer.'

Before Eddy could respond, his companion stood up and walked over to the bar. Eddy watched him through narrowed eyes. Abe was tall and looked brawny in a loose-fitting khaki oilskin jacket. He returned with two more pints.

'Here you go. Now, what do you say?'

Eddy took a gulp. There was no reason for him to feel nervous. All he had to do was keep the conversation going for a short time, while he drank up. As soon as he finished this pint, he would skedaddle. But Abe didn't need to know that. Forcing a smile, Eddy took another swig of his beer.

'Bloody hell, you're a fast drinker! Now, what do you say?'

Abe reached across the table and laid one hand on Eddy's arm, preventing him from lifting his glass.

Eddy hesitated. 'It's good beer in here,' he replied at last.

'You up for it or not?'

Abe was beginning to sound impatient. Eddy had the impression it might backfire on him if he tried to outwit his new acquaintance, but it wouldn't do any harm to string him along for just a few more minutes, just while he finished his pint.

'I'm not sure,' he admitted, doing his best to sound genuinely uncertain. 'How much did you say I'd get?'

He nodded as Abe muttered a figure that was nowhere close to what Eddy needed. He finished his pint. Drinking so quickly on an empty stomach was making him feel woozy. Against his better judgement he was tempted. If he took the job, he might be able to cover one back payment of his rent, retrieve his television, and give something to Luciana to keep her happy. And what was more important, there might be more where that came from. He frowned, puzzling over what to do. He barely noticed Abe fetching him yet another pint. Abstractedly he began to drink it, and realised he was nodding his head.

'Is that a yes?' Abe asked. 'Only like I said, if you're not interested, there's plenty would jump at the chance of such easy cash.'

Eddy hesitated. He wasn't too pissed to think straight. 'Why not someone else then? I mean, why me?'

His companion nodded. 'You're right. I could have spoken to someone else all right. But I hate to see a man down on his luck.'

Eddy bristled. 'Who are you calling a loser? Fuck off and mind your own business.'

Abe leaned forward so that Eddy could smell his stinking breath. 'You need bailing out, mate. Anyone can see that. And I can help you. And the beauty of it is, there's no risk as far as you're concerned. None at all. You'll be parked up the road. If we don't get out you can just drive off, and no one will know you were even involved. You're just the driver. And you're entitled to your cut for being there. We're nothing if not fair. I wouldn't be talking to you if I didn't think you had it in you. Tell you what, Eddy,' he went on, grinning, 'I like to help a mate who's down on his luck. Why don't you take a down payment, right here, right now, and you can have the rest when the job's done?'

As the beer took effect, Eddy warmed to his new friend, who was nothing if not generous. There was something very engaging about his honesty. And it was about time someone started paying Eddy some attention. He got more consideration from a stranger than from his own flesh and blood.

'I'm entitled to a lot more than what you're offering,' he mumbled.

Abe's expression altered subtly, through surprise to irritation. 'Bloody hell, it's a fair whack. You're just driving. Others are taking all the risk.'

'No, no, I'm not talking about that,' Eddy replied. 'Not about your job.'

'Keep your voice down,' Abe said. 'What the hell are you talking about?'

Struggling to present his case coherently, Eddy was filled with self-pity. 'I'm an orphan,' he concluded. 'A poor bloody orphan. I can't even pay my rent and she won't give me a penny.'

Abe had listened thoughtfully. 'What kind of a mother would treat her son like that?'

'She's my stepmother.'

'But she's stealing what should be yours. I feel sorry for you, mate, really I do. She's a monster.'

Eddy nodded, grateful to Abe for his understanding. It was comforting to have a friend he could confide in, and he told Abe as much.

Abe paused before commenting quietly, 'When your stepmother's gone, it'll all be yours, won't it?'

'That's true, unless she decides to leave it all to a bloody charity. I wouldn't put it past her. And in any case, she'll be around for years. The way she looks after herself, she'll outlive me. She'll outlive us all.'

'Unless something happens to her,' Abe pointed out quietly.

Eddy nodded silently. He could certainly do with some help. Meeting Abe might be the answer to all his problems.

32

NOW THEY WERE ALL convinced they were investigating two murders which were related, Geraldine spent a dreary afternoon trawling through paperwork looking for evidence that the brother and sister had a shared enemy. After the initial flurry of activity viewing the crime scene and questioning people who had known the two victims, there was little else to do but await the forensic results.

'That's all policing is, these days,' Ted grumbled. 'Looking things up online. I won't be sorry to leave the job. It's not what it used to be. Even the community links are going because people move around so much.'

'Well said, Sherlock,' Ariadne chipped in, grinning at the speaker.

Someone else cracked a joke about Methuselah.

'Hey, steady on,' Ted grinned, his good humour restored.

Geraldine laughed. 'If you think the population's transient here, you should try working in London.'

'It may be true that there have been a lot of advances in forensics,' Naomi joined in, 'but surely that's all to the good. Think of the number of cases that would never have been solved if it wasn't for forensics.'

'Yes, yes, I know that,' he replied. 'I'm not wanting to turn the clock back.'

'Just as well,' Ariadne said. 'Because you can't.'

'Maybe you should retire to Brigadoon,' a constable suggested.

Geraldine answered Naomi. 'But how many cases are actually

solved by forensic results? Yes, they back up or confute our suspicions, and they supply us with that all important evidence that gets a conviction in court, but most cases are still solved by people like us doing our job. Old-fashioned police work.'

'Hear, hear,' Ted said.

'But what's the point of all that if you don't secure a conviction?' Naomi asked.

'But without us, there wouldn't be anything for the forensic results to prove,' Geraldine insisted.

The conversation continued for a while, but Geraldine's attention wandered. They were just passing the time while they waited. When Ian entered the room, the discussion stopped abruptly as everyone returned to their desks. Geraldine wondered whether her junior officers had reacted to her presence in a similar way when she had been an inspector. It was curious, witnessing her colleagues' behaviour when a senior officer entered the room. Before her promotion, she hadn't been aware that she had behaved any differently when an inspector appeared, but perhaps she had done so unconsciously. There was something compelling about watching her senior officers, now that she had lost that status herself, like picking at a scab.

As she was packing up at the end of a long afternoon, Ian walked past her desk and stopped to enquire whether she was going straight home or if she would like to go for a drink, but she had already arranged to meet Ariadne for a meal that evening. She wasn't sure if she was imagining it, but she thought he looked disappointed by her refusal.

'Another time,' she said.

'How about tomorrow? Only, there's something I want to discuss with you.'

'How mysterious,' she replied, but Ian didn't return her smile.

'Are you ready?' Ariadne called out and Geraldine nodded.

'Tomorrow then,' Ian said.

'I'll look forward to it.'

This time he smiled. Less than twenty-four hours ago she had been pleased when Ariadne had suggested they go out together. Now she regretted making that arrangement. But when she thought about Ian's invitation, she realised he must want to talk to her about his relationship with his estranged wife. There was nothing in that to make her feel excited. She picked up her bag and walked down the corridor.

Ariadne took her to a restaurant in the centre of York with views overlooking the river.

'It's better coming here in the summer when the evenings are longer and you can see out,' Ariadne said apologetically.

'It's nice discovering somewhere new,' Geraldine assured her. 'I know so few places to go in York.'

It was true. Even though she had been there getting on for three months, she had seen very little of the town. The restaurant was airy and pleasant. They took a corner table and spent a few minutes studying the menu.

'So how are you settling in?' Ariadne asked when they had placed their orders. 'It must feel strange, being a sergeant again. Having seen how hard you work, I can't imagine you were happy about it?'

Geraldine paused as she reached for her glass of wine. 'How did you know?' she asked, doing her best to hide her surprise.

'Oh, I wasn't aware that it was a secret.'

Geraldine hesitated, absorbing what she had just heard. Ariadne seemed to imply that everyone at the police station knew all about her demotion.

'Well, no,' she said, registering that her colleague had asked her a question. 'It's not a secret exactly. I just didn't think it was common knowledge. No one's ever mentioned it. I mean,' she stammered, afraid of sounding like a narcissist, 'I mean, of course there's no reason why anyone else would be at all interested in the reason for my relocation.'

'It happens,' Ariadne replied in a slightly dismissive tone. 'You don't have to talk about it if you don't want to.'

'It's not that,' Geraldine hastened to reassure her, although of course she didn't want to talk about it.

But idle speculation might be worse than the truth. With a sigh, she launched into an account of her ruined career.

'It's a long story,' she began.

'I'm listening, but only if you want to talk about it.'

Geraldine explained how she had only recently discovered that she had an identical twin, a heroin addict.

When she had finished, Ariadne raised her eyebrows. 'So you put your job on the line to save your sister's life?'

'Well, that's a rather dramatic way of putting it, but yes, actually, I suppose that is what happened. Although in the end she probably wouldn't have been shot by her drug dealer because he was arrested as she was handing over the money. Only of course it wasn't her, it was me who was doing the handover. She was too scared to face him but if she didn't get the money to him he would have found her and killed her.'

'And he thought he was dealing with her because you're identical, but the police had been tipped off and you were arrested instead of your sister! Bloody hell, Geraldine!' Ariadne stared at her. 'Why did you do it?'

Geraldine had asked herself that question many times. It was difficult to explain that, desperate to convince her screwed up twin that she wanted to help her, she had acted as much for herself as for Helena.

'I wanted to offer her a chance,' she said.

She didn't try to explain that she had wanted to create a chance for both of them to get to know one another and build a relationship. Only that hadn't happened. Not yet, anyway.

'And how has that worked out?'

Helena had gone through a rehabilitation programme and seemed to be coping, but it was early days.

'I'm hoping she'll be OK.'

Ariadne nodded. 'Does she even realise how much you sacrificed for her?'

'I don't know, I really don't. But at least I've given her a chance. No one's ever done that for her before. And I was in a position to help her. I couldn't just stand back and watch her destroy herself without doing everything I could to help her.'

'Bloody hell, Geraldine, I can't make up my mind if you're a saint or an absolute bloody lunatic.'

'Somewhere between the two, I guess, but more of a lunatic than a saint,' Geraldine laughed.

Once she had recovered from her surprise, instead of feeling mortified, she was relieved that her new colleagues had been informed about her demotion. Far from being judgemental, no one seemed bothered by it in the slightest. In fact, no one but Ariadne had even asked her about it, and she was just being friendly. And now Ian wanted to confide in her as a friend. Relocating to York wasn't turning out to be such a bad move after all.

33

AFTER AN EXHAUSTING DAY clearing out her husband's clothes, Charlotte decided to have an early night. She had spent hours packing shoes, trousers and shirts into bin liners, ready for donation to a charity shop. The task was not only tiring, but she had found it upsetting, throwing out all his familiar clothes. First she had emptied his drawers, carting things out by the armful. The most difficult part was when she came to empty out his laundry bin and recognised the smell of his sweat on a jumper he used to wear for gardening. The knowledge that she was inhaling deposits left by his living body made her break down in tears. At last she pulled herself together and, holding her breath, bundled his dirty washing into a black bin liner and tied it firmly closed. Still the smell seemed to linger. In a fury of emotion, she dragged the bag along the landing, bumped it down the stairs, and hauled it outside to the bins. After that, she felt too unsettled to continue, so she closed the door on the clothes still hanging in his wardrobe and took a shower.

Too wretched to do any more she had something to eat and went to bed early, only to be disturbed by a gale rattling around outside. As she came to, she thought it sounded odd, more like a door creaking than a storm. Peering out of her bedroom window, she saw the trees in her back garden were hardly moving. What she had heard couldn't have been the wind. Still, something had woken her up. She lay in bed listening, but couldn't hear anything. She supposed she must have dreamt it. Slightly unnerved, she decided to check all the windows upstairs were shut before going downstairs to check the doors were locked. Before going downstairs she turned off the burglar alarm but when it should have given two long beeps in response to the code she entered, there was only silence. She must have forgotten to set it when she went to bed. Since Mark's death, her own life had been falling apart.

Cautiously she crept downstairs and found all the doors and windows closed. Reassured that everything was secure, she set the alarm and returned to bed, leaving several lights on around the house. But she was wide awake now so she turned the alarm off and went back downstairs to put the kettle on. The noise of the water coming to the boil drowned out the silence. Sipping a mug of tea a few moments later, she told herself she must have been dreaming she had heard noises in the night. There was no other explanation for it, unless the wind had picked up and then dropped again before she looked out of the window. In her confused state of mind, anything seemed possible. Abandoning her tea, she poured herself a large slug of whisky.

If she hadn't been downstairs, she probably wouldn't have heard the faint sound of her front door opening and closing. On the instant her pulse began racing so fast, she thought she was going to have a heart attack. Someone had just entered or left the house. There could be an intruder prowling around as she stood in the kitchen clutching her mug of whisky. The only other person who had a key was Eddy, and he was hardly likely to be visiting her at two o'clock in the morning. Trembling, she hesitated over what to do. It was possible Eddy had walked out on Luciana after a massive row. Never a patient man, he'd always had a short temper. Not only did he have a key to Charlotte's house, but he would have nowhere else to go at that time of night. If that *was* what had happened, as seemed likely, then Charlotte would look pretty stupid calling the police. Moving as quietly as she could, she raced upstairs and grabbed her phone before locking herself in the bathroom. Leaning back against the door, she began to shake. If it wasn't Eddy downstairs, her life could be in danger.

There might be a violent criminal prowling around in her house while she sat on the side of her bath, procrastinating. Her hand trembled as she phoned Eddy, praying that he would answer and tell her that he had just popped in to collect something. He didn't answer; no doubt because he was fast asleep at home. There was nothing else to do but call 999. She couldn't risk waiting any longer to find out who was downstairs. Having summoned the police, she sat staring at the flimsy bolt on the bathroom door, waiting. It seemed to take hours for them to arrive, although in reality it was only about five minutes until she heard banging on her door. Cautiously she opened the window and saw a police car parked outside.

'I'm just coming down,' she called out.

Her legs were still shaking as she crept down the stairs. A police presence on the doorstep was no guarantee she was safe indoors. A drug-crazed maniac might pounce on her at the bottom of the stairs and take her hostage, or stab her to death, before anyone outside had a clue what was happening to her. Reaching the hall, she cast a rapid glance all around before making a frantic dash for the front door and flinging it open. Two young policemen were standing outside.

'Mrs Abbott?' one of them stepped forward. 'We received a phone call from you just now –'

'Yes, yes,' she interrupted him, 'that was me.' She lowered her voice and spoke slowly, aware that her speech was sounding slurred. She needed to be careful or they would never believe her. 'There's someone here.'

The policeman nodded. 'Yes, ma'am, we received your message. Did you get a look at the intruder?'

'No, I didn't see anyone. I just heard the front door open and close.'

The policeman nodded again and gave her a sombre smile. 'The fingerprint officers will be here shortly, so please don't touch the external doors or windows unless you have to before they get here.'

She trailed helplessly behind the two officers as they went around the house checking all the doors and windows. There was no sign of a break-in. The police officers didn't seem surprised when they didn't find anyone else in the house. Charlotte didn't think they believed she had heard anyone, but it made sense that the intruder would have fled as soon as the police began banging on the door. When she followed them into the living room, she frowned. The cupboard doors were open. She always kept them closed. She never left doors open. Mark used to complain about her compulsion for closing doors around the house.

'Someone's been in here,' she stammered.

Her alarm must have shown on her face because the officer gave her a sympathetic smile. 'We'll soon be finished here,' he said gently.

Drawing in a deep breath, Charlotte told him she always closed all the doors in the house.

'It's a habit of mine,' she explained with an embarrassed grin. 'I can't help myself. So you see, I'd never have left those doors open.'

'What about your burglar alarm?'

She bit her lip. 'I must have forgotten to turn it on.'

The policeman took a step away from her. 'We've looked around and there's no sign of a break-in, so I don't think you need to worry, but we're sending a fingerprint officer along. Does anyone else have a key to the house?'

'No, only my son.'

The policeman asked for Eddy's address and telephone number.

'There's no need for you to speak to my son. I can do that myself. If I find out he was here during the night, I'll let you know.'

With no sign of a break-in, and nothing missing, there wasn't much more the police could do but the officer assured her a report would be filed and an incident number issued.

They departed soon after, leaving Charlotte feeling tired and disturbed. The police believed that she had imagined hearing an intruder during the night. The evidence certainly seemed to confirm that they were right. But she knew she hadn't left the cupboard doors open. Although she had already checked the doors and windows were closed, she went around the house checking them all again before she went upstairs to bed. She didn't go back to sleep. She was afraid she was losing her mind.

34

EDDY WAS TEMPTED TO ignore the door bell, but it rang repeatedly until Luciana snapped at him to see who it was. Hastily throwing on his dressing gown, he hurried downstairs in his bare feet. He opened the front door, ready to snarl at the caller to bugger off, and blinked in surprise. He had just been thinking about his stepmother, and now there she was on his front doorstep, as though she had read his mind. Despite his preoccupation with his own problems, he couldn't help noticing that she looked agitated and haggard, as though she hadn't slept. He had a horrible suspicion she had somehow discovered he was tens of thousands of pounds in debt and had come round to challenge him about it in front of Luciana.

'I need to see you,' she blurted out before he could say a word.

He could hardly slam the door in her face. As soon as she closed the front door behind her he turned to glare at her, blocking her from going any further along the narrow hall.

'What's this about?'

'I need to ask you something.'

He scowled at her. 'And this really couldn't wait until later? Listen, why don't you go home and I'll come round and see you when I finish work?'

'It can't wait. Can we go and sit down?'

She looked exhausted but he didn't budge, so she came straight out with it. 'Did you come round to my house last night?'

'Me? Why? What makes you say that?'

'Were you in my house last night?'

'No, of course not. What are you talking about? You'd have known if I was there.'

Behind him, he heard Luciana coming downstairs. Glancing over his shoulder he saw that she was fully dressed, with make-up and everything. It was typical of her to send him down to open the door while she stood in front of the bathroom mirror, getting herself ready. Not that a good-looking woman like her needed so much make-up. Looking at her, he felt a lump in his throat. He still found it hard to believe she was really his wife. One thing was for sure, he was never going to let her down again. Last time she had discovered him gambling, she had threatened to leave him if she ever caught him at it again. He wasn't going to let that happen.

'Who was it? Oh, hello, Charlotte,' she called out as she caught sight of her mother-in-law. 'Is something wrong?'

She joined them in the hall. 'Don't stand around here. Come on in. Eddy, why don't you go up and get dressed? I can keep Charlotte company until you come down.'

Without answering Eddy went into the living room, followed by Charlotte and Luciana.

'So what's happened?' he asked when they were all sitting down. 'Do you want to go and put the kettle on?' he added, turning to Luciana.

'Not until I've heard what this is all about.' She glanced at the time on her phone. 'It must be important to make you come round so early.'

Taking a deep breath, Charlotte launched into an account of what had happened in her house during the night. When she finished, Eddy was barely able to catch his breath, let alone speak, he was so relieved.

'You're telling us you think you had an intruder because you found a cupboard door open?' Luciana said slowly.

Eddy shook his head. 'Mum never leaves doors open,' he muttered. 'She used to drive me and dad mad nagging us about it.'

'There *was* someone in the house. I heard him,' Charlotte insisted.

'But you said there wasn't any sign of a break-in?' Luciana asked.

'That's right.'

'Well, who else has got a key to the house and knows the code for the alarm?' Luciana asked.

'No one. Only me and Eddy.'

'Then if it wasn't Eddy, you must have imagined someone was there.'

Charlotte shook her head vigorously. 'No, I didn't imagine it. There was someone there. I know what I heard.'

While Eddy was trying to decide what to say to his stepmother, Luciana announced she had to leave for work. Without hesitation, Eddy said he would take the morning off to be with his mother. When Charlotte remonstrated that she was fine and he shouldn't stay at home on her account, he insisted. Actually it had all turned out perfectly. He didn't explain that he had been planning to phone in sick so he could talk to Charlotte that morning. He wanted to keep that from Luciana at all costs, for fear she would find out why he was so desperately in need of money. All that remained was for him to convince his stepmother that he was entitled to his share of his father's estate, and all his problems would be over. She would bail him out, and he would be saved from the financial ruin that threatened to destroy his marriage.

With Luciana safely out of the house, he offered his mother a cup of tea, and was disappointed when she shook her head.

'No, no, Eddy, I'd best be getting on. I only called round to find out whether you'd been in the house while I was asleep. I'm fine, really. I appreciate your concern, but there's no need to take time off work on my account. You get going. I'm fine.'

She stood up to leave.

'No. Don't go.'

He spoke more forcefully than he had intended. Surprised, she sat down again.

After an uneasy silence, she reassured him. 'If it *was* you last night, I don't mind. I'd rather know it was you than be left in this horrible uncertainty. Was it you?'

'No, I already told you it wasn't me. Now listen to me, will you? I need to speak to you.'

'Go on then. I'm listening.'

Taking a deep breath, Eddy plunged in. 'I need my money.'

'What do you mean?'

'My money. The money I should have had when dad died.'

'What money?'

'The money that's owed to me.'

His stepmother frowned. 'I don't know what you're talking about. You'd better explain yourself.'

'You know perfectly well what I'm talking about. I was due to inherit a fortune when dad died –'

'Let me stop you right there,' she cut in, her voice cold. 'I was your father's next of kin and his estate came to me when he died. There's nothing complicated or unusual about that. I really don't know why you would think you have any claim to any part of his estate, but you don't.' She leaned forward and her expression softened. 'If you're in trouble, Eddy, I'll help you if I can, you know that. Most of what I own is tied up in the house and I'm not planning on selling it any time soon, if that's what you're thinking. But I've got a small nest egg of my own, and –'

'How much?' he interrupted quickly.

'I'll need to check the exact figure because it's been earning interest, but last time I looked it was just over a thousand pounds –'

'A thousand!'

She smiled, completely misunderstanding his dismayed exclamation.

'I can get my hands on it whenever I want, and I'd like to

give it to you not as a loan, but as a gift.' Her smile broadened as she waited for his expression of gratitude.

He nearly choked on the words. 'Thanks, mum, that's very generous of you, but –'

'But nothing,' she cut in, firm now that she had made up her mind. 'There's no need to thank me. You've been a great help to me, with the funeral, and painting the hall, and everything. I'd have had to pay someone to do the decorating if you hadn't offered. Let's call it a payment for all the work you've done so far, and the work you're going to do for me around the house, and we'll say no more about it. I'll get on to that today.'

Eddy watched her stand up. His mind was racing. This hadn't gone as he had planned, but a thousand quid was better than nothing. With a stake like that, he wouldn't need too many decent wins to recover his losses. Even though his stepmother was a stingy cow, she might have bailed him out after all, and Luciana would be none the wiser.

35

SEEING A MISSED CALL from his stepmother, Eddy dashed to the toilet to speak to her. He could hardly catch his breath for impatience as he waited for her to answer.

'Well?' he demanded as soon as he heard her voice. 'Have you got the cash?'

'Calm down, Eddy –'

'Don't tell me to calm down.' He drew in a sharp breath and lowered his voice in case someone was outside the cubicle, listening. 'Have you got the money, yes or no?'

'Yes, I've got it. I told you I would. You can come round for it whenever you want.'

'I'll be round straight after work.'

After he rang off, he realised he hadn't thanked her. Oh well, that could wait until he saw her in a few hours. Immensely relieved that he had succeeded in persuading her to get hold of the cash quickly, he was impatient to get started. Facing the prospect of a decent stake with which to try his luck made all the difference. Only of course it wasn't luck that sorted the winners from the losers, it was having the bottle to continue when you had suffered a run of bad fortune. What he needed to do now was make a start on recouping his losses that afternoon, hopefully before Luciana noticed he was late home from work.

As he had promised, Eddy went straight round to his stepmother's house after work to collect his cash. Before she had even closed the front door behind him, he reminded her what he was there for. She gave a smug smile, as though she was doing him a favour, when in fact she was giving him only

169

a fraction of what he was entitled to inherit. But he wasn't going to argue with her about that. He just wanted to get his hands on the thousand quid and leave as quickly as possible.

'I was just putting the kettle on,' his stepmother said.

'No, no. I can't stop. I have to get home.'

'But – are you really saying you're going to take the money and leave straight away?'

'Yes, exactly. I'm sorry, but I haven't got time to hang about. So, where is it? I can run and get it if you like. If it's upstairs or –' he broke off, registering her expression. 'What's wrong, mum? You aren't thinking of changing your mind, are you? Only you told me you'd got hold of it. You promised me –'

'No,' she interrupted him coldly. 'I'm not changing my mind. I said you could have it, and you can.'

Scurrying along the pavement five minutes later, with a thousand pounds in his pocket, Eddy glanced around and slipped on the cap which he had remembered to bring with him. His stepmother's parting words didn't bother him in the slightest. He really didn't care that she wouldn't part with another penny to help him out. She had given him a thousand pounds and with some careful tactics he was going to make at least fifty times that amount before the night was over.

He looked around once more before stepping into the betting shop. Although he had seen the weaselly features and large ears of the man behind the counter many times, when Eddy nodded at him the other man's eyes slid away as though he didn't recognise him. Nervously, Eddy fingered the money in his jacket pocket. A thousand pounds was a fair stake to begin with. But although he was in a hurry to get home before Luciana missed him, he had no intention of rushing. This was his moment. He was going to be rich, and no mistake. In any case, Luciana wouldn't care about him coming home late when he told her about the bonus he had been given at work. As for the rent arrears, she would never find out about that. With a rush of wellbeing, he grinned at an old man seated at the table studying the form of the horses about to race.

'Got any tips?' Eddy asked.

The old man merely shrugged his bowed shoulders.

As Eddy turned away, the old man put out a gnarled hand and grabbed him by the arm. 'Just a minute, young man.'

Eddy paused in case the old man had any useful information to share, but he remained silent. 'Well? What is it?' Eddy asked after a minute. 'Oh well, I can't stand around. I've got things to do.'

The old man loosened his grasp and didn't remonstrate when Eddy walked away. He seemed to have fallen asleep. Leaning against the shelf on the far wall, Eddy studied the form of all the horses due to run in the next race. The name of one sprang out at him. He stared at it for a moment, considering, but there wasn't time to think about it for long. The odds were good and the race was due to start. Making up his mind, he marched up to the bookie who nodded at him through the glass. Eddy placed his bet: a hundred pounds on Blue Diamond. Clutching his slip of paper, he waited, immobilised by a familiar sense of anticipation. Time seemed to stand still as he stood there, barely registering voices calling out from the screens, or the old man shaken by a rattling cough, and all the while the bookie was looking down, meeting no one's eye yet somehow aware of everything that was going on.

A familiar feeling of sickening disappointment swept through him. He looked up. Apart from this blow to his hopes, nothing had changed. The man behind the counter didn't react. The old man had recovered from his fit of coughing and was sitting perfectly still, staring into space. Eddy straightened his back and squared his shoulders. He had lost before but he hadn't let that put him off. The important thing was that he wasn't going to lose overall. He knew that he had to win at some point and when he did, he would walk away. It was just a question of putting a large enough stake down at the right time. He stared at the list of horses for the next race, trying to spot a sure winner. He had always avoided going for the favourite, because the odds weren't good enough to make it really worthwhile. On the other hand, the favourite was most likely to win and with a large enough stake he could still clean up. If he patiently bet all his money on the favourite at each race, it might not be the single dramatic win he had been chasing, but by the end of the evening he could be trouble free. It was just a matter of time. He was going to be home late, but he'd deal with Luciana when he got there. Right now, he had some money to win.

Having decided not to worry about being late home, he went a few doors along the road to the pub for a quick beer to bolster his courage. The place was packed with rowdy youngsters all vying to be heard. The racket made Eddy's head reel, as though he had stumbled into a wall of noise. Manoeuvring his way across the packed bar, he struggled to attract attention at the bar. Surreptitiously fishing a tenner from the bundle in his pocket, he waved the note in the air and a plump barmaid came over.

He had to yell to be heard above the noise. The barmaid's dark eyes glinted at him as though they shared a guilty secret while she pulled his pint. Suddenly in a hurry, he didn't even bother to look for a seat. After downing his drink as quickly as he could, he wiped his mouth on the back of his hand and left the pub, pulling his baseball cap lower over his eyes as he scurried along the street to the relative peace of the betting shop. This was it. With a surge of confidence in his new strategy, he strode up to the counter to hand over hundreds of pounds and then watched closely as the bookie counted the notes right in front of him, nearly nine hundred pounds. It was a surefire thing that he would walk out of the betting shop with a lot more money than he had arrived with, because he was no longer hoping to achieve the impossible, but was betting on the favourite. Once that horse romped home, he would do the same for the next race, and the one after that, until he had made as much as he needed.

While he waited to hear the result of the race, he glanced around the room sizing up the other people in there. He would have to be careful. If anyone spotted his haul, they might try to relieve him of it once he was out on the street again. He would probably be wise to take a taxi home. God knows, he'd be able to afford it. He was so wrapped up in his thoughts that he almost missed the announcement. In the act of turning to the bookie with a broad grin on his face, he froze. It took a few seconds for the reality to sink in. He had come out with a thousand pounds in his pocket; he had lost it all.

36

SINCE THE BOOKIE HAD flatly refused to give Eddy any more credit he had been wandering the streets, hoping for a miracle. He had managed to cadge a pint from a sympathetic bar girl but the manager had sent him packing when his credit card was declined. As a consequence he was only slightly drunk, and utterly desperate. It was getting late and he could see no way out of his predicament. He considered going back to his stepmother and begging her for more money, but she had made her feelings clear when she had handed over the thousand pounds. She had accused him of cleaning her out, as though that came even close to the truth while she was still sitting on a tidy fortune, apart from living in the big house Eddy's father had left. When he had pointed out that she could sell the property and move to a smaller place, he had actually thought she was going to hit him. She had as good as thrown him out and he had been glad to go, with the thousand pounds safely stashed in his pocket.

If he had thought he might persuade his stepmother to relent, he would have gone back and thrown himself on her mercy, but there was no chance she would have changed her mind so soon. Besides, she had probably gone to bed and wouldn't appreciate his knocking on her door so late. There was nothing else he could do but go home and face Luciana. Wracking his brains over what to say to her, he made his plans. Somehow he had to fend off her questions until he started working for Abe. Meeting him had been a stroke of luck. After the first job, there were bound to be others, and with the additional income

Eddy would eventually be able to sort out his money worries. It wouldn't have been his first choice, but he was running out of options.

Luciana came bounding down the stairs, calling out his name, as soon as he closed the front door.

'Eddy, where the hell have you been?'

He tried to explain that he had been held up, but she interrupted him.

'Why didn't you phone? I thought something had happened to you. Where have you been? Eddy?'

A host of ideas flew through his mind, many of which he had thought up while he had been walking the streets, none of which now seemed even vaguely sensible. He kicked his shoes off and leaned back against the wall, gathering himself together.

'Are you pissed?'

He shook his head. 'No, no, I'm not pissed.' He laughed bitterly because he was too skint even to get drunk. 'I'm pathetic, Luciana, that's what I am. Pathetic.'

She was in the hall now. He could smell her shampoo. The thought that he might lose her was like a knife stabbing him in the guts. To his dismay, he felt tears in his eyes. That was hardly going to win her round.

'I'm pathetic,' he repeated feebly. 'But I'm going to make it up to you.'

'Come on, love. It can't be that bad. What's happened?'

He shook his head.

'What's wrong, Eddy? Tell me. Are you ill? Are you in pain?'

He shook his head, unable to speak.

'What happened? Speak to me, Eddy.'

As he confessed he was having a few financial difficulties, she drew back with an exclamation of annoyance.

'You've been at it again, haven't you?'

'What?'

'You know what I'm talking about. Have you been gambling?'

'No!' He hoped he hadn't overdone his outrage. 'Of course not. But we've been overspending.' He talked quickly before she could challenge what he was saying. 'But don't worry. I've been offered a job –'

'You've already got a job. I thought you liked working at the builders' merchants?'

On a roll now, Eddy explained that he wasn't planning on leaving his job any time soon, but he had found an extra source of income.

'This one's just an occasional job, to begin with at least. But it'll be cash in hand, and there could be quite a lot of it!'

Although he had resolved not to increase his funds by trying his luck again, it was reassuring to know he had that option if it turned out to be necessary. But he didn't mention that to Luciana. She was asking him about the job and he could tell she was still suspicious. If he refused to say anything about it, she was bound to think he was gambling again.

'It's a driving job,' he said vaguely, 'driving some posh bloke around in the evenings.'

It was partly true. He *was* going to be driving.

'So does that mean we can book a holiday?'

He paused, reluctant to reveal the extent of his debts. But there was no hiding from the rent arrears, or the fact that the television was still missing. It was sheer luck that Luciana had been out when the bailiffs had called round the first time, but the chances were she would be at home when they returned. And if he didn't sort this out, they would certainly be back. At least she was in a reasonable mood. He chanced it and mumbled that he was behind with the rent.

'It's nothing I can't sort out,' he added quickly. 'We'll be able to talk about booking a holiday soon. Just give me a few weeks.'

He nearly asked her to lend him some money, just enough to place a quick bet that could solve all his problems, but he stopped himself in time. It was just as well, because she launched into one of her rants.

'You had me worried there, when you came home so late. Still, as long as you're not gambling again.'

'You know I wouldn't do that. Didn't I promise you? Don't you trust me? Listen, we've got a situation here and we need to contain it. As things are it's barely manageable, but we can just about pull things back from the brink and avoid a complete disaster if we're really careful, for a few months. And with the extra money I'm going to be earning, it might not take that long. Trust me.'

That much at least was true. All he needed to do was have a little run of luck with his first payment from Abe, and he could turn this around. Within a week they could be rich. He had a good feeling about it. Just when he had been really down on his luck Abe had popped up, like a genie from a magic lamp, with an offer of easy money.

He smiled at Luciana. 'Yes, don't you worry. I'm going to take care of everything.'

37

IT WAS STILL LIGHT by the time Charlotte walked back to her car, her prescription sleeping pills in her bag. She knew she wouldn't be able to sleep without them after her argument with Eddy. Preoccupied with thinking about her stepson, she heard the soft purr of an engine before she looked around and noticed a van driving slowly along the street beside her. She told herself she was being needlessly paranoid, and the van couldn't be following her. Nevertheless, she picked up her pace. When she reached her car, she stopped to get out her keys and was relieved to see the van drive past. Fumbling in her bag, she heard a squeal of tyres as the van reversed rapidly alongside her. Drawing level with her, it screeched to a halt and a figure leapt out of the driving seat. She barely had time to gain a confused impression of dark eyes glaring at her from behind a balaclava before the man flung himself at her, and slapped a hand across her mouth. Forcing her head back until she was gasping for breath, he lifted her off her feet, snatched her bag and flung her inside the van, slamming the door on her.

Winded and stunned, for a few seconds she was too shocked to react. By the time she recovered her breath enough to call out, the van had shuddered into motion and they were roaring down the road. The whole incident had taken no more than a few seconds. Jolting along in a strange van, Charlotte tried to understand what was happening. She appeared to have been kidnapped. In a sudden panic, she crawled over to the metal wall that divided her from the driver, and began banging on it as loudly as she could, yelling out for him to stop. The van swerved abruptly causing her to slide across the floor, hitting her head on the side of the compartment. The sudden pain of the impact startled her and she burst into tears, confused and terrified.

While the van rattled on through the streets, stopping and starting as the traffic allowed, she tried to calm down and work out what was going on. All she knew was that she had been seized in the street and thrown into the back of a van, in broad daylight. Her best hope of rescue was if someone had seen her abduction and reported it to the police straight away. It might even have been caught on a mobile phone. At the very least, she hoped someone who had witnessed her capture had made a note of the van's registration number. Even though it was unlikely the van would be registered in her captor's name, there was a chance the police had already been alerted and were looking out for it. She tried to reassure herself that a woman couldn't be grabbed in the street in broad daylight without anyone seeing what was happening, but she had an uneasy suspicion that the incident had been carried out so quickly, it could have escaped notice.

It was dark inside the van. Crawling around blindly, she felt her way cautiously. The floor seemed to be covered in twigs and dry grass, and it stank of rotting vegetation. Apart from the fragments of plants, the interior of the van was empty. Feeling her way along the walls, which felt cold and greasy, she inched her way along to the door at the back. Crouching on her knees and one hand, she moved her other hand sideways across the door, trying to find a way of opening it. Apart from the impulse to escape, she wanted to inhale some fresh air before she suffocated in the stuffy van. With the tips of her fingers she found where the two doors met, but there was no gap between them, and she could find no handle. Resigned to being unable to open the door from the inside, she sat down, leaned against the side of the van, and tried to make plans. If she could somehow lure her captor into the van she would leap out, slam the doors and walk away, leaving him trapped inside. With a shudder she wondered if that was the fate he had planned for her, to die alone in an airless dark space. She scrabbled frantically at the doors again but they wouldn't budge.

At last the van jolted to a halt and she heard the driver's door clang. He was coming to let her out. She held her breath and crouched, ready to leap out of the van as soon as the doors opened, and throw herself at her captor. Only by catching him by surprise would she have any chance of overpowering him. The doors creaked open letting in a wave of light that threw her off balance, momentarily blinding her. Instead of flinging herself at her captor, kicking and scratching like a caged tiger let loose, she cowered back, covering her eyes and whimpering as he reached in and grabbed her by the wrists. She tried to pull him forwards, in a vain attempt to drag him inside the van so she could jump out and shut him in. As he dragged her towards him, she shouted at him to stop, and began kicking out as hard as she could. When her foot connected with the side of his head, he swore and yanked one of her arms so violently behind her back she thought he was going to dislocate her shoulder.

'Stop it, you're hurting me! Please stop!'

'If you don't shut up, I *will* hurt you.'

His voice was so hoarse, she wondered if he was trying to disguise it. Terrified, she abandoned her attempt to resist, and allowed him to pull her out of the van. Before her feet touched the ground, he threw her over his shoulder in an awkward fireman's lift and ran across a paved yard towards the front door of a dilapidated house. From filthy window frames to a weed-covered front yard, everything about it was in need of maintenance. As her captor half turned on the front step, she raised her head and saw a high hedge surrounding the front yard, beyond which lay the street and freedom. Before she could wriggle free, her abductor opened the front door and the opportunity slipped away. With a sinking feeling she heard the front door close behind them.

When he turned to bolt the door, she managed to squirm out of his grasp and landed on the floor with a jolt. She drew away from him. With her back pressed against the wall, she began to scream. At once he spun around and slapped her, hard. She was so shocked she stopped screaming.

'There's no point in shrieking like that. No one can hear you,' he growled.

From inside his balaclava his dark eyes glared coldly at her, seeming to bore into her head. It was impossible to see anything more of his face which was completely concealed. Dropping her gaze, she tried to suppress a whimper but she couldn't help crying out when he yanked her roughly towards him. Seizing her by both elbows he held her tightly, propelling her forwards along the hall.

'No, no! Let me go!'

With one of his arms around her neck propping her upright, and the other clamped over her mouth, he pushed her ahead of him and into a back room. Pulling aside a dirty rug, he wrenched open a trap door and forced her down a flight of steep wooden steps. As she descended, a fetid stench hit her, mingled with a whiff of stale sweat which might have come from her or her captor. They were only halfway down the stairs when he shoved her in the small of her back, so that she stumbled and slithered helplessly down into the cellar. Twisting her ankle as she landed she cried out, momentarily forgetting everything but the excruciating pain in her leg. As she came to her senses, she saw that she was standing in what appeared to be an old coal cellar, a narrow strip of a room with filthy brick walls. Only a faint light reached her from the open door at the top of the stairs, but after being locked in darkness even that was welcome, until she saw what faced her in the cellar.

Her ankle was throbbing, sending spasms of pain shooting up her leg. With a rush of desperate courage, she struggled to her feet. Above her she heard the door slam shut, leaving her in darkness.

'No, no! Don't leave me here!' she shrieked.

Catching her breath, she froze, listening. In the darkness she could hear panting.

'Get away from me!' she cried out.

As she tried to feel her way towards the steps, a guttural growling swelled into a deafening roar that echoed off the walls of the narrow chamber. Her legs felt weak. Disorientated, she shuffled backwards searching for the stairs, and let out an involuntary moan as her shoulder hit the wall behind her. She whirled around, trembling, as the roaring reverberated around the narrow space once again.

38

GERALDINE FELT MORE CHEERFUL the next morning than she had been since her move to York. Without another word being exchanged on the subject, she was relieved to know that her colleagues were aware of her recent history. Until she had gone out to eat with Ariadne, fear of letting something slip about her demotion had kept her on her guard. Now she felt she could relax. Not only did everyone know about her recent history, but no one seemed to care or be at all curious about the reason for her disgrace. The likelihood that Ian had played a role in smoothing the way for her move was an additional source of gratification. For once, she had no reservations about going for a quick drink with her colleagues after work. Whatever had happened to her in London was in the past. She had come to York to stay, and was determined to make the best of her situation. Despite the blot on her reputation she had remained in a job she loved, where she could dedicate her life to serving justice. She couldn't think of anything else she would want to do, or anywhere she would rather be than on Ian's team in York.

'You're looking cheerful today,' Naomi remarked as she and Ariadne joined Geraldine and Ian in the canteen at lunch time. 'Does this mean there might be some good news at last?'

Geraldine glanced at Ian who returned her look with a quizzical expression.

She turned back to Naomi and shook her head. 'No, nothing new, I'm just happy to be here getting on with the job.'

'Not that we're getting anywhere,' Ariadne grumbled.

'Whoever killed Mark and Amanda certainly did a good job of it –'

'In what sense would you call their murders good?' Geraldine asked, raising her eyebrows in exaggerated surprise.

'I meant he's doing a good job of keeping his identity hidden,' Ariadne explained herself although they all knew what she had meant.

'The killer could be a woman,' Naomi pointed out.

'And we don't know for certain that we're looking for just one killer,' Geraldine added.

As though by tacit agreement, the others changed the subject. Geraldine listened in silence for a few minutes as her colleagues chattered inconsequentially. All she wanted to do was discuss the investigation. She had been criticised in the past for having tunnel vision, but she was content with her single-minded dedication to her work. Still, she wanted to fit in with her new colleagues, so she joined in the lighthearted banter as well as she could, competing to make the others laugh. There was some desultory gossip about a retired constable Geraldine had never met, and then the conversation drifted on to Eileen. Geraldine listened closely, keen to discover as much as she could about the detective chief inspector, but she heard nothing specific.

'She's getting crabbier,' Naomi complained.

'She's always had a short temper,' Ariadne agreed.

'I know that, I'm just saying she's getting worse,' Naomi repeated.

There followed a brief debate over whether Eileen's temper was deteriorating under the pressure of a double murder investigation.

'I'm going to miss Ted,' Ian said, putting an end to comments which were becoming increasingly vexatious.

Ariadne agreed that the police station wasn't the same without Ted's cheery face.

'I wonder what he's doing,' Naomi said.

Ariadne replied that a constable had called in to see him and found him busy in his garden. 'He was always a keen gardener,' she added.

'It's so important to have interests outside of work,' Naomi said, and the others murmured in agreement.

Listening to the conversation, Geraldine wondered what *she* was going to do when she retired. She could envisage only empty days stretching ahead of her. She looked forward to spending more time with her adopted sister, Celia, and her family. She hardly saw her niece, Chloe, any more. When she visited these days, Chloe was often out, busy with her friends. And she would be able to see more of her twin who was still virtually a stranger, despite being biologically closer to Geraldine than anyone else could ever be. And she would go and see her friend and former colleague, Sam. But there was no denying that leaving work would leave a gaping hole in her week. More than ever she was glad to have been given the opportunity to continue working as a detective.

Convinced that Ian had taken a hand in persuading Eileen to take her on she smiled at him, but he didn't notice. He seemed to be intent on something Naomi was saying, the two of them engrossed in what appeared to be a private conversation, leaning forward in their chairs, their heads almost touching. Ian left, and a few moments later Naomi stood up and followed him. Geraldine remained behind with Ariadne.

'There's definitely something going on,' Ariadne said, nodding her head, as though she was carrying on an existing conversation. She turned to Geraldine. 'You know Ian, don't you?'

'I used to work with him, years ago.'

'Do you know what's going on between him and Naomi?'

Geraldine raised her eyebrows. 'What do you mean, what's going on?'

'Don't tell me you haven't noticed the way she follows him around all the time, like a little lapdog?' Ariadne laughed.

'They work together,' Geraldine said, smiling in an attempt to hide her irritation.

Although she didn't say that in her opinion such gossip was at best a waste of time, when Ariadne pressed her for an opinion, Geraldine gave a noncommittal grunt, and the conversation moved on. For Ian's sake, Geraldine hoped the speculation about him and Naomi was true. Although not as beautiful as Ian's estranged wife, Naomi was undoubtedly attractive and bright, and she seemed like a pleasant young woman, if rather shallow. If she could make Ian happy, it was no more than he deserved, especially after the way his wife had cheated on him, deserting him to have another man's baby. But the thought that Naomi might supplant Ian's former wife gave Geraldine a cold feeling, as though she herself was being supplanted by Naomi. She knew it was ridiculous of her to resent Ian's relationship with Naomi. He had never said or done anything to suggest Geraldine had ever meant anything more to him than any other former colleague. She had no business feeling disappointed. All the same she felt oddly deflated as she stood up and left. Returning to her desk, she turned her attention back to the more important question of who had a motive to kill both Mark and Amanda, but her thoughts kept wandering back to Ian and Naomi.

39

'YOU READY THEN? EVERYTHING'S in place. I told the boys you're rock solid, so you'd better not let me down.'

Abe's gaze was steady, but Eddy noticed a faint sheen of sweat on his upper lip. As though reading his companion's thoughts, Abe wiped his mouth on his sleeve, muttering. 'It's bloody hot in here.'

Eddy nodded. The atmosphere in the pub was oppressive, with an unpleasant smell of sweat and hops, and piped music blaring out a repetitive beat. A couple of girls were sitting at the next table, their shrill voices raised above the din of the music. Eddy's head felt heavy and he was suddenly so tired he thought he would fall asleep if he allowed his eyes to close even for a second. But of course he couldn't nod off while Abe sat glaring at him across the table.

'I said, are you ready? Jesus, are you deaf?'

Eddy squirmed in his hard seat. 'I heard you.'

'Because if I thought you were getting cold feet –'

Abe broke off, leaving an unspoken threat hanging in the air between them.

'I'm as ready as I'll ever be,' Eddy assured him.

Abe's thin lips twisted in a grin, displaying yellowing teeth. He leaned forward until their noses were almost touching and Eddy caught a whiff of his bad breath. It took all of Eddy's self-control not to jerk backwards. Forcing himself to sit still, he stared back at his companion.

'That's good, because there's no bottling it,' Abe said. 'We've got to be able to rely on you a hundred per cent. This isn't a game.'

'I never said anything about it being a game. If I say I'll do something, I do it.' Although Eddy didn't know exactly what he was getting himself involved in, he had tumbled to the fact that it was illegal. 'What exactly is this job, anyway? I need to know what I'm letting myself in for before I agree to anything.'

Abe's expression darkened and his eyes seemed to burn holes in Eddy's head. 'You already agreed. That means you're committed to seeing it through. It's too late to start asking questions. We're going tomorrow. You're the driver. So you'd better get used to it. Stay cool and clear-headed.' Ignoring Eddy's protests that he was a master of self-control, Abe continued. 'You can't back out now. And you can't fuck it up, or we're all in the shit. Me and the other boys don't take kindly to people who screw things up for us. It's not just a question of the money. If you get us all banged up... well, let's just say I wouldn't want to be in your shoes if that happened. Even in the nick you'd be looking over your shoulder every minute of the day. And once my boys got their hands on you –' he glared at Eddy. 'I'll break your balls myself if you let us down. It's nothing personal,' he added, seeing Eddy's horrified expression. 'But seeing as I introduced you to the gang, I'd feel responsible if you blew it.'

Eddy nodded anxiously. He had an uneasy feeling he was getting himself in too deep, but wasn't sure how to distance himself from Abe. If he tried to walk away, not only would he lose the money he desperately needed, but he'd risk upsetting his new acquaintance, which didn't seem like a good idea. He wasn't sure whether he should be more worried about falling foul of the police or of Abe. Either was enough to give him nightmares.

'So you just take things nice and steady. Do as you're told, and you won't lose –' Abe broke off and his gaze moved slowly across Eddy's face, lingering on each of his eyes as though weighing up how long it would take to gouge them out. 'You won't lose your chance of getting your hands on some easy money,' he concluded.

Eddy licked his lips nervously. 'I won't let you down. Honestly, you know you can rely on me.'

Abe grunted and wiped his mouth on his sleeve. 'Let's step outside. I need a smoke.'

Eddy hadn't finished his pint but he didn't dare refuse. Gulping down a last mouthful, he followed Abe outside.

'It's a lot of money,' he muttered as he caught up with his companion. 'All I've got to do is drive the car? And that's it?'

'Keep your voice down. Yeah, that's all you've got to do. It couldn't be easier. And there's no risk to you. Meet me here at four. I'll give you the keys.' Abe took a long slow drag of his cigarette as he glanced around. 'It's an old black BMW.' He inhaled again and then told Eddy the registration number of the car. 'Make sure you don't forget it.'

Eddy nodded. 'Got it.'

'Go straight to the car. Get in and wait. Watch the pavement on your side of the road. When you see me, start the engine. Don't hang around. As soon as I'm in the car, put your foot down. I'll direct you. That's all you need to know.'

Before Eddy could reply, Abe turned on his heel and walked away. Eddy wandered back into the pub, hoping that his glass would still be on the table. It was. Resuming his seat, he gulped the tepid beer. To be paid so much for doing nothing more onerous than driving a car seemed like a good deal, but the set-up was risky. Abe seemed confident he would get away with enough money to pay Eddy a tidy sum just for driving the getaway car. That must mean he was planning a serious robbery. For some reason that no longer seemed as worrying as it had done just a few minutes earlier. With Abe no longer around, Eddy began to relax.

By the time he had finished his beer, he was feeling quite bold. To make that sort of money, he guessed they must be going to rob a jewellers, or a bank, but he didn't want to think about that too much. All he needed to focus on was driving the car, which couldn't be difficult. Abe had told him it was an old BMW. He wished he had asked to drive it beforehand to get used to the controls, but he supposed it would be no different to any other car, and Abe had made it clear that the less Eddy knew about the job the better. That was fine, because it meant that if anyone gave the police a tip off, Eddy couldn't be suspected of being a grass. And if Abe and his accomplices were caught, Eddy would simply drive away without them. He wouldn't get his money, but even if the worst happened, at least he'd be in the clear.

40

TRACES OF EARTH FOUND on Amanda's body had been analysed. There hadn't been much to work with, but a tiny scraping of mud from her dressing gown had yielded some interesting results. Eileen had gathered the team together to discuss the findings.

'So the soil didn't come from where the body was found?' someone asked.

Eileen merely grunted. The report concluded that the soil had come from a cultivated garden. Microscopic fibres from plants including roses and daffodil bulbs had been found, along with traces of pine bark and evidence of dog waste from a Pitweiler, a cross between a Pit bull and a Rottweiler. The report was unequivocal; the mud couldn't have come from land adjoining the road where the body had been discovered. The findings tied in with the scene of crime officers' judgement that Amanda was already dead when her body had been deposited there.

'She left a single shoe outside her house,' Eileen said. 'Why? She must have known we would find it. Was she trying to tell us something?'

No one answered.

'What about the dog faeces found in the mud?' Geraldine asked. 'Did the victim or anyone living nearby own a potentially dangerous dog like that? If it's a dangerous cross-breed, surely it can't be that common?'

Again the questions were met with silence. The specimen had been carefully analysed but the results were frustrating.

No dog matching that description had been registered with a certificate of exemption anywhere in the area which meant that if the animal lived locally, the owner was keeping the dog illegally. That alone was cause for concern. A trained dog handler at the police station confirmed what they all knew, that such a cross-bred animal could be dangerous.

'These dogs are required to be registered for a reason,' the dog handler explained. 'An animal with that genetic heritage can become vicious if it's not properly cared for and effectively trained. The same is true of any dog, of course, but this kind of Pitweiler typically combines the strength and aggression of a Rottweiler with the temperament of a potentially belligerent Pit bull. If it's being held somewhere in the area, we need to be notified so we can check that appropriate safety measures are in place, like keeping it muzzled in public. And we need to be sure the animal is being well cared for. We have no record of any such animal living in the York area. If you track it down, we need to speak to the owner and check the dog's living conditions are appropriate. It would need to be properly exercised, and well trained, and of course it would have to be muzzled.'

A team was set up to question people who lived near Amanda's house, moving in ever widening circles, searching for information about a large dog being kept somewhere in the area. Despite the slightly baffling evidence, there was an air of renewed optimism in the team as they went about their allotted tasks. They were all aware that if they could only trace the dog, they might find the killer, and an unusually large dog had to be easier to find than an unknown man. Since she had already questioned her once, Geraldine started her enquiries with Moira who had been living next door to Amanda. Moira looked slightly taken aback to see Geraldine on her doorstep, and she hesitated when Geraldine explained she would like to ask a few more questions.

From along the hallway, they heard Geoff's voice calling out, 'Who is it, love?'

'It's that policewoman come back with more questions.'

'You'd better invite her in, then,' he answered.

Still Moira hesitated.

'Is there a problem?' Geraldine asked.

Moira looked uncomfortable. 'It's just that, well, we've been thinking we'd really like to keep the poor thing. But of course, if there's someone who has a claim to it –'

It took Geraldine a moment to work out what Moira was talking about. As soon as she realised, she hurried to reassure her.

'I'm not here to talk about your neighbour's cat. I'm here as part of a team conducting an investigation into Amanda's murder. I can assure you we're not interested in her cat, and I'm sure you're looking after it very well.'

Ironically she had actually come to ask about a dog. When she explained what she was there for, Moira invited her in at once. Geraldine accepted so that she could speak to Moira and her husband, either one of whom might have heard or seen something about a large dog living in the vicinity. But she might as well not have bothered as neither Moira nor Geoff could offer any helpful information although they spent a long time discussing what breed of dog one of their other neighbours owned, finally agreeing it was a corgi.

'Like the Queen's dogs,' Moira said.

'But not a big dog,' Geoff added.

Geraldine continued her enquiries, but even people who tried to be obliging came up with similar useless responses. Returning to the police station, she found her colleagues had also drawn a blank. No one had reported hearing an unknown dog barking at night, and no one had seen a large dog matching the description they were given. Opinions among the officers were divided. Some of the team concluded the dog couldn't be living in the area, while others thought it was being kept somewhere out of sight.

'No one could hide a dog that size,' Ariadne said. 'It would need to go outside to be exercised and then someone would see it.'

'Not if it was only let out at night.'

'But people would hear it barking.'

'Perhaps it's never let out at all.'

'If it's being cooped up somewhere, it'll be going stir crazy.'

But whether the dog was local or not, their failure to trace it was disappointing. Even approaching dog breeders nationwide yielded no result, although if the animal was an illegally produced cross-breed, there was unlikely to be an official record of its existence. The mood around the police station was deflated that afternoon. Eileen marched out of the meeting, frowning, and once she had left the room the remaining officers dispersed quietly. Not for the first time, Geraldine felt that Eileen had let slip a chance to motivate the team with a few encouraging words, although it was difficult to know what she could have said without sounding patronising. Everyone knew they were not getting very far with the investigation. With a sigh, Geraldine returned to her desk to begin writing up her decision log for the day.

41

ABE VANISHED SO QUICKLY Eddy might have doubted he had been there at all, were it not for the key in his hand. He glanced down at a standard car key on an unidentified metal key ring. Slipping the key in his pocket he set off to look for the black BMW. To his relief he spotted it straight away, parked exactly where Abe had said it would be, in a quiet side turning just round the corner from the row of shops. There were cars parked on either side of the road, but no sign of life on the street or in any of the houses along the road as he approached the car. Although a few years old it was still a nice looking motor, if unremarkable, a car that wouldn't attract unwanted attention. Eddy breathed a sigh of relief. He had been worried he might not be able to find the car. As it was, he was going to earn himself a tidy sum driving that set of wheels.

The waiting around had been making him nervous, but now the time had come to do the job, his apprehension melted away. Never one to shy away from a risk, he felt a surge of his characteristic optimism. He just knew things were going to turn out all right. It had only ever been just a question of time before he got his hands on enough money to pay off his debts. Once that was all dealt with, he would be sorted. It was a sign, Abe having turned up out of the blue when he did, just when Eddy had hit rock bottom. And if the job with Abe failed to convert into a long-term money spinner, Eddy still had his back-up plan. Humming very softly under his breath, he sauntered along the pavement, his identity discreetly concealed behind sunglasses and baseball cap. As he approached the car he glanced around. Abe had warned him not to get in if he noticed anyone loitering nearby. But he saw nothing suspicious, no one who could have been a plain-clothes cop watching to see who was going to get in the car.

Even so his hand trembled as he turned the key, and as the door shut, he felt trapped. If the BMW *was* being watched, he would be caught before he had even turned the key in the ignition. He shut his eyes and tensed, waiting for uniformed police to surround the car.

Nothing happened.

He sat motionless for a moment, his eyes closed, waiting. And still nothing happened. After a few minutes his breathing slowed down to a normal rate though his heart continued pounding as if he was running. He opened his eyes. There was no movement in the street. Now all he had to do was wait. That was the difficult part. He didn't dare close his eyes again even fleetingly, for fear he would miss seeing Abe running towards the car. Neither of them had mentioned the jewellers a few doors along from the side turning where the car was parked, but Eddy was sure that must be the target of the robbery. He stared straight ahead, picturing the shop window, its contents twinkling and sparkling in the sunlight. He imagined Abe and another shadowy figure entering the shop, their faces masked, and a terrified shop assistant handing over money and fabulous jewellery.

A shrill alarm startled him, sounding very close by. At the same time he heard a distant clamour of raised voices. He turned the key in the ignition and the engine purred softly while he waited. Two masked figures burst into view, pounding along the pavement. Eddy had a brief glimpse of Abe's eyes glaring wildly from behind his balaclava. His stocky accomplice appeared to be struggling to keep up with him. Reaching the car, they wrenched open the doors Eddy had unlocked in preparation, and hurled themselves into the car, Abe in the front passenger seat and the stranger in the back.

'Go! Go! Go!' Abe cried out as he slammed his door shut.

Before he had finished the first word, Eddy spun the wheel and was pulling away from the kerb while Abe called out directions. They turned left, right, and left again, zigzagging away from the spot where Eddy had been waiting for them. Crossing Lendal Bridge they were forced to slowed down.

'I can't go any faster,' Eddy said, alarmed that they hadn't travelled far from the scene of the robbery, and were no longer able to speed away.

'Don't worry,' Abe said, still panting from his desperate sprint. 'Head towards the station. There's no panic now. We should be OK along here. No one's going to spot us in all this traffic –'

He broke off as a siren rang out above the hum of traffic. Automatically, Eddy's foot hit the accelerator and the car jolted forward but he had to brake almost at once as they drew close to the car in front. The man in the back of the car swore.

'Calm down. They're not looking for us,' Abe said. 'Take that balaclava off, you fucking moron!'

'Of course they're looking for us,' the other man said, his voice shrill with agitation. 'We just robbed a fucking jewellers. Who do you think they're looking for?'

'Sure they're after whoever did it, but they don't know it was *us*, do they?' Abe replied. 'So shut the fuck up, will you? Eddy was parked round the corner, out of sight. No one saw us get in the car. Look,' he went on, raising his voice, 'the street's packed with bloody cars. How are they going to know it was us? Just stay cool and there won't be a problem.'

The man in the back of the car fell silent. Eddy glanced in the rear view mirror and saw that he had pulled off his balaclava to reveal a large square face, still ruddy from his recent exertion. As though sensing Eddy was looking at him, he raised his head. Beady black eyes stared back at Eddy, who shifted his attention back to the road in front. There was something unnerving about the other man's expression. It wasn't just that he was scared, he looked malevolent. For the first time, Eddy began to regret his involvement. Abe had made it all sound so simple and risk-free, but the reality felt very different. Still, it was too late to back out now, even if he wanted to. Wordlessly he drove towards the station, trying to focus on the money he was going to collect when the journey was over, and telling himself it would be worth it in the end. In exchange for a few uncomfortable minutes, he would receive the best part of a thousand quid. It wouldn't solve his problems, but it was a start.

As the wail of the siren grew louder, they left the main road, turning back on themselves. Near the river, Abe barked at Eddy to stop. They waited in the car for a few moments without speaking, until another man approached them.

'Who the fuck is that?' the passenger in the back asked, while Eddy watched the stranger uneasily.

'Come on,' Abe replied. 'This is where we ditch the wheels.'

He jumped out of the car and nodded at the man who had now drawn level with them.

'Give him the key,' Abe told Eddy.

Fumbling, Eddy did as he was told, and they watched the car disappear back the way they had come.

Abe's strained expression relaxed into a broad grin. 'Time to go home,' he said. He pulled off his gloves and slapped Eddy on the back. 'Not a bad day's work.'

He said nothing about paying Eddy for driving the car. All at once, Eddy felt apprehensive. It was awkward having to ask, but he wasn't about to leave without collecting what he was owed. He was entitled to be paid, but all the same his voice trembled slightly as he asked for his money.

Abe scowled. 'What's your problem, Eddy? Don't you trust me?'

The other man laughed, and Eddy forced a smile.

'Sure I trust you. I just thought we weren't going to hang out together for a few days, and if I'm not going to see you for a while, I'd like my money now. I don't want to wait for it.'

He paused, aware that he was talking too much. 'I need it,' he added plaintively.

'Ah, he doesn't want to wait,' the other man taunted him. 'He needs his money.' He turned his head to one side and spat on the ground.

Alone in a deserted spot with Abe and a physically powerful stranger, Eddy was helpless. If they were going to rip him off, there was nothing he could do about it. Slowly, Abe reached into the pocket of his jacket. For a terrible moment, Eddy thought he was going to pull out a gun, but instead he withdrew a grubby envelope which he held out to Eddy who snatched it gratefully.

'Destroy the envelope and change the notes as quickly as possible. Now get lost,' Abe said. 'I'll be in touch when we need you again.'

'Don't you want my number?' Eddy asked.

He was desperate to check how much was in the envelope, but didn't dare to look.

'I'll know where to find you,' Abe said. It sounded like a threat. 'Now fuck off. We can't be seen leaving here together.'

Eddy nodded and hurried away, overwhelmed with relief to be leaving.

42

EDDY COULDN'T WAIT UNTIL he reached home to check the contents of the envelope. Going into the first pub he passed, he hurried to the men's room and locked himself in a cubicle before taking out the dirty white envelope. His hand shook as he counted it. The money was all there, just as Abe had promised, in soiled twenty pound notes. Eddy wondered what kind of stash Abe had made for himself that was worth being so generous to a driver who had been in the car for less than half an hour. But there was no point in speculating. He would probably learn all about the haul in the news the next day. In the meantime, at least Abe had been right about one thing: it wasn't a bad day's work.

Abe had told him to destroy the envelope straight away. He understood the urgency as it would be covered in fingerprints, so once he was outside he slipped into an alleyway, lit a match, and held the flaming paper between his finger and thumb until he was forced to drop the last charred corner. The black scrap floated to the pavement and, with the cash safely stowed in his pocket, he set off for home. He didn't go that way deliberately, but his route took him towards the betting shop. Of course, he knew better than to succumb to that temptation, so instead of continuing on his way, he turned round and went back to the pub to have one quick beer before going home. After a couple of pints, he felt a lot better. He wasn't sure why he had been so worried earlier on. All he had done was sit in a car for about ten minutes and then drive it round the corner. There had been nothing so frightening in that. The fear had been all in his mind. He had done a good job, so there would no doubt be more like that.

He leaned back in his chair and contemplated what to do next. It was a while since he last had so many options to choose from. He could go home, or have another drink, or even take his chances on placing one small bet, just for the hell of it. With getting on for a thousand pounds in his pocket, he could afford to risk losing a single modest stake. On the other hand, a thousand pounds would retrieve the television and go some way towards sorting out his rent. Still undecided, he went over to the bar for one last pint. Mulling over his situation rationally, he realised he would be a fool to let this opportunity pass. Luciana didn't know he had taken the day off work. He had free time and money in his wallet. A chance like this might not come his way again for a while.

The old man seated at the table didn't even look up as Eddy walked past him and placed twenty pounds on the favourite. For once there was no need to feel nervous about the possibility of losing his stake, because he had plenty more cash on him. One tiny flutter, just for luck, and he would be on his way. All the same, he could feel his heart pounding as he leaned against the wall, watching the race on a small screen. With a horrible sinking feeling he saw his horse stumble. It recovered, but not quickly enough to win the race outright. That was it. Reluctantly he turned to leave the betting shop.

The old man reached out a gnarled hand and clutched at Eddy's sleeve as he passed by the table.

Eddy paused in his stride. 'Did you want something?'

The old man nodded, leering up at Eddy. 'I been at this game a long time,' he mumbled.

'So?'

'I know a winner when I see one.'

'How?'

'I make it my business to know. I been studying form all

day, waiting for a good bet, and I'm telling you, son, this is a big one.'

He jabbed at the paper with his knobbly finger, mouthing the name of a horse.

'Here, son.' He held out a greasy ten pound note. 'Do me a favour, put this on for me. I been waiting for a sure bet all day. Go on. Save my legs.' He gestured impatiently with his other hand.

Eddy frowned. 'It's good odds, but it's not the favourite –'

'What's that to you? It's my money. I'd put more on if I had it. I'm telling you that horse is going to win. It's a sure thing. Go on.'

Eddy took the tenner and went up to the counter. He took his own money out of his pocket and hesitated, wondering how much to put down. He would be a fool to ignore a tip from someone who knew how to gauge the odds. He was trembling at being given a credible tip just when he had money to place a bet. If he didn't seize this chance he would regret it for the rest of his life. He glanced back at the old man who nodded eagerly at him, muttering inaudibly. With a rush of adrenaline Eddy turned round, drew his own money from his pocket, and slapped it down on the counter. The bookie's expression didn't alter as he counted the notes. Eddy stepped back, feeling as though he was going to suffocate. He had walked in there resolving to place just one twenty pound bet, and now he had put down all of his money. This was make or break. He held his breath as the race started.

Too late, he changed his mind. He had made a stupid mistake. He shouldn't have risked more than half his money. He knew nothing about the old man. Even if he knew what he was talking about, and the horse wasn't outclassed by any of the others, it might stumble, or have an off day, and he would have lost everything. He could hardly breathe, couldn't watch or even listen to the commentary. When the result was announced, he was so agitated he could hardly hear what was said. In a daze he went to collect his winnings.

Luciana was waiting for him at home.

'Let's book a holiday,' he said, as he sat down.

'A holiday?'

'Yes. We've been so bogged down with the funeral, and my stepmother, and everything, I clean forgot we agreed to take some time off in August. Well, let's book something and go away together, just the two of us. What do you say? I was thinking, you've been so supportive while all this has been going on, you deserve a break. Where do you fancy going? We can go anywhere in the world. Just name a place you want to go and I'll book it up.'

'Are you serious? You want to go away? Can we afford it?'

'Sure, I'm serious. And yes, we can afford it. To tell you the truth, I've been planning this for a while but then with all that trouble with my father I didn't have a chance to tell you, but I've been saving up for ages. You have a think and let me know where you want to go, anywhere at all, and I'll book it up straight away.'

'Italy,' she replied without hesitation. 'I've always wanted to go to Rome.'

'Rome it is then. I'll book it up first thing in the morning.'

43

'WHAT THE HELL'S HE found this time?' Christine said, scowling at the dog. 'He's got something in his mouth. What is it?'

Tom shook his head. 'I can't see, but I don't think it's alive any more.'

'Don't be flippant. Drop it, Benjy. Drop it!' She put her hand over her mouth and shuddered. 'Tom, get it away from him. It could be diseased.'

As Tom stepped forward, the dog backed away from him with a low growl, all the while keeping hold of whatever was in its jaws. Shouting at the dog to drop whatever it had found Christine took a few steps closer to it. The dog backed away again, before turning and bounding off into the bushes. No amount of yelling persuaded it to return. Reluctantly, Tom set off in pursuit, with Christine alternately shouting instructions to him, and summons to Benjy. Neither of them paid much attention to her. Picking his way through the shrubbery Tom searched for Benjy, cursing as he slipped on the muddy ground. Nearby, he could hear the dog whimpering and gnarling, and after a few minutes he spotted its brown and white coat through the foliage. Slowly he approached and stopped in his tracks as he saw what Benjy had found.

'Jesus Christ!' he blurted out.

'What is it?' Christine shouted back from the path. 'What has he found? Is it a rabbit? Get him out of there, Tom. If it's dead it's probably diseased. It could have rabies or something.'

'I don't think rabbits get rabies,' Tom shouted back, before adding under his breath, 'and that's not a rabbit.'

He inched towards Benjy and halted.

'What's going on?' Christine shouted. 'Benjy! Benjy! Get back here now!'

The dog was crouching beside the remains of a person. As Tom took another step closer he saw the mutilated body of a woman. Only her blood-caked skirt revealed her gender as her face had been so badly damaged. It was a shred of her blood-soaked shirt that they had seen hanging from Benjy's jaws. With an exclamation of horror, Tom turned away and threw up. Flecks of pale brown vomit trembled on the leaves of a nearby bush. He was only vaguely aware of Christine's voice calling to him, demanding to know what was going on. Pulling himself together with an effort, he wiped his mouth on his sleeve and yelled at her to stay where she was. Whatever happened, he didn't want her seeing these mangled remains.

'I'll be with you in a minute,' he shouted and paused. 'Chrissie, call the police. I'll be with you as soon as I've got hold of Benjy.'

Hearing his name, the dog growled and thumped his tail on the earth.

'Police? Why? What are you talking about?'

'Just do it!'

Something in the tone of his voice must have got through to her, because Christine stopped fussing, and a few seconds later he heard her talking to someone.

'They want to know what's going on, Tom!' she called out to him. 'What do you want me to say to them?'

Leaving Benjy where he was for the moment, Tom hurried back to her.

'Oh my God, Tom, what's happened? You look terrible. What is it?' She stared closely at him. 'Have you been sick?'

Ignoring Christine's questions, he grabbed the phone from her and gave his name and their location. 'There's a body here, in the bushes. It's the body of a woman. The police need to get here now before any more animals find her.'

As he hung up it occurred to him that the dead woman

must have been lying in the bushes overnight. She might have been there for days, prey to wild scavengers, foxes and rats and goodness knows what else. It was odd that there hadn't seemed to be any insect activity, but he supposed the animals had frightened them away. It didn't do to think about it too much. Meanwhile, Christine was becoming hysterical.

'A body? What do you mean, a body? Who is it? What happened?'

Speaking as calmly as he could so as not to agitate her further, Tom explained that he hadn't recognised the woman. He didn't add that there might be no way of telling who she was, because her face had been mutilated, leaving only a bloody mess of ripped flesh. After that, what with doing his best to calm Christine, and having to remove the strip of fabric from Benjy's jaws, and drag him growling and resisting back to the path, Tom didn't have a second to himself to think any further about his disturbing find. He had just snapped Benjy's lead back on and was scolding him for trying to escape back into the bushes when they heard a siren. A few moments later a couple of uniformed police officers came running towards them over the grass.

'Are you Tom Baines?'

'Yes, yes, it's in there,' Tom replied, stammering with relief that he was no longer responsible for overseeing the body. 'It's – my dog found a body, about three feet away, in the bushes. You can't see it from here.'

He flapped his hand frantically in the direction of the dead woman. One of the police officers began to note down Tom and Christine's details, while his colleague advanced cautiously into the shrubbery.

'I can see it!' he called out after a few seconds.

'What's the status?' the other policeman called back.

There was no reply from his colleague who had disappeared from view.

'She's definitely dead,' Tom answered for him, adding

helpfully, 'your colleague's probably throwing up. I did. It's not a pleasant sight.'

'Don't worry about that,' the policeman replied. 'We're trained to deal with all eventualities.'

As he was speaking, his colleague emerged from the bushes, looking pale.

'She's dead all right,' he said, his voice trembling uncontrollably.

44

GERALDINE WAS DRIVING TO work early on Saturday morning to avoid the traffic, when she received a call about a body that had been discovered lying in the bushes in Museum Gardens, near the ancient ruins of St Mary's Abbey. It wasn't far off her route. Although she was already occupied on a case, she went straight to the park to help contain the scene while the initial assessment team were on their way. Fortunately it was still too early for many people to be out walking in the gardens. The forensic tent had not yet been set up, but an approach path had been established, which meant that Geraldine could walk right up to the body to view it in situ. When it was possible, she really liked to take a close look at the victim of an unlawful killing before they were removed to the mortuary. To do so sometimes yielded useful information that was no longer obvious once the body had been moved.

Slipping on protective clothing, she picked her way carefully over to the body which lay exposed to a grey sky. Storms had been forecast, and the air was heavy with the threat of rain. Officers were scurrying around, eager to erect the forensic tent before the downpour started. Ian arrived, having also been contacted while he was on his way to the police station. Pale and grim-faced, he gave Geraldine a brief nod of acknowledgement as he caught sight of her. She barely glimpsed his tortured expression before he turned away to gaze out across the bushes. She went straight over to him.

'I can carry on here, if you like,' she said quietly as she reached his side.

Although revulsion for dead bodies was hardly useful when working in serious crime, Geraldine sympathised with Ian's sensitivity. So many of their colleagues, herself included, were able to witness gruesome injuries with complete equanimity. In her opinion, Ian's queasiness was a sign of his humanity. She wondered whether he considered her monstrous, because she experienced no emotional reaction when viewing the dead.

But even Geraldine's composure was disturbed by the state of this victim.

As she drew close enough to observe the body clearly, she saw that the woman's head had been badly damaged. What had once been her face was now a bloody mess. Her chest and torso were drenched in blood and one of her legs was severely mangled. Her fists were clenched and a few short hairs were visible in her hands, while more clung to her blood-soaked skirt.

'That looks like animal hair,' Geraldine said.

The scene of crime officer grunted. 'That's what we thought but we'll know for sure once it's been checked in the lab.'

'She bled a lot,' Ian muttered.

Geraldine repeated her offer in an undertone. 'Do you want to go back to the station? I don't mind sticking around for a while, and I can tell you everything they come up with while I'm here.'

He shrugged. 'It's too late now. I've seen it. You can't unsee something like this.'

Geraldine had never heard Ian sound so wound up before, but she resisted the temptation to try and comfort him. No words could soften the horror of what they were looking at. Leaving him to his private struggle, she turned her attention to practicalities and walked over to a scene of crime officer.

'Have you got anything useful to tell us?'

'The doctor's here now.'

He nodded at a lanky young man who had just turned up and dropped to his knees beside the body.

Geraldine waited until the doctor straightened up before repeating her question.

'She was savaged by a large animal,' he replied solemnly.

'What kind of creature was it?'

'My guess would be a large dog. There are vicious bite marks from a large jaw, but no obvious claw marks, so it doesn't look like she was attacked by a wild cat. But that's just an opinion based on the superficial appearance of the injuries. A post mortem will tell you more. She died of –' he shrugged, 'well, of her injuries.'

'When?'

'About twelve hours ago.'

'So sometime yesterday evening?'

The doctor grunted. 'She died between seven and nine.'

Geraldine nodded. She understood it was impossible for the time of death to be pinned down more accurately than that, with the body lying outside for a time.

'I've never seen anything quite like this before,' the doctor admitted. 'Her face is…' he broke off, lost for words, before adding helplessly, 'it's horrendous.'

'The attack didn't take place here,' a scene of crime officer added briskly. 'There's hardly any blood to speak of, the ground beneath her is quite dry, and there's no sign of disturbance.'

'So she was fatally attacked by a large animal, probably a dog, and brought here after she was dead, and dumped in the bushes,' Geraldine summed up.

'Where she might have stayed for a while if she hadn't been discovered by a domestic dog,' the scene of crime officer said. 'She would probably have deteriorated further, demolished by scavengers, foxes, rats, maggots.'

'She hadn't been here very long when she was found, because there's hardly any evidence of insect activity,' another scene of crime officer added.

The forensic tent arrived and the cordoned-off space around the body grew busy. There was little more they could find out at the scene so Geraldine and Ian left. They hardly spoke on the way back to the road. They reached Ian's car first.

'I wonder how old she was?' he said as he reached for his keys. 'At least it's not our case,' he added. 'Much as I hate to say it, I'm pleased we're already occupied on an investigation. I really wouldn't want to be involved in this one.' He gave an exaggerated shudder.

Geraldine nodded. Although she was curious to know more about the creature that had mauled the poor woman to death, they had enough to do, looking into the deaths of Mark and his sister. Another team would be set up to deal with the fatal attack on the victim they had just seen. She didn't envy them.

Engrossed in her work, Geraldine had almost forgotten about the woman who had been mauled to death when Ian summoned her to his office that afternoon. As she arrived, he looked up at her with a sombre expression.

'Looks like we're going to be investigating the woman after all,' he said.

'What woman?'

'The one who was killed by the Hound of the Baskervilles.'

'Ian, what are you talking about?'

But of course she knew.

'I'm talking about the woman who was found in Museum Gardens this morning.'

'Yes, yes, I realised that. How many women have we seen today who were mauled to death by an animal? But why would *we* be looking into it? We're already on a case.'

Ian sighed. 'Because the woman who was killed was –'

'Charlotte?'

'How did you know?'

'I didn't. I mean, I just guessed it from what you were saying.'

'Well, you're right. So someone's got to go to the mortuary, and see her again –'

'I'll go.'

Without waiting for a response, Geraldine turned and left

Ian's office. She hoped he hadn't noticed the expression on her face in case he misinterpreted her gratification at helping him for pleasure at having a chance to view the gruesome corpse again. Nothing could have been further from the truth.

45

THE PATHOLOGIST, JONAH, LOOKED up as Geraldine entered the room.

'Well, hello again, Geraldine. How are you? No Ian this time, I see?'

She shrugged. 'I'm afraid you'll have to put up with me today.'

'That's probably just as well. I have to say I don't blame him for not wanting to look at this. She's a mess.'

Geraldine didn't answer.

'I get the impression your inspector's not keen on looking at dead bodies,' Jonah went on, staring curiously at Geraldine. 'Am I right?'

Uncertain how to answer, she didn't say anything.

'Either that, or he doesn't want to see me,' he added with a grin.

Geraldine returned his smile. 'That must be it,' she replied.

'Aha,' he cried out. 'The ice queen melts. So, I suppose you want to know what happened to this poor woman?' He let out an exaggerated sigh. 'And I thought you'd come here just to see me.'

'I wish that was the only reason.'

With a rueful smile, Geraldine turned to look at the body. It was usually disturbing viewing the corpse of someone she had met while they were still alive, but in this instance it was somehow less disconcerting because Charlotte wasn't easy to recognise. Not merely anonymous, she barely looked human.

'It's self-explanatory,' Jonah began, suddenly brisk. 'She

was killed by physical trauma, shock, blood loss. Her carotid artery was ripped out.' He pointed at the dead woman's ravaged throat. 'She would have bled to death within minutes if she hadn't already passed out from physical shock.' The woman's bloody injuries had been cleaned up and he pointed to bruising on her knees. 'It looks as though she fell to her knees while she was still breathing, if not actually conscious. The first injury appears to have been inflicted here.' He pointed again to the woman's injured throat. 'All this,' he waved his hand at her head and chest, 'all of it was mutilated post mortem.'

'So the attack continued after she was dead?'

Jonah nodded. 'I'd say it went on for a while. Either she was on her own with the animal, or someone else there wasn't able to pull the animal off in time to save her.'

'Or they were watching,' Geraldine added quietly.

Jonah glanced at her and frowned. 'Well, yes, there is that possibility. At any rate, like I said, it appears no attempt was made to stop the attack for a while. Maybe no one else was present. It looks as though the creature was savage, wild even.' He frowned and glanced at Geraldine again, as though weighing up how much to tell her.

'Go on,' she said. 'You were saying –?'

'If that dog is still roaming around out there –' he broke off with a grimace.

'There's no way to hide behind euphemisms when you're talking about something as savage as this,' Geraldine replied. She thought Jonah looked relieved. 'I'm not easily thrown by dead bodies,' she added. 'I've seen a lot of them in my time. I guess there's something about people like us that sets us apart?'

'People like us?'

'I mean, don't you ever wonder how it is we can see things like – well, like this – without having nightmares?'

Jonah looked solemn. 'What makes you think I don't have nightmares? I can assure you I do – and they're always about my wife's credit card bills.' He laughed.

'I'm being serious. Most people wouldn't be able to stomach seeing this kind of thing.'

'It's all part of the job,' he replied casually. 'There are plenty of other jobs I'd have more of a problem with.'

'Such as?'

'I wouldn't want to stick my hand up a cow's backside, and I couldn't operate on a living person. How do surgeons do it? What if they make a mistake? At least with these guys,' he patted Charlotte's bruised knee, 'well, the suffering's over for them, isn't it?'

'Yes, that's what I think,' Geraldine replied.

Relieved that he understood her, she was about to explain that the worst part of her job was dealing with the bereaved families of the victims, but before she could say any more, Jonah continued.

'It was only through her dental records that we were able to identify her. We'll have to try and reconstruct her face but it's not going to be easy for anyone to formally identify her from her appearance. Fortunately, she had a fair bit of work done on her teeth so we've got a definite identification, probably more reliable than visual recognition.'

An hour later Geraldine was back at the police station reporting to Ian about what Jonah had told her. There wasn't really much to add to what they both already knew, as the nature and extent of the victim's injuries had been apparent from their first glance at the body. It didn't take a pathologist to establish the cause of *this* death. But the reason behind it was far from clear. They could be certain only that shortly after Mark died, his sister had been strangled and his wife had been killed by a vicious dog.

'So who stands to benefit from all these deaths?' Eileen asked, once the team had read the report on Charlotte's death.

No one even questioned whether this was another murder.

'Oh my God,' Ariadne blurted out on seeing an image of the dead woman. 'Her face is...'

A few officers groaned and muttered that it was 'gross' and 'disgusting'.

'So,' Eileen's voice cut across the murmuring. 'Who stands to gain from all this?'

Once more, the question was rhetorical. Charlotte had inherited Mark's entire estate which now passed to their only son. It was time to question Eddy again, and Ian was tasked with conducting the interview. Gratified when Ian chose her to accompany him, Geraldine followed his familiar figure along the corridor and out to the car park. It was a bright cold day and they walked quickly.

'You drive,' he said as they reached the car, and she nodded.

Neither of them spoke again, but Geraldine was aware they might be heading towards a defining moment in the investigation.

46

As they waited on the doorstep, Geraldine wondered what it would be like to pursue a career where her arrival was actually welcomed by members of the public, someone delivering parcels perhaps, or pizza. It was increasingly rare for anyone to be pleased to see her outside their front door.

'Do you think anyone's in?' Ian asked, looking around impatiently.

'No one's ever in a hurry to open the door to us,' she replied.

'That's because we're mostly bringing bad news.'

'Or because everyone has a guilty conscience.'

'Speak for yourself.'

She smiled. 'I'd open the door to a police officer any day.'

As she was speaking, the front door opened.

'Edward Abbott?' Ian greeted the man who was frowning at them from the doorway.

'Who wants to know?'

Catching sight of Geraldine, he broke off abruptly and pressed his lips together.

'Edward, we'd like a word with you,' Ian went on.

'It's Eddy, not Edward. My name's Eddy. So, what's the problem?' He swayed slightly as he spoke, his speech slurred.

'Shall we go inside?'

Muttering under his breath, Eddy led them into a small hallway. The threadbare carpet was cluttered with shoes and junk mail.

'What do you want?'

'Shall we go in and sit down?' Geraldine asked gently.

'No. You can talk to me here. What do you want?' he repeated, leaning unsteadily against the wall.

'It's about your stepmother.'

'My stepmother? What's she done?'

'I'm afraid she's dead.'

Eddy's expression was a combination of surprise and shock which appeared genuine.

'So the house... and everything...' he stammered, and paused, taking in what he had just heard. 'You're saying she's dead?'

'I'm afraid so,' Ian replied.

'I didn't know she was – what was wrong with her? What happened?'

'Wouldn't you like to sit down?' Geraldine said gently. 'This must be a shock.'

Eddy glared at her. 'No I wouldn't like to sit down. I'm fine here. And how I feel about the death of my mother is none of your fucking business. She wasn't my mother, she was my stepmother. You know what? A man's entitled to his own private thoughts, isn't he?' They let him continue with his rambling monologue, his voice rising in frustration. 'What is this? You think you can police people's thoughts now? And you think all mothers are so wonderful? If you must know, I did my best to help her after my father died. I did everything she asked me to do, but I never got any thanks for it.' He scowled and waved his hands in the air while he was speaking, as though to emphasise his points. 'She was always tightfisted, and she made no effort to be nice to Luciana. My stepmother only knows one person – only knew one person, I should say. So no, you might not like it that I'm not feeling particularly upset right now, but I can tell you, there's no reason why I should give a damn about her now she's dead, any more than she gave a damn about me while she was alive.' His face twisted into a smile. 'So I'm the heir to my father's estate now? You can look as disapproving as you like, but you can't tell me you wouldn't be pleased if you suddenly came into a load of money. It's money I'm entitled to, and she kept it from me.'

'Sit down,' Ian said quietly, steering Eddy through the door into the living room.

For an instant it looked as though Eddy might be considering squaring up to Ian, but the detective towered over him, waiting until he sat down abruptly, muttering, 'I want you to leave.'

Geraldine and Ian exchanged a glance.

'The thing is, your mother didn't die of natural causes,' she said softly.

Eddy scowled at her. 'What difference does it make how she died? She's dead, isn't she?'

Geraldine repeated what she had said.

'What's your point? You came here to tell me she's dead, which means her house belongs to me now. And now I want to be left alone. I've got a lot to think about.'

'You'd better come with us,' Ian said heavily. 'There are a few questions we need to ask you.'

Eddy's expression altered. All at once he looked frightened, as he finally grasped the implications of his mother's death.

'No! What do you want with me? Just get out and leave me alone.'

'Come along now,' Ian said. 'You'll only make things more difficult for yourself if you resist.'

'I told you to bugger off and leave me alone. I've not been arrested. You can't make me go anywhere. Now get lost.'

'If you had nothing to do with your mother's death, there's no reason why you would refuse to help us,' Geraldine pointed out. 'Surely you want to help us find out what happened to her?'

'What *did* happen to her?'

Geraldine hesitated.

'She was attacked and killed by a dog,' Ian replied shortly.

'A dog? Bloody hell. What sort of a dog?'

'A dog big enough to kill a grown woman. Do you know anyone who owns a dog like that?'

219

Eddy looked startled. 'No. You've got my mother confused with someone else. She never even had a dog.'

'What about you?'

'What about me? I haven't got a dog, if that's what you mean. I never had a dog. My wife isn't keen on them.' He paused for a moment, frowning. 'Aren't you supposed to do a formal identification? How can you be sure it's her?'

When Ian explained that his stepmother's body had been identified through her dental records, Eddy shook his head.

'You met her, didn't you?' he asked Geraldine, turning to her. 'Why didn't you recognise her? What's the deal with her dental records? What's going on?'

Reminding herself that Eddy had a strong motive to murder his stepmother, Geraldine batted his question away. She couldn't afford to feel sorry for him at this stage in the investigation. True, he had just lost his stepmother, but it was looking as though he had murdered her himself.

'Come along,' Ian said. 'Let's go along to the police station.'

'No way.'

'We can talk more easily there.'

'We can talk here,' Eddy replied doggedly. 'I'm not going to the police station. You'll have to arrest me first.'

Without any evidence to suggest he was a suspect, they couldn't insist on Eddy accompanying them to the police station. Eddy's face was sweaty and very pale. He wiped his forehead with his sleeve and gave a worried smile.

'Go on then,' he said. 'What happened to her?'

Ian answered him with another question. 'We'd like to know where you were yesterday evening.'

'What?' Eddy asked. 'Why yesterday evening? Is that when it happened?'

'Your stepmother was attacked by a dog,' Ian repeated. 'We need to work out where it happened, and why, and we need your cooperation so we can make sure whoever's responsible is apprehended.'

'Yes, you find out what happened,' Eddy responded, with growing agitation. 'This is my mother you're talking about. You've come here to tell me she's been killed and I want to know who did for her!'

'That's what we're trying to find out,' Geraldine said. 'Now, perhaps you'd like to start cooperating. So, where were you yesterday evening?'

He hesitated. 'I was here.'

'Can anyone corroborate that?' Ian asked.

'What do you mean?'

'Was anyone else here at home with you yesterday evening between around seven and nine?'

'I was here with my wife all evening, from about half past five. She'd tell you that herself only she's not here, but she'll be home in about an hour if you'd like to come back and speak to her.'

Eddy appeared to have sobered up and now seemed to want to be helpful. Geraldine wondered how genuine his alibi was, but in the meantime they couldn't sit around for an hour waiting for his wife to return. Once they were back in the car, Geraldine traced Luciana's mobile number and called it but there was no reply so they decided to go straight to Luciana's place of work. They were keen to speak to her before she saw Eddy.

'You don't think he'll get to her first, do you?'

Ian shook his head. 'She's probably not answering her phone because she's still at work. I can't see how he could have spoken to her yet, but there's nothing we can do about it if he has. Find out where she works and we'll go straight there.'

47

THE DOOR CLOSED ON the two detectives, and Eddy ran to find his phone. He had to persuade Luciana to agree to tell the police that they had spent the previous evening together. As long as he spoke to her first, he was home and dry. He didn't really harbour any serious doubt that she would back him up. She was his wife, after all. But until he had explained the situation to her, he would be on tenterhooks in case the police questioned her before he had a chance to speak to her. He thought quickly. He could call her, but there would be a record of his having done so. With a flash of inspiration he remembered the pay as you go mobile phone Abe had given him.

'Take this in case we need to make contact. I bought it for cash so there's no way the police can trace it back to me. Only call me if you have to.'

There had been no need for Eddy to use it, until now.

He ran to the bedroom and rummaged in his underwear drawer, tossing socks and pants on the floor in his desperate hurry to get his hands on the phone. Praying that Luciana would pick up, he dialled the shop. He didn't call his wife's mobile in case the police saw that she had received a call from an unknown number immediately after they had spoken to him. To his immense relief, she answered.

'Luciana, it's me. Don't speak, just listen. Make an excuse to leave work early and come straight home. Don't speak to anyone, and don't answer your phone to anyone. I'll explain when you get here.'

'Eddy, what –'

'Just do it, will you? Come home now.'

'Are you all right?'

'Yes, yes, there's nothing wrong, but I need to speak to you right now. Come home, please.'

'Have you been gambling again?'

'No, no, it's nothing like that. Listen, the police were here just now.'

'The police?'

'Can you stop interrupting me to repeat everything I say! My stepmother's dead –'

'Your stepmother? Oh my God, I'm so sorry. What happened? It's not another –'

'Never mind all that. The thing is, I think I could be in trouble –'

'What do you mean?'

'It's complicated.'

'Eddy, tell me what's happened.'

'Come home and I'll explain. And don't talk to anyone!'

'Tell me what's going on.'

Eddy groaned. This was taking too long. While they were talking, the police could be on their way to speak to his wife.

'She was murdered,' he said, his voice rising in panic. 'Just come home, will you?'

Luciana spoke so softly he could barely hear what she was saying. 'Did you do it, Eddy?'

'What?'

'Your mother, did you –'

'What? God no! But the police seem to think I did, just because I'll now inherit the house and everything.'

'Jesus.' He heard her gasp and then she asked briskly, 'What do you want me to do?'

'Don't speak to the police before I've spoken to you.'

'I won't.'

He realised if his wife left work early that might also arouse suspicion. In the meantime, they had been talking for so long, it was possible the police were already there. He would have to explain the situation to her right away.

He spoke quickly. 'Listen, they might be there any minute. It's probably not a good idea for you to leave early. It might look suspicious.'

'What do you mean, suspicious?'

'All you have to do is tell the police that you were with me, at home, yesterday evening. You came straight home from work, I was here, and we were both in all evening. Have you got that?'

'Yes, but –'

Afraid the police might arrive and see her on the phone, he rang off, cursing her for having kept him talking for so long. He should have told her what had happened and what to say to the police straight away, instead of messing about like that. But when he looked at the phone he saw that they had actually been talking for less than a minute. He turned the phone off and removed the sim card. There was no way the police would be able to discover he had spoken to Luciana after they had called at the house. He found a bottle of beer in the kitchen and went into the living room. The beer wasn't as cold as he would have liked, but he flung himself down in a chair and gulped it down anyway.

'Do your worst,' he muttered. 'Go on, knock yourselves out. She's my wife and you can fuck off with your questions and your suspicions of a poor orphan.'

Then he began to laugh because he wasn't poor. Not any longer. His stepmother had saved him, after all, in spite of herself. He remembered his real mother with an overwhelming feeling of warmth and laughter, recalled holidays on the beach, and her taking care of him when he had been ill, but he could picture her face only as a series of still photographs. After her death, which had been quite sudden, he had been looked after by another woman he hadn't liked at all. She had been very strict and never laughed. With hindsight he guessed he had resented her for not being his mother. When his father had remarried a year later, he had been young enough to accept his stepmother without too much trouble because he felt she had saved him from the hated nanny. They had got on well enough while he was a child. And now she was dead.

He gazed around his cramped living room, slowly registering that everything in his life was about to change. The carpet in the living room was stained, the curtains threadbare, and the paper was peeling off one wall near the ceiling. He had promised Luciana he would redecorate the room when he had time.

'You've got time to decorate Charlotte's hall,' she had pointed out, scowling.

He had no answer to that. His stepmother had been on her own, in a state of shock after his father's death. He had felt bound to help her.

'It's not that I'm putting her first,' he had tried to explain to his wife.

Now he wouldn't have to bother with decorating, because they would be moving out. They had a proper house to live in, with a nice garden, and an en suite bathroom, and a kitchen large enough to accommodate a table and chairs, and a separate dining room as well. Or they could sell his parents' house and buy another one of their own. Life was changing, all right, and everything had turned out for the best in the end, as he had always known it would. He was going to make sure his stepmother had a proper send-off, as long as it didn't cost too much. That was the least he could do for her. And best of all, he would be able to conceal the extent of his debts from his wife. He knew from his stepmother's experience that he would have to wait for the lawyers to do their messing around before he could get his hands on the money. In the meantime, he just needed a small win to tide him over until his inheritance came through.

He had known his run of bad luck couldn't last forever.

Emptying his wallet he counted out two five pound notes and nearly ten pounds in change. It wasn't much. There was only one thing for it. He wouldn't have raided the holiday money if his stepmother hadn't croaked, but knowing it was only a temporary measure changed everything. Pocketing the lot, he set off, whistling. To his relief the old man was sitting in his usual seat, eyes closed. Eddy went over to him and tapped him on the shoulder. The old man let out a loud snore but didn't stir.

'Hey, wake up!' Eddy whispered, shaking him vigorously by the shoulder.

The old man's eyes fluttered open and he glared at Eddy.

'What's your problem? Can't a man get a bit of shut-eye around here?'

'I need another tip,' Eddy said, pulling up a chair. 'And you're going to give it to me. Come on, mate,' he went on, in an attempt to cajole his new acquaintance into obliging him. 'You know the horses. Tell you what,' he went on when the old man didn't respond. 'I'll put a fiver down for you, how about that? No, a tenner. Just give me the name and I'll do the rest. It doesn't have to be the next race. I can wait. Just give me another winner and we both cash in. What do you say?'

The old man stared at him. 'You'll put a tenner down for me?'

'Sure. That's the least I can do.'

Eddy's hand shook slightly as he handed over all his money. He watched, mesmerised, as it was counted. The bookie gave him a curious look and asked him to wait while he made a call. Eddie nodded uneasily and watched as the man picked up a phone. After a brief exchange, the man hung up and nodded at him to indicate his bet would be accepted. Eddy leaned against the wall and waited, telling himself that his troubles were finally over. The old man had already proved his tips were sound and Eddy only needed him to come good one more time.

When the race ended Eddy turned to the old man, barely able to contain his fury. Until that moment it hadn't seriously occurred to him that he might lose the lot.

'You told me this was a sure thing!' he yelled, only vaguely aware of a voice calling to him to 'keep it down'.

The old man cackled, revealing toothless gums. 'A sure thing,' he repeated, nodding his head.

Eddy could have wept. He had thrown nearly three thousand pounds away on a useless tip, and Luciana was bound to notice that the holiday money had gone. Resisting the urge to lash out and wipe the silly grin off the old man's face, he restrained himself, aware of the bookie's watchful eyes.

'You told me Bright Vista would win! You said it was a sure thing.'

'You can never rely on a horse,' the old man replied, tapping the side of his nose with one finger.

'You don't want to listen to Bob,' the bookie called out, hearing what Eddy had said. 'He's totally lost the plot. Thinks he's got a crystal ball. I don't remember him backing many winners.' He laughed. 'Isn't that right, Bob?'

The old man's smile didn't waver. 'I know how to pick a winner,' he mumbled. 'Golden Nugget in the next race is going to come in first. I can always tell a winner, every time.'

'You lost your tenner,' Eddy snarled.

The old man grinned up at him. 'Wasn't mine to lose.'

48

THEIR ROUTE TOOK THEM into the centre of town where Ian dropped Geraldine off. They had agreed a female detective on her own might invite confidence, and the more low-key the encounter remained, the more likely Luciana was to speak freely. By the time Geraldine walked up the hill and reached the bridal shop where Luciana worked, it was nearly closing time. She went inside and looked around. A skinny girl with highlights in her hair was standing behind a pale pink counter, surrounded by rails of long white dresses. All around her Geraldine saw white and cream lace, organza and tulle, satin shoes, and wreaths of silk flowers. With a faint pang she remembered Celia's wedding, an extravagant affair where Geraldine had been obliged to wear a frilly dress designed for a much younger woman.

'Can I help you, Madam?'

'I'm looking for Luciana. Is she here?'

The girl nodded. 'One moment.'

She disappeared, and a moment later she returned with Luciana in tow. Eddy's wife frowned when she saw Geraldine.

'Yes? I'm sorry, is there a problem?' She glanced at her colleague and gave a slight nod, as though to say she would deal with this customer.

Geraldine took a step closer to Luciana. 'I'd like to ask you a couple of questions.'

'What about?'

There was little point in trying to pretend this was a casual enquiry, so she launched straight in and asked where Luciana had been on Friday evening. Without any hesitation, Luciana replied that she had gone home after work on Friday, as she usually did.

'Not that it's any business of yours,' she added with a sour expression.

Geraldine pressed on, ignoring Luciana's scowl. 'And what time did you get home?'

Luciana shrugged one shoulder. 'About half past five, I suppose. I didn't make a note of the time.'

'Were you at home alone, or can someone confirm what you just told me?'

'Why do you want to know?'

'Please, just answer the question. Was anyone else there at home with you from half past five? Can anyone confirm that?'

Luciana's expression altered very slightly. The sardonic smile that had been playing around her lips vanished, and her expression grew wary.

'You want to know if anyone can vouch for *me*?' she said, sounding indignant. 'Why? What do you want to know that for? Why is that any of your business?'

Her colleague glanced up and looked away again. All at once, Geraldine felt so tired she could scarcely be bothered to listen to Luciana's indignant posturing.

'You got home about half past five?'

'Yes. That's what I just said.'

'And then what?'

'What do you mean?'

'It was Friday evening. Did you go out?'

Luciana shook her head. 'I was at home all night.'

'Were you on your own?'

'I spent the night in bed with my husband, actually. Do you want me to give you graphic details about what we did?'

Geraldine ignored the sneer. 'Did your husband go out at all? Popping out to the shops, or –'

'No, he didn't go out anywhere. Neither of us left the house.

I told you, we were at home all evening from sometime before six when we both got home from work. I can't remember who was home first,' she added quickly. 'Sometimes it's me, sometimes it's him gets in first. Like I said, I didn't make a note of everything that happened that evening. Why would I?'

'So you were both at home all evening?'

'I just said so, didn't I? Do you want me to say it again? I was at home, all night, with my husband.'

There was no point in prolonging the encounter so Geraldine went home and wrote up her notes. It all seemed conclusive, but the following morning Ian called to tell her that Eileen had sent a car to bring Eddy into the police station for questioning. As she had been to see Luciana, Eileen wanted Geraldine to be present when Eddy was questioned. She sighed as she listened to this latest development, but it wasn't her place to question her senior investigating officer's decision.

Walking along the corridor behind Ian, she noticed his broad shoulders looked slightly stooped. She had already observed that he had developed a slight paunch since his wife had left him, although in other respects he had scarcely changed since she had first met him as an eager young sergeant. His blond hair was as thick as ever, and his face was barely lined. Only a melancholy expression in his eyes betrayed how much he had altered from the young man she had once known, who had lived and worked with such enthusiasm. He still had as much energy as before, but he wasn't the same.

'Here goes,' he muttered as they entered the room and sat down side by side.

His smile was so strained, she wanted to reach out and reassure him that everything was going to be all right. Telling herself that he was tense only on account of the pending interview, she turned to face the two men who had just entered the room and were taking their seats. Eddy shuffled and fidgeted in his chair, while a grey-haired solicitor sat motionless at his side as Ian read out the obligatory preamble to the interview. It went on for a long time. Geraldine studied Eddy who squirmed under her steady gaze. At last Ian finished.

'So, Eddy,' Ian said pleasantly, 'let's go through this once more.'

He waited but Eddy didn't say anything.

'Where were you on Friday evening?'

'I told you, I was at home with my wife.'

'What time exactly did she come home?'

Eddy looked uncomfortable. 'I can't say,' he admitted. He glanced at his solicitor who gave an almost imperceptible nod. 'I was having a kip,' Eddy added.

'Having a kip? Hadn't you just come home from work yourself?' Ian consulted his notes. 'According to your boss, you left the builders' merchants at five and you boarded your bus at five fifteen, arriving at the top of your road at five forty.'

Eddy looked startled. 'How the hell do you know that?'

'So you must have fallen asleep pretty promptly because your wife told us she arrived home sometime before six.'

'I was tired.'

'It's not an offence to fall asleep in one's own home,' the solicitor pointed out in a low voice.

'True, but it sounds like the kind of thing someone might say when trying to fudge the truth,' Ian replied.

The solicitor laughed. 'Can you remember exactly what time your wife arrived home two days ago?'

Although Ian's face remained impassive, Eddy gave a sly smile, as though he sensed that his lawyer had somehow managed to rile the police inspector.

'What happened then?' Ian asked.

'None of your fucking business,' Eddy replied. He turned to his lawyer. 'I don't have to tell him what I do with my wife in my own house, do I?' He looked straight at Ian with a curious grin. 'Or are you one of those perverts that likes to spy on other people?'

'You still haven't told us what you and your wife did once she came home on Friday evening.'

'Well,' Eddy replied, leaning back comfortably in his chair as though he felt unassailable, 'we stayed in all evening, just the two of us. Ask Luciana. She'll tell you. It was a good evening.' He grinned.

Ian continued to question him for a while, but far from crumbling under the pressure, Eddy appeared to be enjoying himself. There was nothing to be gained from keeping him any longer. Ian was fuming, but they were powerless. All they could do was keep him in for one night to allow Geraldine time to speak to Luciana again knowing her husband wouldn't be present. But there didn't seem to be much hope that she would change her story backing his alibi.

'It's so frustrating,' Ian said, 'knowing he's guilty but still scratching around for proof.'

'We know that how?'

He looked at her in surprise. 'Now he gets to inherit the lot, doesn't he? Think about it, he killed his father for his inheritance. His stepmother took it all, so he got rid of her too. Who else stood to gain from these deaths?'

Geraldine held back from criticising him for jumping to conclusions. Instead she asked about the dog.

'So he got hold of a dog from somewhere,' Ian replied. 'It's not so difficult to get hold of a dog, is it?'

'Well, we haven't been able to find it.'

Ian grunted. 'Keep looking.'

49

GERALDINE DROVE ALONE ALONG streets that were already beginning to look familiar, in a city that had begun to feel like home. The sharp edge of regret she had initially felt about her move had blunted to nostalgia for the lively streets of North London where a cosmopolitan population roamed, and anonymity was the norm. York, with its quaint medieval streets and its modern shops and hotels, was smaller and friendlier. Yet despite its air of quiet decency, Geraldine knew there was at least one evil individual hiding in the city, someone prepared to murder for reasons known only to the killer.

Eddy's terraced house was situated halfway along a side turning, not far from a Salvation Army headquarters on the main road. Drawing into the kerb, Geraldine jumped out of her car and hurried across the narrow front yard hoping to catch Luciana before she left for work. It was a few minutes before the door opened. Luciana looked surprised to see Geraldine on the doorstep.

'Where's Eddy?'

'He'll be home when we've finished with him. Can I come in?'

After a brief hesitation Luciana opened the door. 'You're here now, aren't you?'

Geraldine stepped inside.

'You haven't told me when he's coming home,' Luciana repeated.

Cautiously Geraldine hinted that the police had reason to believe Eddy and Luciana hadn't been together all Friday evening when his stepmother had been murdered, as they had both claimed. When she tentatively issued threats about obstructing the police in their enquiry, she could see that Luciana wasn't cowed. She probably knew that as Eddy's wife she couldn't be compelled to give evidence against him in court. Her black hair swung around her pale face as she shook her head vehemently.

'No, no,' she insisted. 'We were here together, just like I said. And now I need to get to work.'

'I want you to think very carefully. Are you sure you have nothing else to tell me?'

Luciana remained adamant that she and Eddy had both been at home on Friday evening, and Geraldine left soon after that. By the time she had finished writing up her report, she was ready for lunch. She made her way to the canteen. While she sat toying with a salad, Ian came over and joined her. At first slightly surprised, but very pleased, she caught sight of his expression and put her fork down.

'What is it?'

Ian's eyes were bright with excitement. 'Just listen.'

She nodded, catching his enthusiasm. 'What's happened?'

'I've been looking into Eddy's finances.' He paused. 'He's in a lot of trouble.'

'What sort of trouble?'

'He's got debts running into tens of thousands –'

'Bloody hell. Still, that doesn't really help us. I went to see Luciana again this morning, and she's sticking to her story that they were at home together from about five thirty and there's nothing we can do about it.'

'Do you believe her?

Geraldine thought for a moment. 'No,' she said at last. 'No, I don't think so. But –'

'I know,' he interrupted her. 'We can't force her to retract her statement. Oh well, that's how it is then.'

Staring into his troubled blue eyes, Geraldine had to resist the urge to say something comforting. There was nothing she could say. They both knew they would have to let Eddy go, now that his wife had given him an alibi. Without any evidence, there was no longer any chance of a successful prosecution.

Eileen frowned at this development. 'We could try to put pressure on him, but his lawyer knows he's got an alibi.'

'But she's his wife,' a young constable protested. 'No one's going to take any notice of what she says.'

'She's still a witness,' Eileen replied shortly. 'And we don't have any proof that Eddy was involved in the murders. All we can say for certain is that his financial problems would give him a motive. But that's all. We can't send someone to court accused of having a motive for murder.'

Knowing what they did about Eddy's financial situation, Ian suggested it might be worth challenging him about his debts in front of his wife. It was possible he had been concealing the extent of his problems from her. By springing the details of Eddy's financial situation on his wife, they might provoke a spontaneous response.

'Marriage is no guarantee of loyalty,' he concluded sourly.

'Assuming she was lying about them being together all Friday evening, that could swing it,' Eileen said when they told her what they had in mind. 'And if she subsequently changes her mind again, she'll be dismissed as an unreliable witness.'

Having released Eddy, Ian and Geraldine agreed to wait until the following evening to pay their suspect and his wife a visit. Until then, they could only focus on writing up reports and checking whether there had been any new developments.

'At least there've been no more bodies today,' Ian said, with an attempt at a smile, as they left the building together that evening. 'So it could be worse.'

When she reached home, Geraldine phoned her brother-in-law. He didn't answer so she left a message, and about an hour later he returned her call.

'How's the baby?'

'He's great. He's beginning to try and turn his head!'

Geraldine sighed. She wondered what else she was going to miss in his life as he grew up.

50

STEPPING CAUTIOUSLY THROUGH THE low doorway, he tightened his grip on his cosh. Even after all this time he trembled in the presence of the beast. He wasn't sure how to go about getting rid of it, so he did nothing. Sooner or later it would die and he would be able to throw the carcass out. In the meantime, as long as it was alive he intended to make use of it.

His girlfriend was constantly nagging him to let the creature out of the cellar.

'It's not natural,' she said. 'You can't keep it locked up down there all the time. It'll go nuts.'

He laughed. 'That ship sailed a long time ago.'

'That's so cruel. Why would you want to drive a poor dumb creature nuts? Anyway, what about us?'

'What about us?'

'We've got to live here, haven't we? That filthy animal makes the whole place stink.'

'You want to clean it up?' He laughed again. 'Go on, be my guest. I won't stop you. Get down there and shovel the shit. But don't expect me to come down after you – or what's left of you by the time my dog's finished with you.'

That shut her up.

Torch in one hand, truncheon wrapped in barbed wire in the other, he descended, one step at a time, stopping halfway down the staircase out of reach of the animal's snapping teeth. With a howl it sprang towards him and halted abruptly as the leash tightened around its neck. Even though he knew the chain would prevent it from reaching the steps, he could feel his legs shaking. If he slipped, his throat would be ripped out and he would be torn apart. He stayed where he was, out of reach of the powerful jaws. Shining his torch down into the cellar he saw the beam of light quiver in his grasp, and swore. He wasn't used to experiencing fear.

The beast drew back and crouched down, gnashing its teeth, glaring at him, waiting for him to move closer. Beneath one of its front paws he could see a bone the colour of parchment, stripped of flesh. Splinters of another bone lay on the floor beside it. The creature's top lip rose in a snarl and the beam of light from the torch was reflected back from its eyes when it raised its massive head to look at him. With a roar it leapt and he almost dropped the torch in alarm.

'Down, boy!' he shouted. 'Do as you're told! Now! Down!'

Conscious that his mastery over the beast was a sham, he brandished his truncheon. If the animal hadn't been tethered, it would have attacked him. Arm raised, he took a step down, careful to remain out of reach of its slobbering fangs. He swung the cosh in front of him as he descended, and the animal retreated, glaring and snarling, dragging the bone along the filthy floor as it went. Delving into the bag he was carrying, he tossed a rotting chop down on to the floor as far into the corner as he could. While the vicious brute was distracted by the rancid meat he darted down, dropped the tub of water he was carrying, and raced back up the steps. With one bound it was at the bottom of the stairs, but he was already halfway up and out of reach. With a snarl, the animal returned to its feeding.

Reaching the door at the top of the steps, he turned and shone his torch down into the cellar. In spite of the stench, and the potential risk involved, he would be a fool to let the animal die while it was still strong enough for him to use.

'Until next time,' he called down.

As he closed the door, he heard the beast growling.

51

JUST AFTER ONE THE following day, Geraldine was thinking about stopping for lunch. The sun was out, and she fancied leaving the police compound and stretching her legs. She was about to go across the road for a sandwich when she received a message that a woman called Jill had come to the police station with information regarding the investigation into Charlotte's death. Postponing her lunch she went along to the interview room, where she saw a skinny woman with thick make-up and highlights in her hair, wearing jeans and a blue jumper. Although she couldn't place her, Geraldine thought she looked vaguely familiar, and as soon as the woman began to speak, Geraldine remembered where she had seen her recently.

'I work with Luciana,' she said, adding, 'Luciana Abbott,' as though there might be more than one woman with that first name involved in Geraldine's investigation.

Geraldine nodded. 'I saw you in the shop with her.'

'Yes, that was it. I thought I'd seen you before. The thing is, I couldn't help overhearing what you were saying. I mean, I wasn't listening, not deliberately.'

Geraldine waited but the woman sat silently gazing at the floor.

'What did you hear?'

'It's about Luciana.' She hesitated and Geraldine waited. 'I didn't mean to eavesdrop or anything, but I was right there and I couldn't help hearing what you were saying.'

'Go on.'

The woman shifted in her seat and crossed her arms, tapping one upper arm nervously.

'Why have you come to see me?' Geraldine prompted her gently.

Jill shook her head. 'No,' she muttered, half rising to her feet. 'I shouldn't have come here. It was a mistake. I haven't – I can't – I don't know what I was thinking of, coming here like this. I'm sorry to have wasted your time.'

'What is it you wanted to tell me? You had a reason for coming to see me. What is it?' She leaned forward. 'Do you know something that might have a bearing on our investigation?' She paused. 'A woman's been brutally murdered. We need to find the killer and stop him from carrying out any more attacks. So if you know anything that could help us, anything at all, you have to tell me.' She paused to allow her words to register with the other woman. 'As long as the killer remains at large, any one of us could be his next victim. Imagine how you're going to feel if you hear that the killer has claimed another victim, while you've been keeping quiet about information that could have helped us to track him down.'

While Geraldine was talking, Jill settled down in her chair again, a worried expression in her face.

'All right,' she conceded. 'You're right. There is something. But I don't know if I should say anything. It's probably nothing.'

'Go on.'

'I might have got this all wrong, but I thought I heard Luciana tell you she was at home on Friday evening. I thought she said she went straight home from work on Friday.'

'Yes, that's right. That's what she said.'

'Is this important?'

'It could be.'

'Well, she didn't.'

'Are you saying she didn't go straight home?'

'Yes, that's what I'm saying.'

'How do you know?'

'Because she was with me.'

With some prompting, Jill explained that she and her colleague had gone out for a drink on Friday evening.

'Was this something you do regularly?'

'Now and again. Does that make a difference?'

Geraldine shook her head. 'Probably not. So, whose idea was it for you to go out together last Friday?'

Jill said she couldn't remember. 'We just kind of agreed.'

'So you left work together?'

'Yes.'

'And what did you do then?'

'We had a couple of drinks and then went for a Chinese.'

'And were you together the whole time?'

Jill looked surprised. 'Yes. I mean, we might have gone to the loo –'

'And what time did you finally part company?'

Jill shrugged. 'I can't remember exactly. We must have packed up around half past five when the shop shut, then we went to the pub for a couple of pints, and then we had something to eat. We left the restaurant around nine. I remember her saying she wanted an early night.'

'So she didn't get home until after nine?'

Jill shrugged. 'I don't know what time she got home, do I?'

'But you know you were with her, in the Chinese restaurant, until about nine?'

'It must have been around nine, I suppose. But I can't be sure. Look, I've told you everything I know. Can I go now?'

There was clearly nothing more Jill could tell them, but it didn't matter. The restaurant would have records of payment, and possibly CCTV footage, to confirm what time the two women had left. Geraldine thanked her and assured her she had been very helpful.

Before they could act on Jill's testimony, they wanted to gather as much corroborative evidence as they could. Currently, they had Jill's word against Luciana's. Admittedly, if Eddy had been alone on the evening his mother had been attacked, his wife had an obvious motive for concealing the truth, and there was no ostensible reason for Jill to lie. But the situation was not necessarily as clear-cut as it appeared. As yet, they knew nothing about Jill, other than that she worked with Luciana. Reasons might emerge for dismissing her as an unreliable witness, and Eileen felt the case was too flimsy to try and pursue a prosecution.

Naomi and another constable were despatched to the pub and the Chinese restaurant to retrieve information, and by the end of the afternoon evidence had been logged that confirmed Luciana had indeed gone out with her colleague on the preceding Friday evening. They had been recorded on CCTV entering a pub at five forty, and leaving at ten to seven. Ten minutes later they arrived at a Chinese restaurant. At five to nine they settled the bill by credit card, paying half each, after which they left the restaurant just before nine fifteen. At nine thirty-five, Luciana boarded a bus which would take her to the corner of her street.

With evidence that Luciana was lying, it was time to arrest Eddy. Before sending a car to pick him up, Geraldine suggested she and Ian challenge him about his financial difficulties in front of his wife. If Luciana could be persuaded to withdraw any support for him, prosecuting him might be simpler. Eileen agreed with her proposal, and Geraldine and Ian set off together. It wasn't until they were driving away from the police station that Geraldine remembered she had missed lunch.

52

THERE WAS A DISTURBANCE in the hall.

'Shut it, will you?' Eddy called out, 'I'm trying to watch the telly here.'

'Guinness?' a man's voice said softly, as the bottle of beer was lifted out of Eddy's hand. 'There won't be much of that where you're going.'

Eddy spun round. Seeing the police inspector, he leapt to his feet. 'What the fuck? Give that back!'

He struggled to hide his apprehension as the detective approached him.

'What the fuck are you doing here?'

'We'd like to ask you a few questions concerning the murder of your stepmother on Friday evening –'

'That's nothing to do with me. I told you, I was here, with my wife, all evening. You tell them!'

Luciana began to gabble her way through the story, but the detective held up his hand to silence her.

'Unfortunately for you, we know that's not true,' he said.

'We have evidence you were away from home on Friday evening, at the pub and then out for a Chinese meal,' his female colleague added.

'What are you talking about?' Eddy asked.

'That bitch Jill,' Luciana burst out. 'She's the one who's lying. I came straight home on Friday –'

'Who's Jill?' Eddy shouted. 'Shut up, Luciana! Don't say anything! Me and my wife were here all evening.'

'Not according to the CCTV footage we have,' the detective replied.

She listed details of Luciana's movements on Friday evening, with the exact times she entered and left the pub and restaurant and boarded the bus.

While she was speaking, Luciana's shoulders dropped, and she looked helplessly at Eddy.

'Tell them they're wrong,' he called out in panic, 'tell them I was with you. Tell them, Luciana! I was here, with you, all evening!'

Ignoring his protests, the detective repeated they wanted to ask him some questions.

'Before we go,' the female detective said, 'there's something we think your wife might like to know.' She turned to Luciana. 'Are you aware of the extent of your husband's gambling debts?'

Luciana's eyes narrowed. 'What?'

'Don't listen to her,' Eddy cried out. 'They're lying. They're trying to turn you against me. It's not true. I haven't placed a single bet since I promised you I wouldn't.'

The policewoman shrugged and gave him a pitying look. 'Your husband currently owes over fifteen thousand pounds in gambling debts. He's maxed out on several credit cards. And of course the loans are all accruing interest.'

'It's lies,' Eddy cried out. 'It's all lies.'

In a panic, he attempted to push his way past the policeman who promptly slapped him in handcuffs and led him out of the house, resisting all the way. He fell silent as the car drove them to the police station. Although he wanted to bawl and struggle, locked in a car and handcuffed, there was no point in trying to escape. The next few hours passed in a blur. His shoes were taken away, while a cheery officer in uniform removed his handcuffs and his wallet and phone, and asked him a host of questions before leading him along a corridor.

'This is all wrong,' Eddy insisted. He was nearly in tears.

'You've got this all wrong. I had nothing to do with any of it.'

'Come along, sir, and don't worry, you'll have plenty of opportunity to prove your innocence. This way, and be careful not to touch the walls as you go or you'll set off the alarm.'

After that, Eddy seemed to be sitting for hours on a hard bunk in a cramped cell, fretting and worrying. At last, just when he thought he couldn't bear the solitude any longer, the door swung open to admit a thin man with a face that resembled a weasel. In a whining voice he introduced himself as Jonathan Randall, the duty solicitor, and explained that it was his job to protect Eddy's interests.

'If you really want to help me, get me out of here,' Eddy said. 'This is all a mistake. You have to make them understand, I had nothing to do with my stepmother's death. You have to believe me. She was like a mother to me. Why would I want her dead?'

The lawyer stood perfectly still, his head on one side, listening.

'The point is,' he replied at last when Eddy fell silent, 'your stepmother left a considerable estate, which you are due to inherit. In fact, you're her sole heir. You do know that, don't you? And it's not helping your cause that you've incurred such a substantial debt. Since you have a motive, the police are investigating whether it's possible you could have been responsible for her death. But they haven't arrested you, and as long as you stay quiet, I'll have you out of here in no time. Just leave it to me, and don't worry. It's my job to get you out of here, and I will. There's no need to make a fuss. They can't hold you.'

He led Eddy along a maze of corridors to an interview room where the two detectives who had brought him there sat facing him across a small table. With a nod at Eddy, the lawyer dropped into a chair beside him. The detective asked Eddy again what he had been doing on Friday evening. Muttering curses under his breath, Eddy repeated that he had been at home with his wife.

'How many times do I have to tell you, for fuck's sake?'

'You're going to have to do better than that,' the female detective said.

She repeated what she had already told him about Luciana's movements on the evening of his stepmother's murder.

'What do you mean?' he blustered.

'It means you can stop telling us you were with your wife on Friday evening, because we all know that's not true. We have proof, so you're not helping yourself by lying.'

When he tried to bluff his way out of it, the lawyer leaned over and warned him to stop talking, then requested a break.

'They have evidence your wife was out with a friend on Friday evening,' he explained when he was alone with Eddy once more. 'We'll have to come up with another line of defence.'

Eddy shook his head. 'What can I do?'

'I think the only approach now is to confess, and then we can take steps to convince the jury you weren't in your right mind when it happened.' He frowned, thinking. 'Were you drunk at the time? Certainly you were in a rage. It wasn't a straightforward killing, was it? She must have –'

'No,' Eddy cried out in a panic. 'No, that's not true. You're supposed to be on my side.'

'I am. But the problem now is that you lied to give yourself an alibi. That's not going to sit well with a jury –'

'Never mind that, the point is, I didn't do it. I've never killed anyone.'

'So you say, but you can't prove it, and now you've lied to the police –'

'I *can* prove I didn't do it, because I wasn't on my own on Friday evening. I was –' he broke off, uncertain whether to trust the lawyer.

'Go on.'

Eddy bit his lip. If he said anything about his movements on Friday evening, the police would want to speak to Abe to confirm Eddy's alibi. Even if Abe agreed to cover for Eddy, which was highly unlikely, the police would easily discover that Eddy hadn't been in the pub with Abe at all, and they might unearth what the two of them *had* been doing on Friday evening. Not only would he still have no alibi, but once Abe knew his name had been given to the police, Eddy's life would hang by a thread. The worst the police could do to him would be to lock him up. Abe would kill him.

'Nothing,' he muttered. 'It's nothing. I didn't do it, that's all.'

'You said you were with someone else on Friday evening. Who was it?'

Eddy shook his head. 'No one,' he mumbled. 'It was no one.'

The lawyer gave him a quizzical look but said nothing.

53

THE MOOD AT THE police station was purposeful, but good-humoured. Only the previous day everyone had been speaking in hushed tones, with solemn expressions. Today Geraldine heard her colleagues chatting and laughing together. No longer ensconced behind her desk, Eileen walked around with a broad smile plastered across her face. Although Eddy hadn't yet confessed to murdering his father, aunt and stepmother, the case against him was beginning to look watertight, his false alibi seeming to clinch the case against him. When Geraldine pointed out that the collapse of his alibi didn't prove his guilt, no one paid serious attention.

'Why do you think he lied about being with his wife if he didn't have something to hide?' Naomi asked.

Geraldine frowned. 'I'm not saying he's not guilty. He could well have been up to something that Friday evening. But we have no evidence to confirm he was killing his stepmother. He could have been doing – well, something else that evening. Maybe he was seeing another woman and he doesn't want his wife to find out. And there's nothing to link him to a dangerous dog.'

'Let's examine the spate of murders in this family,' Eileen interrupted. 'First, Eddy had access to his parents' house where his father was hung. Killing him would have taken not only physical strength, but knowledge of the house and its structure. There was no forced entry and the execution of the hanging was fast and efficient. Whoever hung Mark knew about the position of the banisters, and was able to gain access to the property to set up the murder before it actually took place. Second, we know that Eddy might well have wanted his stepmother dead because he was in serious financial difficulties which he was desperate to keep hidden from his wife. So not only did he have a compelling and urgent motive for eliminating both his parents, but it now turns out he's unable to provide a credible alibi for his movements at the time of either murder. So he had the opportunity. Finally, Amanda was convinced her brother was murdered, and she was also murdered. She was in her slippers when she died, miles from home, so although she wasn't attacked where she lived, she must have left the house with someone she knew well. She would hardly have gone out in her slippers if she was with a stranger. Everything points to Eddy.'

Geraldine bowed her head. She was doing her best to suppress her reservations about Eddy's guilt. What Eileen was saying made sense. It certainly appeared that all three victims had been killed by someone they knew, and the list of possible suspects was short. As time went on, the case against Eddy seemed to be growing stronger. But just because there was no other obvious suspect didn't make it any more likely that Eddy was guilty.

That afternoon, the custody sergeant contacted her to say that Eddy wanted to talk to her. Promising to report back to Ian as soon as she had spoken to the suspect, she made her way down to the cell where she found him lying on his bunk with his arms behind his head, apparently asleep.

'Eddy?' she called out softly.

He grunted without opening his eyes.

'Eddy, sit up and talk to me.' When he didn't stir, she added, 'I'm not convinced you killed your family, but I can't help you if you refuse to talk to me.'

He sat up at that. 'What do you mean you're not sure I did it?' he asked, his eyes narrowed in suspicion. 'Why don't you let me go home, then?'

'It's not that simple.'

'It never is with you people,' he grumbled, but he didn't lie down again.

'You do know you're accused of killing three people,' she began, but he interrupted her.

'I know. That's the reason I want to talk to you. I thought this was just going to be about my stepmother. If it was just one murder, I might have been tempted to take it on the chin, go for a light sentence, you know, say we had a row or something, and go down for a few years. Only now that lawyer is saying you're trying to pin all three murders on me. Three? I'll never get out, will I? They're going to send me down for life. So I've been thinking, and I've decided. I'd rather be done for robbery.'

Geraldine was puzzled. 'You need to explain to me what you mean by that.'

He glanced around. 'There's no recording going on in here, is there?'

She shook her head.

'Look, when my dad died, I was at work, see? But there was no one else with me. And when my aunt died, I can't remember what I was doing. It's not like I keep a diary of everything I do. Anyway, it didn't matter then because no one was accusing me of killing them. But when my stepmother died, suddenly I'm the number one suspect. But the crazy part of it all is that I do know where I was when *she* was killed. I was in a car, driving, with a bloke I know. So it couldn't have been me killed her. So I'm not your killer.'

He leaned back against the wall and crossed his arms.

'Who was with you when Charlotte was killed?'

He shook his head. 'I can't tell you that.'

'Eddy, if you don't give me the name of whoever you were with, then you don't have an alibi.'

'Are you calling me a liar?'

Geraldine sighed. 'A jury isn't going to take your word for it, and neither is my boss. Without a witness, you don't have an alibi.'

'I can give you details of the robbery I was involved in, if you like.'

He reeled off times and places, including details of the robbery, and the exact spot where he had been sitting in a parked car, waiting for his accomplices.

'We need to know who you were with, or this won't stand up as an alibi.'

After a momentary hesitation, Eddy shook his head. 'I can't say any more. If I tell you his name, he'll kill me.'

'Who's going to kill you, Eddy? Tell me his name. You're going to have to, sooner or later. Unless you want to be sent down for a long time.'

'At least I'll be safe in prison.'

54

SHE LAY PERFECTLY STILL, listening. A car revved outside, and far away a siren wailed. Rigid with fear, she tried to block out all the noise from the street below so she could hear if there was any sound in the house. Apart from occasional creaking and groaning in the pipes, all seemed to be silent. She wished she had thought to check the cellar door was closed before he'd gone out, but she was too scared to go into the living room now, knowing there was no one else in the house – no other humans, at least. This was getting too much for her to cope with. If she had anywhere else to go, she'd be out of there in a flash.

Telling herself that the animal wasn't loose in the house, and couldn't get through the door to the bedroom if it was, she sat up and reached for her cigarette papers. Her fingers trembled as she rolled a clumsy spliff. It didn't matter that shreds of weed were spilling out of one end, or that the papers hadn't stuck together evenly. Her mother used to say life was a competition so she should always try to do things well, but that was bullshit, just like everything else her mother had said. Maybe winning was important to some, but for people like her it was just a question of survival. It didn't matter if the spliff was a mess. Once she'd smoked it, the untidy reefer would no longer exist. He would slap her face if he found out she was smoking in bed, but he wasn't there. She scraped her tangled hair off her face and took a long drag.

By the time she finished her smoke, her brain had woken from its icy fear and she had worked out that her best course of action was to drag the chest of drawers along the wall until it blocked the door from opening. That way, even if the dog somehow managed to get loose, it wouldn't be able to force its way into the room. After pinching the end of the roach to make sure it was extinguished, she clambered off the bed and crouched down beside the chest. It was surprisingly heavy. Only after she had removed all the drawers was she able to propel it along the floor. The carpet puckered as she pushed the chest along, making it even more difficult to budge, but at last she had it in place across the door. When her boyfriend returned, she would have to push it back across the room, so she wasn't sure what to do about the drawers in the meantime, but she decided to replace them. The dog was a powerful beast. The heavier the chest was, the safer she would feel.

It was exhausting work, and when she had finished she fell on to the bed, ready to fall asleep. Then she realised she needed the toilet. She glared miserably at the chest of drawers that she had laboured so hard to move, but there was nothing for it. Removing the drawers, she pulled the chest aside far enough to allow the door to open sufficiently for her to slip out, and raced to the bathroom, almost tripping over in her haste. By the time she returned to bed, with the chest of drawers securely in position again, her back was aching. She rolled another joint to calm herself down and relax her muscles, and dropped a moggie to help her sleep through the pain.

She was woken by a loud banging. In her confusion, she thought the dog must have escaped from the cellar. It was a few seconds before she registered a voice was yelling her name. The curtain was open, and it was still dark outside. Glancing at her phone she saw that it was five in the morning. He had been out for most of the night, leaving her alone in the house with the animal. She could have been torn to shreds if she hadn't taken steps to keep herself safe.

'What the fuck are you doing? Open this door before I kick it in!'

She couldn't help sniggering. He'd have a tough job forcing

that door open. The chest jolted and shifted. There was another loud thud and it jerked forward another inch. Eventually he would push it far enough to get in. Alarm galvanised her.

'Hang on!' she shrieked, leaping from the bed. 'I'm coming!'

'What the fuck are you doing? Open this door!'

In a panic, she tugged all the drawers out, spilling underwear and stained T-shirts on the floor. Kicking the clothes out of the way, she crouched down and heaved the chest away from the door. It burst open and he came in, his face red with exertion, or rage. Probably both. She retreated to the other side of the chest and they faced one another across it.

'What are you playing at, shutting me out like that?' he fumed.

He wasn't sober, but there was no way she could dart past him while he was standing in the doorway.

'I wasn't shutting you out. I was protecting myself from that bloody monster you're keeping in the cellar.'

'You know perfectly well the dog's chained up and the cellar door's shut. How do you think it's going to get out? Huh?'

He glared at her, his face still red with fury, and shoved the chest, forcing her to take a step backwards.

'But what if it got out? I'm scared, I'm really scared. You go out all the time, leaving me alone here in the house with a beast that could tear my throat out with one snap of its jaws –'

'You stupid cow.' He pushed the chest another inch towards her. 'I'll teach you not to shut me out.'

'No, no! I wasn't shutting you out.'

He lowered his head and pushed the chest until she was trapped, pinned against the wall.

'Stop it! You're hurting me!'

With a loud burst of laughter he leapt on to the bed and bounded towards her. For a moment everything seemed to happen in slow motion. A bead of sweat crawled down his forehead towards eyes blazing with fury, as his fist came crashing down.

55

'SHE MAY DRIFT OFF to sleep at any time,' the nurse warned her. 'She's on a high dose of pain relief, and talking tires her out. We don't know her name yet, so let us know if you manage to find out anything at all. You can have a few minutes with her. She looks worse than she is.'

If her condition had been worse than it looked, she would probably be dead, PC Jane Matthews thought, as she approached the patient. She leaned over the hospital bed and listened attentively, but it wasn't easy to understand what the injured woman was trying to say. Her breath came in whistling gasps through broken teeth, and her jaw was strapped so tightly she could barely move her chin to talk. One of her eyes was concealed by a pad while the other one was so swollen it hardly opened as Jane addressed her.

'Can you hear me?'

'Yes.'

'I'm a police officer. We want to find out who did this to you. What's your name?'

The woman's eyelid flickered but she made no attempt to answer.

'Do you know who did this to you?'

The woman shook her head and winced, mumbling incomprehensibly.

'Can you describe your assailant?'

The woman muttered too softly for Jane to hear what she was saying.

'Can you repeat that?'

As the nurse came over and tried to usher Jane away, all she could make out from the patient's garbled message was something about a dangerous dog.

Jane nodded to the nurse. 'One moment, please.' She turned back to the injured woman. 'Did you say your attacker had a dog? We need to be very clear about this. Is there a dog involved?'

'Yes,' the woman hissed, her lips hardly moving. 'Savage dog. Could've killed me. That's why I was scared. That's why...' her voice petered out and her swollen eye closed.

Jane turned back to the nurse. 'Was she attacked by a dog?'

The nurse spoke quietly. 'No. She's confused. Her injuries were inflicted by a person. She was punched repeatedly in the head and kicked in the abdomen, causing her spleen to rupture. From the bruising on her abdomen it looks as though someone may have stamped on her.' She lowered her voice still further, until she was almost whispering. 'She also has multiple cigarette burns, only some of which are recent, and her X-rays show several past fractures. She refuses to answer any questions about what happened.'

There was no need for the nurse to add that for some time the patient had been living with a violently abusive partner.

'Piecing it together, we think on this occasion she suffered severe injuries in the course of an attack at home. This took place during the night and she was then carried out on to the street where a passerby found her, unconscious, the following morning. That was yesterday morning. If she'd been left there for a few more hours, she might not have survived her injuries.'

Jane nodded. 'I'll make a full report.'

She turned back to the patient to reassure her that her situation would be investigated by the police, but the woman was asleep. Thoughtfully, Jane returned to the police station. As soon as she had written up her report, she went to find the detective chief inspector, but she was in a meeting. Jane's next thought was to speak to an inspector involved in the murder enquiry.

She found Ian in his office, talking to the new sergeant.

'Come in,' he said, looking up with an encouraging smile. 'What's up?'

Jane smiled back. She liked the inspector, who was always ready to listen to her suggestions. She wasn't so comfortable talking to the new sergeant from London. Geraldine struck her as very cool and distant, and Jane hesitated to share her discovery in front of her, not wanting to be dismissed as a fussing time waster.

'I wasn't sure if this could be significant,' she concluded. 'I know you've been looking for a dog that might have been cross-bred illegally, so I just thought maybe I ought to tell someone what the victim said. It's all in my report so you'd have seen it anyway, but –'

'You did the right thing bringing your concerns to our attention straight away,' Geraldine interrupted her. 'Are you sure she mentioned a dog?'

'Yes. It was difficult to make out what she was saying, but she definitely mentioned a savage dog. She said it could've killed her, and she was scared of it.'

'Where does the injured woman live?' Geraldine went on urgently. 'We need to go round there right away and see what's what.'

'Hang on a minute,' Ian said. 'There's no need to go rushing in blindly. Let's speak to the victim first and see what she has to tell us.'

'Don't be stupid, Ian, that's the last thing we want to do.'

Geraldine spoke so disrespectfully to the inspector that Jane was startled. They glared at one another, and seemed to have forgotten she was there.

'This woman has a history of violent abuse,' Geraldine went on. 'If she hasn't reported her assailant before, there's no reason to assume she'll do so now. Think about it, Ian. If we risk alerting her to our suspicions, we'll give her a chance to warn her abuser. There could be an illegal dog on the premises, which could potentially be the one we're looking for. We should go there first, before he learns we even know about it. And we don't want to give him time to move it elsewhere.'

Ian frowned. 'I think you're jumping a few steps ahead,' he said slowly. 'Let's speak to Eileen.'

Geraldine shook her head. 'If the dog's there now, and if it *is* the one we're looking for, we should go round there right away before he discovers we've been told about it. You know I'm talking sense, Ian.'

Jane had the impression Geraldine was frustrated by Ian's refusal to comply with her suggestion immediately. But she was only a sergeant, and he was an inspector. She shouldn't be questioning his decisions so openly, or addressing him so rudely.

'Come on, let's find Eileen straight away and see what she has to say about it,' was all he said.

Jane wondered how he might react if *she* spoke to him in the tone Geraldine had adopted. There was something slightly off-key about the conversation. She mentioned her impression to another constable later that day.

'Oh, you're talking about Sergeant Steel?' her colleague replied. 'Geraldine Steel?'

'Yes.'

'She's the one who came to us from London where she was a DI. You do know she was demoted, don't you?' she added, lowering her voice.

'Oh yes, that's right, I remember now. I hadn't realised it was her. I was just taken aback by the way she spoke to him. What was she demoted for?'

Her colleague shrugged. 'Search me, but it must have been something bad. Insubordination perhaps?' he added, with a sly smile.

56

EILEEN LISTENED CAREFULLY TO what Ian was saying.

'So we need to go round there and check whether the dog she was talking about is the same dog that attacked Charlotte,' Geraldine added. 'And we need to do it before the owner gets wind of our suspicions.'

Eileen nodded. 'I see where you're coming from, but what's important now is that we're not distracted from searching for evidence that Eddy could have been present when these murders were committed. We know he lied about being with his wife at the time of his stepmother's murder. We can't be sure he isn't giving us another trumped-up alibi.'

Geraldine could hardly insist they forget about Eddy and focus on searching for the dog. Seemingly convinced Eddy was guilty, the detective chief inspector had been sceptical of the alibi he had given Geraldine.

'Granted there was a robbery in town that evening, that's still hardly conclusive. He could have seen it on the local news, or read about it in the paper. While his wife was out, he could have gone to visit his stepmother without anyone knowing. His aunt's unlikely to have left her house with a stranger, in her slippers, so she was presumably killed by someone she knew. And the most compelling thing pointing to him having killed both his parents is that we know he's in serious financial difficulty, and with them out of the way he stands to inherit a sizeable estate. Whichever way you look at it, everything points to Eddy.'

Even so, Eileen had agreed it was also important to pursue

the new line of enquiry. Given that Charlotte had been killed by a dog, and that traces of faeces from the same animal had been discovered near Amanda's corpse, it was clear that the killer either owned a dog, or else knew someone who did. After the meeting with Eileen, Geraldine drove straight back to the hospital. When she introduced herself and explained the purpose of her visit, the nurse she was speaking to shook her head.

'I'm afraid she's not regained consciousness since this morning,' the nurse said. 'We'd like to contact her family, but we don't know who she is.'

'Haven't we checked her dental records?'

'It looks as though she hasn't had her teeth looked at for decades, if ever.'

Geraldine took a DNA sample from the patient so she could check for a match on the police database. 'We're also interested in discovering her identity.'

She didn't add that the reason the police wanted to know the woman's identity was that they were keen to search her home, hoping to find a dangerous dog and, hopefully, a killer. At last she was on her way back to the police station with the victim's DNA sample. There was no match for it on the database, so that was no help. It was time to question Eddy again. He was adamant that when his stepmother had been killed he had been driving the getaway car after a theft. All the details he had given them tied in with an actual robbery but they needed something more conclusive than that if his alibi was to be believed.

Geraldine glanced at Ian who was sitting silently staring straight ahead. She was concerned about him. For a few days he hadn't been looking like his usual cheerful self. He put on a jaunty show when other people were around, but Geraldine had known him for a long time, since he was a young sergeant, and she could tell he was troubled. She wondered if he was ill. With a sideways glance at him, she stepped in and took control of the questioning.

She leaned forward and spoke firmly. 'Eddy, you do understand that without any names your alibi's useless?'

'I told you his name. It's Abe. That's all I know.' His voice rose in a whine. 'I'm telling you the truth. I wasn't on my own, so you can't say I haven't got an alibi because I have.'

It took her a while to worm out of him that Eddy had first met the man he called Abe in a betting shop, after which they had gone to a pub and then met on the street. A team was immediately set to work, checking CCTV, to try and piece together Eddy's movements on the evening of his stepmother's death, and to establish who he was with. They began by viewing the film from the evening when Eddy claimed he had first met the man he called Abe. No one by that name was known to the police. Vice, drugs squad, and borough intelligence had all checked their records and drawn a blank. No one by that name had even been given a parking ticket or speeding fine. By the following morning the Visual Images, Identifications and Detections team had scrutinised hours and hours of film footage. Eddy was recorded entering a betting shop, just as he had described. He left there just over two hours later in the company of a tall man. Even with image enhancement it proved impossible to make out any of his features hidden in shadow inside his black hood.

'He's keeping his back to the camera,' one of the VIIDO officers told Geraldine, who was leaning forward looking at the screen. 'We've been through this section of film again and again but there's no sight of his face, and no other clue to his identity.'

The same thing happened when Eddy and his companion were picked up again about ten minutes later, entering a local pub. Eddy's face was clear enough to recognise but the other man must either have been very lucky or else he knew the position of the security cameras, because he had his back to them the whole time. There was no other sighting of the two men on camera that they had been able to find yet.

'We'll keep searching,' the VIIDO officer assured Geraldine. They both knew it was likely to be pointless. They were hardly likely to catch a chance glimpse of Eddy on CCTV again, with his hooded companion's face visible.

'We'll just have to put pressure on him to talk,' Eileen said when she was brought up to speed. 'His alibi is suspect, to say the least, and we know Amanda was killed by someone she knew. A woman of her age wouldn't go out in her dressing gown and slippers with a stranger. Only someone she knew could have persuaded her to go out like that.'

'I wonder why anyone would want to do that,' Geraldine muttered.

She glanced at Ian but he didn't respond to her helpless shrug.

'We need someone else, a witness, to corroborate what you're telling us,' Geraldine repeated to Eddy.

He scowled at her. 'You don't believe me, do you?'

'It's not a question of whether or not we believe you,' Geraldine said wearily. 'A jury won't take your word for it. If you don't have a witness…' she broke off with an exaggerated sigh. 'Let's just say I wouldn't want to be in your shoes.'

'But this is ridiculous!' Eddy burst out. 'I'm telling you the truth. I didn't kill my stepmother. I didn't go anywhere near her on Friday. Why would I want to kill her, anyway?'

'Money,' Ian said curtly, speaking for the first time.

As though Ian's contribution was his cue, the lawyer joined in. His narrow features were pinched with exasperation, while his voice seemed devoid of energy.

'You have to tell the police what they want to hear. If you don't, they're going to think the worst.'

'You don't know that,' Eddy objected, casting a glance of supplication at Geraldine. 'You can't assume they're all bad, just because they're cops.'

'They want a conviction, Eddy. That's their job. And mine is to protect you, so I have to warn you, if you don't tell the police everything they want to know, you'll risk being convicted for murder. Three murders in fact. It doesn't matter whether or not you killed anyone. All that counts is what a jury are going to believe. And refusing to cooperate with the police isn't going to help your case. You have to tell the police the name of your witness.'

Eddy's dark eyes glared helplessly around the room. He was sweating.

'Abe's the only name I know. That's what I called him. Abe.'

The lawyer called for a break and they left the room.

As they walked along the corridor back to the offices, Geraldine approached Ian quietly.

'Are you all right?'

'Why shouldn't I be?'

She shrugged. 'I don't want to pry, but you haven't seemed like yourself for the last few days.'

He frowned. 'Is it that obvious?'

'Only to someone who knows you really well.'

He looked surprised by her answer and she felt her face grow hot.

'I mean, we've known each other for a long time,' she added. 'Tell me to get lost and it's none of my business if you like, I won't mind, but if there is something wrong, I thought you might like to talk about it with a friend.'

They were nearly back at his office when he paused in his stride and turned to face her. In a low voice he told her that his ex-wife had asked to see him. Momentarily nonplussed, Geraldine hesitated. She didn't think it would be right for Ian to be reconciled with his wife after the way she had cheated on him and deserted him, but she wasn't sure she could trust herself to give a sensible response. In wanting him to reject his wife, she was afraid she might be motivated by self-interest.

'Do you want to see her?' she asked before the silence could become awkward.

'She left me because she was having another man's baby,' he

replied sourly. 'Why would I ever want to see her again?'

He turned and disappeared into his office, but not before Geraldine had seen the hurt in his eyes. She wanted to follow him and say something comforting to him but she continued walking steadily back to the office, maintaining an appropriately calm expression.

57

IT WAS ALL OVER apart from finishing the paperwork and tying up a few loose ends to make the case against the suspect as watertight as possible. Eileen was satisfied the Crown Prosecution Service would go ahead with a prosecution and was walking around the police station with a complacent smile on her face. Keeping her reservations to herself, Geraldine tidied up her reports and tried to look cheerful. Ian was the only one of her colleagues who knew her well enough to see through her façade of good humour, but he was too preoccupied with his own affairs to notice her.

Before setting off on the long drive to Kent to see her sister, Geraldine went along to the canteen for a late breakfast. Spotting Ian sitting on his own, she joined him.

'How's your sister?' he asked, nodding a greeting without looking up.

Convinced that he was avoiding meeting her eye, Geraldine smiled uneasily.

'She's fine, and the baby's doing well –' she paused, seeing Ian's puzzled expression. 'Oh, you meant Helena, didn't you?' He was one of the few people Geraldine had confided in about her twin, the recovering heroin addict. 'Sorry, I thought you were asking about my adopted sister, Celia. She's been on my mind a lot lately because she's just had a baby –' she broke off in confusion, remembering that Ian's estranged wife was also expecting.

Lowering her voice sympathetically, she asked him whether he had decided what to do about Bev. He looked up from his coffee, still without looking directly at her, and shook his head. She waited, uncertain whether to change the subject.

'I suppose I ought to see her and find out what she has to say for herself,' he replied at last. 'Although I think it may be better to leave it to the solicitors.'

'You think she wants a divorce?'

He shrugged his broad shoulders. 'What else could it be? We haven't had any contact for months, and suddenly she wants to see me. It's the only thing that makes sense, isn't it?'

Geraldine hesitated to suggest that his estranged wife might want to explore the possibility of a reconciliation. It would be cruel to raise his hopes if that wasn't the case.

'Who knows what she wants?' she replied vaguely. 'Has she given birth yet?'

'I've not heard anything, not a word, but why would she tell me? Her bastard baby's got nothing to do with me.' He took a gulp of coffee and grimaced. 'So, how is your sister?'

'Which one?'

Before Ian could answer, Naomi came over to their table and asked if she could join them.

Ian stood up abruptly. 'I was just leaving. Time to get back to work.'

He turned and hurried away without so much as a backward glance at them.

'Was it something I said?' Naomi asked, with a bark of laughter that was obviously fake.

Geraldine laughed too, relieved that her awkward conversation with Ian had been interrupted. 'Ian just wanted to get back to work.'

Naomi glanced down at Ian's mug, as though checking whether he had finished his drink. Geraldine pretended not to notice.

'He's been a bit off with me lately,' Naomi blurted out.

'Off?'

'Oh, you know. I mean, there's nothing going on between us, but – well, I thought he liked me…'

'Why wouldn't he like you?' Geraldine responded more sharply than she had intended.

Her young colleague shook her head miserably. 'He used to be so friendly, but just the last few days he's – oh, I don't know. He's changed.'

'What do you mean?' Geraldine asked, deliberately obtuse.

Naomi hesitated. 'It's nothing. He just doesn't seem so friendly any more, that's all. I wondered if I'd done something to annoy him. I don't suppose he's said anything to you about me?'

'No. He hasn't mentioned you at all.'

Geraldine left soon after that. When she arrived at her sister's house, her brother-in-law opened the door. With old-fashioned good looks, he was at his most handsome when lost in his own thoughts and looking faintly worried. Now his face creased in a lively smile as he saw Geraldine. They pecked one another on the cheek and she went in. The house was very quiet, until Geraldine's niece came bounding down the stairs.

'Shh, they're both asleep,' Sebastian said.

As he was speaking, they heard a faint mewling sound.

Sebastian laughed. 'Not any more. Come on, they're in the lounge.'

Having given her niece a quick hug, Geraldine followed him. Her sister was sitting on an armchair, with her feet up on a footstool, a bundle of white lacy fabric in her arms. The baby was no longer crying and as she drew near, Geraldine heard a sniffly squeaking sound.

'He's feeding,' Celia whispered.

'He's always feeding,' Chloe explained. 'All he does is feed and sleep. I should know.'

'That's what babies do,' Celia said.

'And poo,' Chloe added. 'He does these tiny little yellow poos and the most massive wees! You have to be quick changing his nappy.'

They all laughed.

'Sounds pretty healthy to me,' Geraldine said.

LEIGH RUSSELL

Sebastian and Chloe disappeared into the kitchen to prepare lunch, leaving Geraldine alone with her sister and her new nephew.

'Would you like to hold him?'

It was a strange experience, holding such a tiny creature in her arms. Her training had prepared her for all kinds of situations, but knowing this was Celia's son made the experience both daunting and exciting. She would watch this small bundle of humanity as he grew and developed into an adult.

'He'll be taller than us one day,' she said, and Celia smiled.

'I still can't believe it,' Celia said. 'Do you think that's why pregnancy lasts so long, to give us time to get used to the idea of having a new life to nurture?'

'I think it's to give the baby time to develop physically enough to survive independently.'

'He's hardly independent.'

'Well, no, but he can breathe and function on his own.'

'He can't.'

'You know what I mean.'

Chloe came in to summon them for lunch, and Celia held out her arms to receive the baby.

'Thank you,' Geraldine said, and Celia smiled.

The time seemed to pass very quickly, until it was time for Geraldine to leave.

'I'll come out to the car with you,' Celia said. 'He's fast asleep and I could do with a breath of fresh air.'

Opening the front door, she stooped down and placed a shoe inside the door frame to stop the door slamming behind her. But while they were on the front path, a sudden gust of wind blew it shut, nudging the shoe on to the front step.

Geraldine started forward. 'Oh my God!'

'It's OK,' Celia laughed, 'they'll let me in again.'

Geraldine grunted, but she wasn't listening to her sister. She was thinking about another solitary shoe that had been discovered outside another house.

58

'YOU NEVER THOUGHT EDDY was responsible,' Ian said curtly. 'I can't see what difference this makes anyway. I'm not even sure what you're talking about.'

This was so unlike the Ian Geraldine knew that if she hadn't known about his marital difficulties, she might have been quite put out. As it was, she tried to explain, as patiently as she could.

'It just means that Amanda might never have intended to leave the house in her slippers. We've taken that as indicating she knew her killer, because unless she was with someone she knew well and trusted, why would she have gone out with him without getting dressed? But the point is, she might not have known her killer. She could have put one shoe in the door -'

'Put a shoe in the door?'

'Yes, exactly, put a shoe inside the door frame to stop the door from closing when she went out.' She paused. 'To save her having to go and find her key.'

'Yes, yes, I understand what you mean, but this is mere supposition. The DCI's not going to listen to it, and even if she does, she certainly isn't going to take it seriously.'

'Which is why I'm here in your office, talking to you and not her.'

'Because you know you're talking nonsense?'

'No. Because Eddy had no reason to kill Amanda –'

'She might have known something about the other murders.'

'And she could equally well have been killed by a stranger,' Geraldine continued, ignoring Ian's interruption, 'so the other two victims could have been killed by someone else as well. I know Eddy had a motive for killing his father and stepmother, but if a stranger could have killed Amanda, why not them as well?'

Ian shook his head. 'Geraldine, I don't understand what you're talking about, really I don't.'

'Do I at least have your permission to pursue this?'

'Pursue what? I have no idea what exactly you're proposing to do with this hare-brained theory you've just come up with for no reason other than that you decided Eddy wasn't guilty, and now you're clutching at straws trying to prove you were right and everyone else was wrong.'

He sounded so irate that Geraldine made her excuses and left the room. There was no point in talking to him if he wasn't even prepared to listen to her. But she was determined to find out more about the circumstances of Amanda's death, and her house seemed the best place to start her enquiries. After a fruitless hour searching around Amanda's house and talking to her neighbours, Geraldine went to the hospital hoping to fare better there. This time she was in luck. Learning the victim of the attack had just woken up, Geraldine hurried to her bedside. If anything, the woman looked worse than previously, with her two eyes blackened, and her nose red and swollen above her bandaged jaw. But she was conscious. Glancing at her notes, Geraldine read the name: Angie. She was forty-two. The list of her injuries was extensive. She only glanced briefly at the notes before turning her attention to the supine woman.

'What's your name?' she asked gently. 'Can you tell me your name?'

'Angie,' the woman muttered. 'I already told you, it's Angie.' Her inflamed eyelids fluttered. 'Are you the doctor?' she lisped.

'Angie what?' Geraldine asked. 'I'm here to help you,' she added, 'but I need to know your name.'

'Angie. Just Angie.'

'OK Angie, that's OK. Where do you live?'

'Why?' The woman's eyes opened wider. 'Are you going to

get rid of it? I can't go back, not while it's there.'

'Are you talking about the dog?' Geraldine guessed, and was rewarded with another flicker of recognition in the woman's eyes. 'Yes, we can arrange to get rid of it so you can go home.'

'Thank you.' The woman closed her eyes. 'It's a vicious brute, and it stinks the place out.'

'But I can't sort that out for you unless you tell me where you live,' Geraldine added quickly, afraid that Angie would drift off to sleep again before telling her what she wanted to know.

Angie mumbled an address as her eyes closed. With a quick nod at the nurse behind the desk, Geraldine left. She called the police station to log her movements, summoned immediate back-up, and on impulse also phoned Ian to let him know what she was doing. He advised her not to enter the property where Angie lived until back-up arrived, including a trained dog handler.

'Don't worry,' she assured him. 'I'm not going to do anything stupid. I've no intention of risking being mauled by a savage dog.'

'Just be careful.'

His insistence irritated her. She was hardly a fresh-faced young officer with something to prove. She had helped to train him when they had both been less experienced. Without answering, she hung up and set off. There was no real urgency, but she put her foot down, speeding unnecessarily along Gillygate. Leaving the hospital, she forked off to drive parallel with the River Foss to her right. The address Angie had given her was in a side street off Haxby Road. She pulled up outside the end of terrace house and glanced around. The patrol car hadn't arrived yet but a quick check showed that it was on its way and would arrive within a few minutes. There was no need to wait for it. On the contrary, a discreet approach might reveal more, before anyone was alerted to police interest in the residents.

She hurried to the front door and rang the bell. There was

no response. She tried again. This time, the door swung open slowly, with a chain across. An aged face peered suspiciously up at her. She introduced herself and held up her warrant card for inspection. The old man nodded his head, mumbling to himself, but didn't remove the chain from the door.

'And what is it you'll be wanting with me?' he demanded in a marked Irish accent.

'Do you keep a dog on the premises?'

'That I do not.'

Geraldine considered. The old man looked extremely frail. She doubted he would be able to control a sizeable dog.

'Does anyone else live here with you?'

'No.'

'What about Angie?'

'Who?'

Patiently Geraldine described the woman in hospital.

'Oh, that'll be her next door,' the old man said, jerking his head to indicate the side of the property. 'This is number 7. You'll be wanting 7a. They live downstairs.'

With that, he slammed the door. Walking along the side of the house, Geraldine wondered fleetingly how the old man managed the stairs to the first floor, and whether she ought perhaps to report his conditions to social services.

Number 7a had no bell so she knocked on the door, gently at first, then hammering loudly when no one answered. A few seconds later she heard footsteps and the door was flung open. She recognised the cadaverous face staring at her with a curious intensity, as though he too was trying to work out where he had seen her before.

'What?' he demanded. 'Is this about her?'

'Do you mean Angie?'

'Where is she?'

'She's still in hospital.'

He scowled, muttering angrily about the stupid cow having fallen down in the street.

'She drinks,' he added, with a sly glance at Geraldine. 'I told her to be more careful. It was an accident waiting to happen. She's badly hurt, isn't she?'

She nodded. He seemed to think she worked at the hospital. So much the better. His guard would be down. Just then her phone vibrated and she heard a car pull up in the street. Back-up had arrived.

'Do you keep a dog on the premises?' she asked, determined to unearth as much as she could before the man's suspicions were alerted.

The man's eyes narrowed. 'No,' he replied, a shade too quickly.

'Are you sure you never have a dog here? Perhaps you look after it for a neighbour?'

He gave an exclamation that was half spitting, half laughter.

'It's not the sort of thing you forget. You can come in and take a look if you don't believe me.'

Out of the corner of her eye, Geraldine saw movement around the corner of the building. Her colleagues must be at the neighbour's door. Reassured, she nodded and stepped inside. As the man reached across to close the front door behind her, she noticed an unpleasant smell. The narrow hall was almost blocked by a muddy lawnmower. The man manoeuvred his way past it and she followed him, taking care not to soil her trousers on the mower. When he opened a door at the far end of the hallway, the stench grew stronger. Momentarily uneasy, Geraldine paused, but her colleagues would arrive at any minute. Once the man saw uniformed officers at the door, all hope of catching him unawares would be lost. Taking a deep breath, she followed him into the back room.

A pair of threadbare upholstered armchairs and a couple of miscellaneous upright wooden chairs were arranged around a low coffee table on which were several packets of cigarette papers, an opened packet of hand rolling tobacco and a bright red plastic lighter. Shreds of tobacco had spilled on the table

273

and on to a grubby rug. The man crouched down and jerked the edge of the rug back to reveal a trap door. As he wrenched it open the putrid smell grew stronger, engulfing her in a wave of hot damp air. Before she could stop him the man seized her by both arms and pushed her through the door on to a staircase she could barely see in the darkness. She slid down the first few steps with the man propelling her downwards. In a flash, she spun around but she was too late to save herself from falling.

'Dinner's arrived!' he yelled.

Below her, in the darkness, she heard an answering growl.

59

'I DON'T KNOW WHAT we're supposed to be looking out for,' Police Constable Max Parker said to his colleague.

Micky shrugged. Although he was a constable in uniform, he had been in the job for a long time, neither seeking nor gaining promotion. Nearing retirement, he had seen more than his fair share of dodgy characters who had deliberately chosen a life of crime, and nut jobs too crazy to know when they were breaking the law. There wasn't much petty crime going on in the city that he hadn't come across at one time or another. On this particular occasion, he had been summoned to help a sergeant who was checking out an illegal dog. The dog handling team had been alerted but Micky and his young companion had been patrolling the area and were first on the scene, apart from the sergeant who had put in the original call for back-up.

'We're here to see a man about a dog,' he replied breezily. 'It's fine by me. I like dogs. Got one myself at home. I'd have another one, but the missus doesn't want any more.'

Max looked worried. 'Dogs aren't all the same, you know.'

Micky snorted. 'I've had dogs all my life, son. They're nothing to be scared of.'

'So what about that illegal fighting dog that's loose somewhere in the city without a muzzle? Don't you think we should wait for the dog handlers?'

Micky laughed. 'We're not after catching a savage animal. That's not our job. We're just here to provide back-up for a sergeant who's on a fact-finding mission. Don't look so worried. It'll turn out to be a false alarm. Happens a lot. A neighbour gets the needle about some dog that keeps barking and reports it as dangerous and it turns out to be a little pooch that wouldn't hurt a fly.'

'But what about the murder investigation? You know, the woman who was attacked and killed by a dangerous dog.'

'No need to go jumping to conclusions. You're putting two and two together and coming up with five. This is just a report of a dog causing a nuisance.'

Max frowned. 'Did you read the report of that victim?' He shuddered.

'Listen, we had a call to come over here to act as back-up, that's all. You can stay in the car if you like. We're here as a police presence at the scene. We don't deal with murder cases. If you're looking for that kind of drama, you need to get yourself moved to the MIT. As long as you're with me, you're just a bobby on the beat. We get enough excitement on the streets on a Saturday night without looking for more. Come on, let's go. We're here. Are you coming or not?'

They rang the bell at number 7 but there was no answer. After waiting for a few minutes, Max tried again. At last the door was opened on the chain by an elderly man.

'What is it now?' he snapped, seeing them on the doorstep. 'Can't you people leave me alone? It's up and down them stairs like a jack-in-the-box you'd have me, is it?'

The door slammed.

Max turned to Micky with a helpless shrug. 'We'd better try again?'

This time the old man didn't shut them out but stood scowling at them through the half open door.

'What is it you're wanting? If it's that girl, I told you already, you've come to the wrong house. I don't keep a girl here more's the pity of it.' He leered at them with toothless gums. 'And before you ask me, I don't have a dog here, neither. No, it's the house next door you'll be after. That's where she lives, her and her fellow. But I haven't seen a dog there, not for a while. So if that's all you'll be wanting, perhaps you'll leave an old fellow in peace now and not have me up and down them stairs for nothing all day long.'

Still grumbling to himself, he closed the door.

Without a word, the two police officers exchanged a quick glance and set off around the side of the building to knock on the next door. After a few minutes it was opened by a tall, thin man.

'Yes, officers, how can I help you?' he enquired pleasantly enough, although Max thought there was something shifty about the way he stared fixedly at them as if he was trying to psych them out.

'We're responding to a call,' Micky said. 'Do you keep a dog here?'

'A dog? No. Why?'

'We had a report that you're keeping an unlicensed dog here.'

The man shook his head slowly. 'You must have the wrong house.'

There was nothing more they could do, short of forcing their way in without a warrant.

As Max and Micky rounded the corner of the house, they recognised a detective inspector striding towards them.

'The old guy at number 7 says there's a woman living next door,' he called out.

Briefly Micky explained what had happened when they had spoken to the residents of number 7 and 7a.

'So there isn't a dog anywhere on the premises, at number 7 or 7a. We've checked them both. False alarm,' he concluded cheerily. 'What did I tell you?' he added, turning to Max,

'You said we'd find a harmless dog that barked a lot,' Max reminded him.

'Well, either way, there's nothing for us to investigate here.'

'Did you go inside either property?' the inspector asked, his blue eyes glittering.

'There didn't seem to be any need. Both householders assured us they don't keep a dog, and we had no reason to suspect either of them was lying to us. I didn't hear any barking when the door was open, did you?'

Max shook his head. 'I didn't hear anything.'

With a curt nod, the inspector asked them to wait while he made a call. After pacing up and down the pavement for a minute or so, phone pressed to his ear, he dropped his hand and shook his head.

'There's no answer.' He hesitated, casting an anxious glance at the house as though he wanted to peer through the brickwork. 'Let's go and take a look around. Come on.'

Micky shrugged and nodded at Max. Together they followed the inspector back along the side of the building.

'I told him there aren't any dogs here,' Micky muttered. 'What's got into him, do you suppose?'

60

UPPERMOST IN GERALDINE'S MIND had been the need to prevent herself from toppling any further down the stairs, but keeping her footing wasn't easy as she wrestled with her assailant. It didn't help that the steps were narrow and steep. Desperately she had struggled to reach into her bag for her cosh and strike back, but the man was holding her so tightly she was unable to free either of her arms. As they tussled, the back of her forearm hit a metal rail. Twisting her wrist painfully against his powerful grip, she had contrived to grasp hold of it. With the man still trying to force her backwards down the stairs, she clung on to the rail with all her strength.

A clattering noise had reached them through the open trap door. At the sound, her assailant had let go of her so abruptly she had stumbled and nearly lost her balance. Lunging at her, he had seized her by her shoulders and given her a vicious shove before he turned and disappeared through the door. In her panic she was barely aware of her knees and shins bumping against the steps. Only her determination to keep hold of the rail prevented her from tumbling headlong down the stairs. Hanging on by one hand she scrabbled to pull herself up into a sitting position, nearly tripping again in the darkness, and hitting her head against the wall as she hauled herself up.

Dazed, trembling with shock and fear, she focused on breathing slowly and trying to think clearly. With every breath a sour taste of vomit rose in her throat at the smell, which seemed to be a mixture of excrement and rotting flesh. In spite of her training, it took her a few seconds to regain her composure. Meanwhile she sat perfectly still, dizzy and nauseous, breathing through her mouth, trying to block out the foul odour which seemed to seep through her skin and make her eyes sting. More than anything, she wanted to go home and shower, and wash the stench from her hair and clothes.

Enveloped in darkness, she turned and shuffled cautiously towards the trap door, pressing her palm against the wall to keep her steady. Even leaning against the cold clammy wall, it took her a while to clamber back up the stairs. Shaking, she pulled at the catch, and found the trap door was locked. Fighting back her panic, she took out her phone but there was no signal. She tried switching it off and on again, but it made no difference. Furiously she rattled the catch, but it wouldn't open.

She banged against the trap door with her fist, yelling to be let out. 'I'm a police officer. I didn't come here alone! You can't keep me here!'

After a few minutes she stopped shouting, exhausted, and sat down on the top step. Recovering her breath, she decided her best course of action was to conserve her energy and wait as patiently as she could. Her colleagues knew where she had been heading, and her car parked in the street was evidence that she had arrived. Back-up would be with her very soon, if they hadn't already turned up. In fact, she thought the noise she had heard before the door to the cellar slammed shut had probably been the police at the front door. Luckily, she had spoken to the neighbour at number 7 who would confirm where she had gone straight after speaking to him. If a patrol team was initially turned away from the house where she was being held captive, it wouldn't be long before her disappearance was investigated, and then she would be found. It was just a matter of time. She hoped she would be released soon, because the smell was making her gag. In the meantime, she just had to remain strong and wait to be rescued. There was nothing to worry about because her colleagues weren't going to walk away once they realised she must still be on the premises. They were bound to come looking for her, and when they did there was no way they would leave without finding her.

Closing her eyes, she was doing her best to ignore the smell, when she was disturbed by a noise. She listened. An animal was growling nearby. Instantly alert, she switched on her phone torch to assess the nature and extent of any immediate danger. Still seated on the top step, she shone the beam of light around slimy brick walls and a ceiling that appeared to be concrete. She turned her attention to the entrance. Probably not much sound would penetrate the solid door unless someone was standing quite close to it on the other side. As she banged on the door again, the snarling grew louder until it broke into the deep-throated bark of a large dog. She stood up, still holding on to the rail, and shone her torch downwards. At the bottom of a steep staircase she could see a narrow cellar. At one end of it, half hidden beneath the stairs, a huge muscular dog was gnawing at a bone. Geraldine shuddered. It looked as though she had found Charlotte's killer.

Taking her cosh from her bag, she shone her torch all around but could see no means of exit other than the locked door behind her. The beam of light from her torch fell on the dog once more as, with a guttural snarl, it dropped the bone, rose to its feet and then crouched. Points of light shone at her from its eyes, which were fixed on her. She tried not to look at its huge yellow teeth as she tensed to repel its assault. Aware that the huge dog would easily knock her off her feet, she gripped the rail firmly with one hand. Her grip on her cosh tightened as the massive creature leapt forwards to the bottom of the stairs.

61

WITH THE TWO UNIFORMED officers at his heels, and a dog handler on the way, Ian paused before knocking at the door of 7a. The resident at number 7 claimed to have sent a detective answering Geraldine's description to see his neighbour in 7a. Since then no one had seen her, and she wasn't answering her phone. She had simply disappeared. It looked as though she must still be at 7a. At the very least, Ian thought he had sufficient grounds to go in and look for her. And if he overstepped the mark, he would deal with the consequences later. His priority right now was finding Geraldine.

The resident at 7a said that he had never owned a dog. The old man at number 7 had told a slightly different story, saying he hadn't seen any sign of a dog at 7a recently. Ian had no way of knowing whether a dog *had* actually been kept there illegally at some point and, if so, whether the dog was still there or not. Either way, if there were any grounds for suspecting a dangerous dog was being kept in the house, they would have to go in. The sensible course would be to wait for a dog handler to arrive. If they were denied access to the property, it would be safer to force an entry accompanied by a specialist trained to restrain a dangerous animal. But the situation was complicated by the possibility that Geraldine might already be in the house, and perhaps at risk. By waiting, he could be exposing her to more danger. He remembered the woman who had been mauled to death by a vicious dog, and shivered at the thought that Geraldine might be in danger inside the house while he was procrastinating outside.

Casting a swift glance over his shoulder at the two constables, he knocked at the door. After what felt like a long time, the door was opened by a lanky man who stared at him, his gaunt face twisted in an expression that could have been insolent or wary. The man caught sight of the two uniformed officers, and his eyes narrowed.

'What do you want?'

As he spoke he shifted the door a fraction, as though he was about to shut it. Ian put his foot forward to prevent him from closing it any more, and the man scowled at him.

'Get off my property, arsehole.'

'No need to be abusive,' Ian replied softly. 'We just want to have a word with you.'

'What do you mean, a word? A word about what?'

'May we come in?'

'Why? What do you want with me?'

'You won't help yourself if you argue. Now, can we come in please?'

'Have you got a warrant?'

Holding the man's gaze, Ian frowned. 'Let me get this straight. You're saying you want us to go and get a warrant before we can come in? That leads me to think you're stalling us, which can only mean you want to prevent us from coming inside just now. So, why might that be? You're making me think you've got something to hide here.'

'Bullshit.'

'So you say, but you're behaving as though you've got something here you don't want us to see, which gives me grounds for suspecting you're harbouring something illegal. So, if you refuse to stand aside, you'll have to come along to the station. And either way, we'll be coming in to have a look around.' He glanced at the uniformed constables and then looked back at the tall man. 'Now are you going to step aside?'

The man hesitated, then nodded uneasily and moved back to allow Ian to push his way past.

'What's your name?'

The man scowled. 'Will. Now can we get this over with, because I want you out of my house. You've got no business here. How long is this going to take?'

Ian shrugged. 'As long as it takes.'

The first room Ian entered had barely enough space for a double bed and a wooden chest of drawers. A duvet lay untidily on the bed. As Ian manoeuvred his way around it, he caught a whiff of stale body odour. But he found no dog hairs, and no traces of dog food. Next he went into the kitchen where a tap was dripping with a faint plink plink sound, and there was a faint smell of cabbage and sausages. He stood for a moment staring around at a few unwashed dishes and pans on the draining board beside a food encrusted hob, and a cracked plastic dustpan without a brush on the grubby floor.

'Are you satisfied now?' the man snapped.

Ian didn't answer.

'If you tell me what you're looking for, I might be able to help you.'

Without answering, Ian checked through the fridge and cupboards. Among bottles of beer and a mouldy loaf of bread, tins of beans and boxes of cereal, there was no meat, and nothing resembling dog food. After looking in the narrow hall, he went into the back room. There were some chairs arranged around a scuffed coffee table, a large television on another table, heavy grey curtains and a worn rug lying on bare floorboards. There was no sign of a dog, no dog hairs visible, and no scratches on the furniture. Pulling back a grimy curtain, he looked out at a back yard.

'What do you keep out there?' Ian asked.

'What? Nothing. Nothing at all.'

His insistence aroused Ian's suspicions. 'I'd like to take a look outside.'

The man shrugged. 'Be my guest.' He led Ian to a back door at the end of the hallway. 'Go and see for yourself.'

At first there was nothing to see outside, apart from a row of overgrown shrubs along one side of a paved yard and tall weeds flourishing between dirty paving stones. Once again, there was no sign of a dog, but Ian noticed a shed hidden behind the bushes that had not been visible from the house. With a thrill of excitement and fear, he crossed the yard. All was silent but as he reached for the door he paused, aware that there might be a vicious dog inside. He knew he ought to wait for the arrival of the specialist dog handler who would have been trained to restrain a dangerous animal. Taking a deep breath, he yanked the door open. Inside he saw a wheelbarrow, a lawnmower, rakes, hoes and various other gardening tools. There was no dog, and no sign of Geraldine.

Walking back to the house, he noticed a foul smell that grew stronger as he approached the building. With a shudder he recognised the stench of rotting flesh.

'Is that it then?' Will asked when Ian went back inside. 'Are you done with your snooping around? Because if so, you can fuck off now and get out of my house.'

There was no reason for the three police officers to stay there any longer. But Geraldine hadn't been seen since she had spoken to the old man at number 7, after which she had allegedly gone to see Will. Ian couldn't just walk away. In desperation he tried Geraldine's number again, but there was still no answer. Striding around the house again, he noticed the foul odour was strongest in the back room.

'We need to take this room apart. Something stinks in here,' he said.

'What the fuck are you talking about?' Will demanded, his face turning red with anger.

'You heard what I said.'

'Fuck off out of my house!'

Ian nodded at the uniformed constables who moved into position, ready to restrain Will.

'We're going to take this room apart inch by inch,' Ian said slowly. 'We're going to rip up the floorboards, and strip the walls if we have to, but we're not leaving until we find out what you're hiding here. Now let's get on with it. Get *him* out of the way. I'm sending for a search team.'

'What the fuck?' Will burst out, starting forward. 'Don't you touch my property. You can just fuck off!'

One of the constables reached out and took him by the wrist. With a roar, Will tore himself free and made a dash for the door. At a nod from Ian the constable lunged forward, seized Will by his arms, and handcuffed him.

'Get off! What the fuck do you think you're doing? Leave it out!'

'Take him away,' Ian snapped. 'We need to get started.'

Taking out his phone he called Eileen. To his relief, he got through to her straight away, but she was sceptical.

'You're saying you think this man has an illegal dog hidden in his house?'

'Yes, ma'am.'

'And you want to search for it because you think it might be the dog that attacked Charlotte?'

'Yes, ma'am.'

'But you didn't actually see any evidence that there's a dog there now?'

'Ma'am, this is urgent. Geraldine was last seen going to this house, and now she's disappeared. There's every reason to suppose she might still be here. If she isn't, I don't know where she's gone because her car's parked in the street outside. And I think he's got a dangerous dog here that no one knows about. There's a chance it's the same dog that killed Charlotte.'

As soon as Eileen grasped the situation, she agreed to obtain a warrant urgently and have Will's premises searched, but it would still take time to organise. Hanging up, Ian despatched Will to the police station with the two officers in uniform who dragged him to the police car, resisting and yelling obscenities. His violent reaction made Ian more determined than ever to discover what he might be hiding. Closing the front door on the ruck outside, he returned to the back room and paced up and down across the dirty floor for a few seconds, thinking. It didn't take him long to decide what to do. While he was standing around waiting for permission, Geraldine could be in danger.

62

IF GERALDINE'S GRIP ON the torch hadn't tightened with an involuntary movement of her hand, she might have dropped it in shock when the dog leaped at her. The beam of light quivered in her grasp as she shone it around. The dog was on the floor of the cellar. Slavering and straining to get at her, she saw that it was tethered by a chain that rattled as it struggled. Whichever way the massive body twisted, it couldn't break free. She hardly dared move, but her legs were trembling too violently for her to stay on her feet. Slowly she sat down. As long as the dog remained tied up, she was safe. If the chain snapped, she would be torn to pieces by its powerful jaws.

Below her in the shadows the dog began to whine. As calmly as she could, Geraldine weighed up her options. She had to decide what to do if the chain broke. If she remained seated it might be more difficult for the dog to barge into her and knock her down the stairs. On the other hand, sitting down would make it more difficult for her to beat off the animal if it attacked her. Torch in one hand and cosh in the other, she stood up and leaned against the rail, watching and waiting, while below her the chain rattled and the dog snarled. Every time the animal made a lunge for the bottom of the stairs, the chain around its neck pulled against its throat until it choked, forcing it to fall back again. It tried several times before it subsided, growling angrily, and at last fell silent.

Sitting very still, Geraldine heard faint grunting and slurping. Very quietly, she shifted over to the edge of the stairs and looked down to see the dog lying on its stomach, gnawing at the bone.

She slid sideways until she was leaning against the wall. It felt as though she had been locked in there for days, although in fact it was only half an hour. She tried to block out the stench, telling herself her colleagues would soon come and rescue her, but it was impossible to ignore what was happening. Not only was the edge of the narrow step digging into her backside, but she couldn't forget about the dog. Even when the animal was quiet, she could smell it. Now that she no longer felt under immediate threat, she began to wonder how long the animal had been imprisoned there. Even if it had savaged a woman to death, the dog could hardly be held responsible for what had happened. Whoever had chained the dog down there had thrown a woman down the stairs, and she had every reason to suspect it was the same man who had tried to push her down the stairs too. He had murdered one woman that she knew about, possibly more, and had done his best to kill her too. And she was the only person who knew he was guilty.

Unable to remain patient any longer, she turned and hammered against the trap door with her cosh, yelling as loudly as she could. Below her in the darkness, the dog began to bark so ferociously she almost missed another sound that reached her very faintly. Something was scraping and banging above her head.

'I'm here!' she shouted as loudly as she could. 'I'm in here! The door's locked and I can't get out! Help!'

Below her the dog resumed its deep throated barking. If it succeeded in breaking free of its chain, she would be dog meat by the time she was found.

Above her she thought she heard someone calling.

'Hurry!' she shouted, as loudly as she could, 'I'm down here with a vicious dog and it might break free at any moment. Let me out! Help! Let me out!'

There was a rattling sound, and the trap door shuddered. A few seconds later it flew open and a familiar voice called out.

'Geraldine? Is that you?'

'Ian!' she shouted, fighting a sudden urge to cry. 'Ian! Thank God! Get me out of here!'

A large hand reached down to her as she stuffed her cosh and phone back in her bag. She grabbed Ian's wrist and scrambled up out of the dark cellar.

'Jesus!' he said, 'what a stink! What the hell have you been eating?'

Geraldine sank into a chair and leaned back, closing her eyes. She sat for a moment, shivering, and filled her lungs with relatively fresh air. When she opened her eyes, she gave Ian a weak smile. Catching sight of the open trap door, she waved one hand at it, and shuddered.

'Close the trap door for Christ's sake. Shut out that damn smell.'

'What's he got down there? Rotting bodies?' Ian asked as he shut the door with a clunk.

She shook her head, closing her eyes again. 'It's not dead, not yet.'

'What are you talking about? What's not dead?'

'The dog in the cellar.'

Ian's confusion seemed to clear. 'Sorry,' he blurted out. 'I was so preoccupied with worrying about you, I forgot about everything else...' he faltered, flustered. 'So there *is* a dog down there?'

She nodded. 'We can't just leave the poor beast where it is, but I'm not going anywhere near it. And nor are you,' she added.

'We don't need to. A dog handler's on his way. He should be here soon.'

'Thank goodness.'

'You don't seem very keen on dealing with this dog?'

'Dog? It's a vicious monster. Ian, it would have ripped me to pieces if it hadn't been chained up. It's not safe to go near it.'

'OK, don't worry. We'll leave it to the dangerous dog handler.'

'I think it's the one that killed Charlotte...' Geraldine flinched. 'But it's not the dog's fault, is it?' She started to her feet. 'Where's the man who lives here? Where's he gone? We need to find him –'

'Don't worry,' Ian interrupted her. 'He'll be at Fulford Road by now. Tell you what,' he added, taking a step back as Geraldine came towards him, 'why don't you pop home and I'll meet you at the police station in an hour and we can get going questioning him. In the meantime, I'll wait here for the dog handler, and you can go home and clean up.'

'Do I smell that bad?'

Ian didn't answer.

'I'll be off then,' she said.

Her legs and back ached as she left the house, and she felt momentarily almost too tired to walk away, but the fresh air of the street soon revitalised her. She drove home in a daze, and it wasn't until she undressed for the shower that she realised how badly bruised her legs were, black and yellow where she had hit them on the stairs. The shower was glorious, and by the time she had dressed in clean clothes, she felt a lot better. Eileen had told her to take the rest of the day off and then see how she felt, but Geraldine decided to go straight back to the police station. There was nothing to be gained from hanging around at home, and she didn't want to miss the conclusion of the investigation that had been occupying all her waking thoughts for more than five weeks.

And she wanted to face the man who had tried to kill her in the most horrible way imaginable, by having her physically ripped apart by a dumb animal.

63

'I MUST SAY I'M surprised to see you here.' The detective chief inspector's response was ambiguous, her reprimand tempered by an expression of approval, possibly even admiration. 'Are you certain you feel up to continuing? I would have expected you to take at least a few days off.'

Geraldine smiled. 'Not while we still have a killer to nail.'

Eileen stared at her until Geraldine grew uncomfortable under the intense gaze.

'Very well,' Eileen nodded at last, as though satisfied with her scrutiny. 'If you're sure you're ready to come back to work.'

Geraldine didn't point out that she had never left. She had only gone home to shower and change.

'I'm quite sure. Thank you for your concern, but I'm fine, really. Nothing happened, and I wasn't in any danger because that poor dog was chained up the whole time.'

'That "poor dog" savaged Charlotte Abbott to death,' Eileen said. 'I wouldn't waste any sympathy on it.'

'It was hardly the dog's fault,' Geraldine protested. 'It's the owner we need to see convicted for murder.'

To begin with, Eileen flatly refused to allow Geraldine to be present while Will was interviewed, but Geraldine finally managed to persuade her senior officer to relent.

'If you're sure you can face him and remain professional,' Eileen said.

'Nothing affects Geraldine's professionalism,' Ian said. 'She's not a human being, she's a detection machine.'

Geraldine wasn't sure whether to be pleased by Ian's response or not.

'The dog had to be put down,' Ian told her on the way to the interview room.

'I'd like to say I think that's a shame,' Geraldine replied. 'It doesn't seem fair to blame the dog. It couldn't help having been bred to be aggressive, and then it must have been half starved, and had probably gone insane after being cooped up in that stinking cellar for God knows how long. What kind of a man could do that to an intelligent, sentient living creature?'

'Let's go and find out,' Ian said grimly.

'I think we already know. He's the kind of man who'll treat a dog with careless cruelty, and kill his fellow human beings without any qualms. He's a psychopath. Callous. No conscience and no feelings. If there is such a thing as an evil man, then Will is one.'

Ian stopped and turned to face her. 'After all you've seen in your career so far, can you really still question whether people can be evil?'

Ian seemed so annoyed that Geraldine hesitated before answering. 'People commit evil acts, yes. But does that mean the person is actually evil? I mean, I don't buy into all that BS about people being damaged by their upbringing and all that. There are plenty of people who suffer the most terrible abuse yet grow up to be perfectly decent and kind. I'm not saying people shouldn't be held responsible for their actions. But an evil man? I don't know. Psychopaths lack the capacity to feel empathy, but to say he's evil makes him sound like a pantomime villain. And we both know that real people are far more complex than that.'

They had reached the door of the interview room. With a solemn nod, Ian opened the door and stood back to allow Geraldine to enter. Once they were seated, and the convoluted introduction had been given, Ian glared across the table at the suspect.

'Why did you do it, Will?' he asked. 'What do you stand to gain from all this?'

Will shrugged and looked askance at his brief as though he wasn't sure what to say.

'We're going to need an answer at some point,' Ian went on, 'so you might as well stop wasting our time. We know from the forensic evidence that your dog attacked and killed Charlotte Abbott. We also know from the bloodstains in your cellar that she was killed there, where you kept that poor animal locked up.'

'He had to be locked up,' Will said. 'He's a vicious brute. They never told me –'

'We'll come to where you got the dog from later. Right now we're concerned with the murder you committed.'

'I never murdered anyone!'

'You threw a woman into your cellar where your dog savaged her to death. Who do you suppose a jury are going to hold responsible? The dog?'

'It was an accident. I didn't know she was in the house. She should never have gone down there. I couldn't have stopped him, even if I had been there, which I wasn't.' Will protested. 'You can't pin that on me. You can't even prove I was in the house when it happened.'

'But you moved the body, the remains, afterwards, didn't you?'

'I didn't want them to take my poor dog away. He'd have been put down and it wasn't his fault some woman went down there, without my knowledge, while I was out.'

'What was she doing in your house?'

'How the hell should I know? She was an intruder. She got what she deserved. She had no business breaking into my house. I'm the victim here!'

'Why did you kill her, Will? What was her connection to you?'

The suspect shrugged.

'My client has already told you he didn't know the victim and has no idea what she was doing in his house while he was out. His only crime was to conceal the death and he's already explained he did that to protect his dog. A lot of people love their dogs, Inspector.' He smiled at Will. 'A jury will sympathise with that.' He turned back to Ian. 'You must be aware that you have no grounds for accusing my client of murder. This is a deliberate attempt at intimidation.'

'Oh, bollocks,' Ian muttered under his breath. Aloud he said, 'Your client is the one who intimidates other people. In fact, you have a history of violent bullying, don't you, Will?'

'What the fuck are you talking about?'

'Angie told us about how you beat her, regularly,' Ian fibbed. 'And how you used your dog to threaten people.'

'She's lying!' Will's eyes blazed with sudden fury. 'She's always lying.'

The lawyer's tone was even, but he looked irritated. 'Do you have any evidence to support these allegations, Inspector? Or are you just throwing out wild accusations in an attempt to discredit my client's character?'

'You won't get far with that,' Will said.

'My client took in a stray dog and looked after it,' the lawyer said. 'He also cared for a recovering drug addict, whose accusations against him can't be taken seriously as she's not a reliable witness. In addition, he helps out his neighbours doing odd jobs for them without expecting anything in return. He is a decent and upright citizen and he refutes these slurs on his character.'

'I've got people can tell you I help them out with odd jobs, out of the goodness of my heart,' Will added.

'What sort of odd jobs?' Geraldine asked. 'You need to be more specific. What exactly do you do and who are you working for?'

She threw a quick glance at Ian and cleared her throat, hoping he would follow her lead.

'I don't work for anyone. I just help out. That's the kind of bloke I am. Soft hearted. I like to help. I don't suppose that's something you people can understand.'

'So what do you do, when you're being helpful? What sort of jobs?'

'All sorts. Whatever needs doing.'

'Would those jobs include gardening?' Geraldine asked.

'What? No, not really,' Will replied. 'I'm not much of a one for gardening.'

'Really? I noticed a lawn mower in your hall.'

'So what?'

'It's not an offence to own a lawn mower,' the solicitor said.

'What else do you do, if you're not gardening?'

'You keep gardening tools in your shed,' Ian interrupted, finally realising where her questions had been heading.

Although he sounded bored, Geraldine understood him well enough to know that was far from the case. They had worked together so many times, she knew he had picked up on the reason for her interest.

'I saw hoes and rakes,' Ian went on thoughtfully, 'and a lawnmower and a pretty heavy-duty leaf blower, and now I come to think of it you had a hedge trimmer there as well, even though your yard is fenced in. I remember wondering what you used all those tools for.'

Will shrugged. He looked faintly uneasy but had the sense to remain silent while he waited to see where this was going.

'As I recall, the tools had been used recently. There was fresh grass on the lawnmower blades. Of course we can easily get that checked,' Ian went on.

Geraldine and Ian exchanged a quick glance, and Will frowned.

'Since when was gardening a crime?' the lawyer enquired blandly, but Geraldine detected a flicker of uncertainty in his expression.

'Yeah, so I like to garden sometimes,' Will admitted. 'So

what? I do a bit of gardening at home. I like to look after my place. I'm a –'

'Your garden's quite small, I believe,' Geraldine said, turning to Ian.

'More of a yard than a garden,' Ian agreed. 'In fact, apart from a bank of overgrown bushes along one fence, it's all paved over. No grass to mow there.'

Will squirmed uncomfortably in his seat.

'So you must have done some gardening for other people?' Geraldine suggested.

When Will didn't answer, she gestured to Ian to turn off the tape. 'It could go against us if he helped out his neighbours,' she said softly. 'Especially if he helped old people.' She turned back to Will. 'The tape's been turned off so you can tell us, off the record. Was it a community service order, or were you doing it for money?'

'I wasn't doing community service and I wasn't paid anything,' Will replied quickly. 'I just helped out. I like helping people. I do it out of the goodness of my heart. That's who I am,' he went on, becoming more expansive as he spoke. 'I'm a dog lover, and I like helping people. No jury's going to condemn me for that.'

He grinned uncertainly at his lawyer, as though to say he had the situation under control. The lawyer didn't appear to share his client's view but watched Geraldine with a wary expression.

She nodded at Ian to turn the tape on again. 'You just told us you do casual gardening jobs to help out your neighbours?'

'That's right,' Will replied, glancing nervously at the tape which was running again. 'And I'm a dog lover and all. I found my poor mutt abandoned and wandering the streets and I took him in and looked after him. That's the kind of person I am. You don't want to believe what Angie says. She's a sad case.' He shook his head, sighing.

'I know how helpful you are,' Geraldine said. 'In fact, I

witnessed it myself. You helped Mark Abbot with his garden, didn't you? You're the gardener who took the body down when his wife found him hanging there. That's why we didn't find anyone else's fingerprints or DNA at the scene. Because there *was* no one else there. It was you all along. You were the one who hung Mark, and then you waited in the garden until Charlotte called for help, at which point you rushed in, which explained why your fingerprints and DNA were all over the body and the banister. Ingenious! We never questioned why your fingerprints and DNA were found at the scene, because you were there pretending to try and save the man you had just murdered. Perhaps you wanted to make sure he was really dead.'

Will had gone pale. 'I don't know what you're talking about. Why would I kill anyone?'

'You'll have to tell us that yourself. Why did you kill him? And Amanda? Did you look after her garden too?'

'I never went to her house, and you can't prove I ever did. I don't even know her.'

The lawyer stirred. 'You brought my client here on suspicion of owning a dangerous dog which is alleged to have attacked and killed Charlotte Abbott. He has not been accused of murdering Mark and Amanda Abbott.'

Ian looked grim. 'He has now.' Ignoring Will's protestations, he charged him formally.

'Why?' Will blurted out. 'Why would I want to kill them? Any of them? What possible reason could I have?'

His voice rose in an emotional crescendo, but the question was rational enough.

'We need to take a break,' the lawyer cut in, raising his pale hand to silence Will. 'I'd like to talk to my client.'

64

IAN AND GERALDINE WENT to see Eileen together to discuss the turn the interview had taken.

'We don't know if Will actually knew Amanda,' Geraldine said, 'but they were both at Mark's funeral.'

'Did they speak to each other?'

'Not that I saw. But it doesn't matter whether Amanda knew him or not, because she could have left her house with a stranger.'

'So you're saying you now think Will, and not Eddy, is a serial killer?' Eileen asked.

Geraldine didn't point out that she had never believed Eddy was guilty of murdering his parents, but no one had listened to her opinion. As an established inspector, her views had been given serious credence. Since her demotion she had grown accustomed to being doubted. She had almost come to expect it. While she was determined to rebuild her reputation, in the meantime she accepted that she had to tolerate her senior officer's scepticism of her judgement. But she didn't like it.

'Everything so far seems to point to Will having killed them all,' she replied doggedly. 'Will was there when Mark was hung, traces of his dog's faeces were found on Amanda's clothes, and we know it was Will's dog that killed Charlotte.'

Eileen nodded. 'That can't all be coincidence. So you're saying we have a new suspect in the frame for all three victims?'

Geraldine tried to conceal her impatience but it seemed to her that the detective chief inspector was being unnecessarily obtuse. 'Yes, obviously.'

'But the question remains, what motive could he have had for killing even one of them? He didn't stand to gain anything by their deaths, did he?'

'That's the problem,' Ian replied.

Eileen shook her head. 'No, the only person who might have wanted to get both Mark and Charlotte out of the way was Eddy. He stood to gain a tidy estate when they were both dead. He must have killed Amanda because she knew too much. But the fact remains, we know Eddy had a strong financial motive for killing his father and his stepmother, but Will had no such reason. Why would he have wanted them dead? It doesn't make sense. Just because he could have killed them doesn't mean he did.'

'Eddy and Will could have been working together,' Geraldine suggested. 'Maybe they arranged for Will to kill Eddy's father and stepmother and share the proceeds between them. Or perhaps the killer wanted Eddy out of the way as well, and set things up to make sure he was the obvious suspect for the murders.' Ignoring Eileen's gathering frown, Geraldine pressed on. 'With Mark and Charlotte both dead, and Eddy locked up for murder, who would benefit from the estate?'

'His wife.'

There was silence for a moment while Eileen and Ian considered Geraldine's theory.

'So, you're suggesting Will was in collusion with Luciana to plan the deaths of her father-in-law and mother-in-law together, knowing Eddy would go to prison for murder, leaving her with all the money?' Eileen asked. 'And so you're saying Will killed them all, but Luciana instigated the murders?'

Ian nodded. 'It's possible Luciana could have talked him into it, for money or love.'

'Or both,' Geraldine added.

Eileen looked concerned. 'Geraldine,' she said gently, 'you seem convinced that Will's guilty. Are you sure you're not allowing yourself to be swayed by an emotional response to your experience at his house? It would be perfectly understandable. You could easily have been killed when Will threw you into his cellar. In fact, if it hadn't been for Ian, you might have died down there.' She smiled at Ian who looked at the floor and shrugged.

Geraldine did her best to conceal her anger at this accusation of subjectivity. She had always prided herself on her integrity. In fact, until recently she would have been confident her own feelings would never influence her judgement. But after her humiliating demotion, she had to accept that she hadn't always acted professionally. She was further irritated when Ian appeared to agree with Eileen.

'Luciana couldn't have known that we'd arrest Eddy,' he said. 'It wouldn't be a very sensible plan, when you think about it.'

'Is premeditated murder ever sensible? But if Luciana knew about her husband's gambling, she'd realise we were bound to discover it too, and then we'd be fairly certain to suspect him. A man desperate for money has to be a suspect, where he stands to benefit so considerably.'

'Would she be sufficiently confident of that to risk killing her in-laws?'

Once again, Geraldine hid her impatience as well as she could. 'She wasn't really taking a risk, not if she had Will carrying out the murders for her. If it all went wrong, she'd be ready to distance herself from it. And in any case, if Will was prepared to kill her in-laws, as a last resort they could have arranged to kill Eddy as well, perhaps staging another suicide.'

'That makes sense,' Eileen agreed slowly.

'It's the only theory that *does* make sense.' Geraldine said.

'So how do we test this theory?' Eileen asked.

At least the detective chief inspector was prepared to accept as possible something that seemed obvious to Geraldine. But as she walked back to her own desk, Eileen's comment bothered her. Thinking back over her career, she could only think of one situation where she had acted unprofessionally.

Admittedly it had been a serious misdemeanour. She had been demoted and relocated as a consequence of acting illegally to protect her drug addict twin. Eileen knew about it. But it hardly seemed fair of her to judge Geraldine's professional integrity on the basis of one, albeit serious, offence. The trouble was, when Geraldine put herself in Eileen's place, she came to the same harsh conclusions as Eileen had reached. It was difficult to acknowledge that she was no longer an officer whose objectivity could be relied on.

65

THE INTERVIEW RESUMED. WITHOUT turning her head to meet Ian's eye, Geraldine introduced her idea. They both watched Will closely, hoping for a reaction, but he didn't seem concerned when she told him that Luciana had been to the police station. He appeared blasé, but Geraldine thought she detected a glint of interest in his eyes.

'Luciana Abbott,' she repeated slowly. 'Eddy Abbott's wife.'

'I don't know anyone called Luciana,' he replied, a trifle too quickly.

Although he returned her gaze levelly, she noticed him shift uneasily in his seat. She couldn't be sure, but she thought he was aware that she had noticed he was jumpy because he looked down.

'Well, that's strange,' Ian said. 'Because she certainly seemed to know all about you.'

When Will looked up his eyes were glowing more brightly and his face looked flushed, as though he was suffering from a sudden fever.

'What was that name again?'

'Luciana Abbott.'

He shook his head. 'Perhaps she's one of the women I've done odd jobs for,' he suggested. 'Yes, that must be it. She must be one of the neighbours I've helped out.' He gave a sheepish smile that Geraldine guessed was intended to charm her. 'I can't remember all of their names. I help a lot of people. Like I said, that's the kind of person I am.'

'You can't come across many women called Luciana,' Geraldine said.

All this while, his lawyer had been sitting very still, listening. Now he spoke.

'What's the significance of this woman, Luciana?'

'I think Will knows perfectly well what this means,' Geraldine replied.

'My client has already told you he knows no one by that name.'

'He's lying.'

'Can you substantiate that accusation? Or even explain to me why that might be true?' the lawyer replied.

Will shook his head, muttering that he had no idea what the police were talking about.

'Luciana was the one who started all this, wasn't she, Will?' Geraldine asked. 'She put you up to it, didn't she?'

The lawyer leaned back in his chair and nearly closed his eyes. 'Put him up to what, exactly?'

Ignoring the interruption, Geraldine pressed on. 'She told us it was all your idea, but that seems unlikely. The Abbotts weren't your family, were they? You didn't stand to gain anything from their deaths, did you?'

'What are you talking about?' Will spluttered. 'I've no idea what you're on about. I don't know anyone called Abbott.'

Finally rattled, Will turned to his lawyer and hissed, 'Get me out of here!' He was sweating with indignation, or perhaps fear.

Geraldine smiled to herself. Now they had riled Will, he might start making mistakes. With any luck he would condemn himself and do their job for them. The lawyer shifted in his seat. The same thought must have occurred to him.

'Just keep calm,' he muttered to Will. 'Leave this to me. That's what I'm here for, to defend you.'

'But they're saying I've committed a murder. Can't you stop them?'

'Three murders,' Geraldine muttered.

'I'm not sure why you're getting so agitated,' Ian said. 'If you're innocent, as you claim, then you should have nothing to worry about.'

Will scowled. 'You think it's nice sitting here being accused of all sorts of things I never did? You're trying to stitch me up.' He glared at his lawyer. 'They're trying to frame me. It's all lies what they're saying about me.'

'My client is feeling harassed,' the lawyer said. 'We need to take a break.'

'Another one?' Ian retorted, before he announced he was stopping the tape.

During the break, Geraldine and Ian went to the canteen for a coffee. Seated at a corner table, they spoke in undertones. While they were in agreement that it was time to increase the pressure on Will, they were not quite certain of the best way to proceed. Within the parameters of allowable conduct, Eileen had given them a free hand to do whatever proved necessary to establish the truth. Geraldine had already suggested they hint to Will that Luciana had accused him of carrying out the murders.

'If he's innocent, he's hardly going to say he committed three murders, is he? It's not as if he's easily cowed. We're only going to plant the suggestion that Luciana has implicated him. We're not going to actually come out and say it. He doesn't have to admit anything. But if he *is* to blame for three murders – which he must be, considering the part his dog played in at least one of them, not to mention the fact that it could have killed me – if he *is* to blame, it's our responsibility to see him brought to justice, and make sure he can't kill anyone else.'

Luciana had been questioned, but so far she had given nothing away. She had denied knowing anyone called Will. But he hadn't been told that. If Geraldine hadn't been convinced Will was guilty, she probably wouldn't have pushed to go ahead with a plan that implied something they knew wasn't true. As it was, she had succeeded in overcoming Ian's objections by pointing out that Will didn't have to cave in. Only now, sitting in the canteen with a mug of tea and a bun, was she able to take a step back and acknowledge that her determination to see Will convicted possibly went beyond the realms of appropriate response. She was afraid she had allowed her reaction to be coloured by resentment at the way she herself had been thrown in the cellar to die.

When she voiced her reservations, Ian was irritated. 'It was your idea in the first place to tell him Luciana informed on him. Now you're saying you don't think we should.'

'I'm just wondering if what we're doing is – well, ethical?'

'Like you said, we're only raising a possibility. We can't put words in his mouth.'

Ian sounded almost as though he regretted the restrictions on police activity, put in place in the nineteen eighties to protect the public from maverick police officers.

'Come on then, let's do this,' he said at last.

Geraldine followed him along the corridor in silence. It seemed she was committed to going ahead now. But she felt a frisson of unease as she followed Ian back into the interview room.

'We've spoken to Luciana.'

'I told you, I don't know anyone called Luciana.'

'Stop playing games,' Ian snapped. 'We've spoken to Luciana and she's told us everything.'

'Everything?' the lawyer repeated, with a sceptical grunt.

'She's told us what you did.'

The lawyer leaned over to Will and hissed at him, loudly enough for everyone in the room to hear. 'They're just fishing. If they had anything to use against you, they'd be more specific. They don't know anything. Leave this to me.' He turned back to Ian. 'What exactly has she told you?'

Ian shook his head, smiling. 'You know very well we're

not obliged to tell you what she said.' He looked at Will. 'But you know what happened, don't you? And now we know too, because we've spoken to Luciana.'

Will stared at Ian. 'I don't believe you,' he said flatly.

'You don't believe she spoke to us about you? Really?' Ian laughed. 'Why do you think she came to see us then?'

'She'd never talk to filth like you,' Will blurted out angrily. 'She's got too much sense.'

'I thought you didn't know who she was,' Geraldine said softly. 'So I wonder how you would be in a position to make that judgement.'

'Exposing the first lie is just the start,' Ian said, speaking to the lawyer. 'This is where his whole story will start to unravel.' He turned back to Will. 'So, we've established that you know Luciana. You know her well enough to state with confidence how she might behave. We also know she stood to gain a fortune from killing off her husband's family and framing him for the murders.'

'And we know that you are in possession of a dangerous dog that killed Luciana's mother-in-law,' Geraldine added.

'A dog you used in an attempt to kill my colleague here.'

Although he said nothing, the lawyer was clearly startled by this revelation. 'I need a moment with my client,' he said.

'You've had enough moments,' Ian replied. 'I take it that during one of your moments so far your client described how he pushed my colleague into a cellar with a dangerous dog, the very same animal that savagely killed Charlotte Abbott?'

'This is harassment. He's entitled to take advice,' the lawyer stammered, wide-eyed with shock.

Will interrupted him. 'It's all lies. A pack of lies.'

'Do you deny owning a dangerous dog?'

'Yes, I do.'

'We found him chained up in your cellar.'

'Poor Buster wasn't dangerous. He wouldn't hurt a fly. You could leave him to watch over a newborn baby and it would be perfectly safe. He was the gentlest dog I ever saw. It's a lie to say he was dangerous.'

'When I saw him – after you locked me in your cellar with him – he was ferocious. The dog handler assessed him as a danger to the public. He mauled Charlotte to death and, if his chain had broken, he would have killed me too.'

There was something truly bizarre about sitting in an interview room calmly talking about how she had almost been savaged to death by a dangerous dog.

'What a load of nonsense! Poor Buster wouldn't have hurt you. He barks a bit, but he never bites.'

'I found my colleague locked in the cellar,' Ian said sternly.

'She went in there to look at Buster,' Will replied, appearing to dismiss the implied accusation. 'When you lot came barging in, the door must have slammed shut on her. How could I have known she was trapped in there, after you dragged me out of my own home and carted me off here? If she'd starved to death in the cellar, that would have been *your* fault.'

'The carpet had been replaced over the trap door,' Ian pointed out.

'It must have fallen back,' Will replied calmly.

'What you're saying doesn't tie in with what we've heard from Luciana,' Geraldine said.

She was trying to hide her disappointment at Will's refusal to confess. He was proving difficult to perturb.

'Perhaps your witness is lying,' the lawyer said. 'You have no evidence my client was involved in any criminal activity.'

'Haven't you been listening to a single word we've been saying?' Geraldine burst out. 'Your client locked me in a cellar with a dangerous dog and left me there to die!'

'An accusation my client has refuted. Now charge him or let him go.'

66

IT HAD PROVED IMPOSSIBLE to disturb Will's presence of mind. Without a confession, and in the absence of further evidence of his guilt, the most they could charge him with was assaulting a police officer and owning an illegally bred dangerous dog. It was beginning to look as though he could escape a conviction for murder, and their case might remain unsolved. It was maddening. They were convinced they had found the murderer they were after, yet they were powerless to prove it.

'He locked me in the cellar,' Geraldine protested for the twentieth time.

'He insists we dragged him away before he had a chance to realise what had happened to you,' Ian said. 'And he claims it was a terrible accident, his dog attacking Charlotte. The infuriating thing is, his story's just feasible. Granted, we don't believe him, and the quantity of Charlotte's blood in the cellar suggests she was killed there, but we're not his judge and jury, more's the pity. A clever barrister could cast doubt on what happened.'

She sighed. 'We have to find another way.'

It seemed their only hope was for Luciana to tell them what they wanted to know. They agreed their best chance of getting to the truth was if they could frighten her. Will had refused to be intimidated into making a confession. Perhaps she would be easier to break. It was nearly dark by the time they drew up outside her house. She didn't answer the door straight away and when she did open it, she had put the chain on.

'What do you want?'

'We'd like to talk to you.'

'It's late. I was going to bed.'

'This can't wait,' Ian replied.

Muttering, she opened the door and let them in. 'What do you want? You know I'm here all on my own now, while Eddy's away. When are you going to let him go?'

'That depends on a number of things,' Geraldine lied. 'We're not here to talk to you about your husband. We want to talk about Will.'

'Who? I already told your people I don't know anyone called Will.'

'That's not what he says.'

'Who?' she asked quickly. 'What are you talking about?'

'Will seems to think he knows you,' Geraldine said. 'He seems to think he knows you very well.'

'It must be a mistake.'

'Do you think he knows another woman called Luciana? Now that would be a coincidence. It's not as if Luciana's a common name, is it?'

Luciana's wary expression hardened. 'What do you want?'

'The truth.'

'I don't know what you mean. What do you want to know?'

'Can we come in so we can talk?'

With a show of reluctance, Luciana led them into the living room.

'Tell us about Will,' Ian said, as they all sat down.

'Look, I've already told you I don't know anyone called Will –'

'Yet we've met someone called Will who says he knows you. So, one of you is lying.'

Luciana hesitated, and Geraldine could see she was wavering.

'Oh Will,' she said at last. 'Yes, of course. I know who you mean. But I hardly know him –'

'Well, he seems to know you,' Ian told her. 'He told us he's been doing a few jobs for you.'

Luciana gave a noncommittal grunt and looked away.

'You do know he's been arrested?'

Luciana frowned. 'Why would I know anything about that? I hardly know the guy.'

'Which means we'll be releasing your husband.'

'My husband?' she frowned. 'What's this got to do with him? I don't understand. What do you mean?'

'It seems we suspected the wrong man. It was Will who committed the murders in your family, not Eddy. But of course you knew that, didn't you?' Geraldine said.

'What do you mean?'

There was no ignoring her anxiety. All the colour seemed to have drained from her face, and her lips twitched uncontrollably.

'Will has told us all about it.'

'About what? What are you talking about?'

Geraldine spoke very gently. 'It's over, Luciana. You can stop pretending you don't know Will. We know what you did. Will's told us everything.'

Luciana shook her head. 'I really don't know what you're talking about.'

'We know Will killed three members of your husband's family. And since you're the only person who stands to gain from the deaths and Eddy's arrest, it wasn't difficult to work out who put him up to it, and why. If he'd tried to deny it, we might have looked for more evidence, but he's made a full confession. He's told us it was all your idea.'

'That's a lie!' Luciana cried out. 'None of this was my idea. Will came up with the whole plan, from beginning to end. I thought he was just messing about, trying to make me feel better, because I was upset when Mark told Eddy he'd changed his will. There was no argument or anything, Mark just said it would all come to Eddy in the end anyway, but he was changing his will to make Charlotte feel secure. So I was complaining about it to Will and he came up with this crazy plan. He wanted me to tell him when and where it would be safe to find them alone. But it was just talk. I had nothing to do with what happened. Nothing! It was Will's idea all along. And

I never for one moment thought he was serious.'

'We'd like you to accompany us to the police station,' Ian said, moving to block the door so Luciana couldn't try to leave the room.

Her eyes widened in panic. 'What? Why? I've told you it was all his idea. We were just talking. He came up with the idea that if anything was to happen to Mark and then Charlotte, Eddy would inherit everything and then if Eddy had an accident, it would all be mine. Will planned everything. He said I could help him by telling him when Mark was there on his own, and letting him into the house, because Eddy had a key and it was easy for me to get hold of it and make a copy without anyone knowing. He said he knew how to make it look as though Mark had killed himself, but I told him there was no point because there was a suicide clause in Mark's will.'

'Which you knew all about, didn't you? Including when it ran out,' Geraldine said quietly.

Luciana stared at her, realising she had admitted to knowing too much. 'The suicide clause wasn't a secret. Mark told Eddy about it when he told him he had changed his will. He read it out to Eddy, and Eddy told me. But I never said anything to Will about the details of Mark's will. We weren't that serious about it; at least, I wasn't. We were just talking. It was all talk. That's all it was. We were only messing about. I never thought he'd go ahead with it.'

'You gave Will a key so he could get into the house and take Mark by surprise and hang him from the banister.'

'No, no, I didn't do anything. It was just talk.'

'You waited, and once the suicide clause ran out you told him when it was safe to go ahead, didn't you?'

Still insisting she had done nothing to help Will, Luciana broke down in tears. 'It was Will's idea. It was all Will's idea,' she insisted.

'That's for a jury to decide,' Geraldine replied as she handcuffed Luciana and led her to the car.

67

EDDY WAS LYING ON his bunk when Geraldine entered. He turned his head to look at her without stirring from his prone position.

'What now?' he asked. 'Can't you leave me in peace even in here? I'm not talking to you without my lawyer. Not that he's much use.' He turned his head towards the wall. 'You can go now. I'm not going to talk to you.'

'I came to tell you that we don't want to talk to you any more.' He turned back to look at her. 'You won't be going home just yet, not until you've been tried as an accessory in a robbery. You've already confessed to your part in that, of course, so the courts will probably be lenient, especially if you change your mind about revealing the identities of your accomplices. I'd advise you to tell us everything you can, but your lawyer's the one to advise you what's best for you to do. I came here to tell you that you're no longer being charged with the murders of your parents and your aunt.'

Eddy sat up, rubbed his eyes with his knuckles and stared at her in obvious disbelief.

'What's going on? What trick are you trying to pull? I told you, I'm not talking to you without my lawyer present.'

'I thought you might be a little more pleased than that,' she replied, smiling. 'It's not every day you're told the police believe you're innocent of murder.'

His eyes narrowed in suspicion. 'How come you've changed your minds for no reason?'

'Who said it was for no reason?'

'What do you mean?'

'You're free to go because we now know it wasn't you who killed your parents or your aunt. You didn't kill anyone, Eddy.'

'I know that, but I don't understand what made you change your mind.'

'We know it wasn't you, because we know who it was. We've caught the real culprits.'

Eddy nodded but he still looked puzzled. 'Culprits?'

'The people who did it.'

'Yes, I know what the word means. So, who was it?'

'Will Donovan killed them all, along with his dog.'

'Who the hell's Will Donovan? And why did he kill his dog?'

'No, no, he didn't kill his dog. His dog was part of – part of his plans.'

'Who is he? What are you talking about?'

'Will Donovan was your father's gardener.'

'Oh, that Will.'

'Yes, that Will.'

Eddy sat in silence for a moment, shaking his head. 'I don't get it,' he said at last. 'Why are you telling me all this?'

'I'm telling you because it's the truth, Eddy.'

He gazed at her and nodded, seemingly convinced. 'But why would he do it? Why kill them? It doesn't make any sense. What had they done to him?'

Geraldine sighed. 'He wasn't acting alone.'

'Who else was in on it?'

'Who stood to gain with your parents both dead and you framed for murder?'

He shook his head. 'How the hell should I know?'

Geraldine wasn't sure if he was being deliberately obtuse.

'Your wife,' she said softly.

'My wife? What's any of this got to do with her?'

'The two of them were in it together. Will and your wife. They planned the murders together.'

'My wife? Luciana?' Eddy leapt to his feet, staring wildly

at her. 'What the hell are you talking about? Don't you dare accuse her –'

'I'm afraid your wife put Will up to it. She was planning to get her hands on your family's money.'

'That's ridiculous. I know my wife. Luciana didn't have anything to do with any of this.'

Geraldine sighed. 'I'm afraid she did.'

'You have no proof –'

'She framed you, Eddy. She made sure she had an alibi for the night your mother was murdered, and then agreed to give you an alibi, knowing we'd expose her lie and leave you unprotected, with herself in the clear. It would have worked, if we hadn't already realised she was working with an accomplice.'

'I don't believe it,' he insisted. 'Luciana wouldn't hurt anyone. She's not like that.'

'She didn't actually kill anyone herself, but she organised the whole affair and promised Will a generous fee for carrying out her wishes.'

'That's a lie. You mustn't believe him. He's a conman. He's lying –'

'She's confessed, Eddy.'

'Let me speak to her. Please,' he begged. 'Let me see my wife.'

'She'll only tell you what she told us.'

'Please, she's my wife. Let me see her.' He was crying now, tears sliding down his cheeks, his voice almost incoherent with sobs. 'I need to see her.'

'You'll be able to visit her.'

Struggling to control his crying, he stammered, 'Tell her. Tell her I know she didn't do it. She couldn't have. Tell her I love her.'

Geraldine stared in surprise. 'Do you really think she'll care how you feel about her, after all she's done?'

'I know she will. She loves me, and she needs to know I still love her.'

'How can you say that, knowing she framed you for murder just so she could get her hands on your parents' money?'

'I don't believe you.'

'She told us herself.'

He shook his head. 'It makes no difference. You don't stop loving someone just because they do something wrong.'

'You would have gone to prison for life, Eddy. She set you up to save herself.'

'I can't help how I feel,' he replied with a helpless shrug. 'I love her. Please, let me see her.'

It was Geraldine's turn to shrug helplessly. 'I'm sorry, there's nothing I can do. Maybe they'll let you attend her trial. You might even be able to sit in the public gallery, depending on how long you get for the robbery. Are you sure you want to protect your accomplices' identities, Eddy?'

'I don't know their names,' he replied, his sobs subsiding. 'All I know is that one of them called himself Abe. That's all I know. I want to see my wife,' he repeated, as Geraldine turned to leave. 'I want to see my wife. Tell her I still love her. Tell her I'll wait for her, however long it takes.'

Geraldine turned back in the cell doorway. 'You're going to have a long wait,' she said. 'But once you've had time to think about what she did, I'm sure you'll feel differently about her. She wasn't the woman you thought you knew, Eddy.'

68

GERALDINE SMILED AT IAN. They had been too busy lately for her to enquire about his meeting with his estranged wife, or for him to ask after her sisters. Now they were at the pub, with time to take an evening off and chat, only they were surrounded by their colleagues, all celebrating the successful conclusion to their investigation. They were standing with Naomi and Ariadne and not far away Eileen was talking to a group of constables, young and eager enough to listen to their senior investigating officer telling them something they already knew. Eileen cracked a joke and her audience laughed loudly.

'So there were two of them all along,' they heard her say.

'Three if we count the dog,' Ian said, too quietly for anyone beyond their immediate circle to hear.

Naomi heaved a sigh. 'Poor animal. I think it's a shame it had to be put down.'

'It had mauled a woman to death,' Ariadne said. 'And it nearly killed Geraldine!'

'It wasn't the dog's fault,' Naomi replied. 'It's always a person who's to blame, not a poor dumb animal.'

Geraldine nodded. 'Naomi's right.'

'So who *was* responsible?' Ariadne asked. 'Will or Luciana?'

'It was both of them,' Naomi replied.

'But someone must have had the idea first,' Geraldine added. 'I wonder which of them was the first to think of it. They're both so busy blaming each other, I don't think we'll ever know who started it.'

'I wonder who really did think up the idea first,' Naomi said.

'It must have been Luciana. She was the one who stood to gain from the deaths,' Ariadne replied.

'But he's the psychopath,' Naomi said. 'Who else would have come up with the idea of killing them? I mean, anyone might speculate about ways to get their hands on their inheritance, but most people would never dream of committing murder, let alone actually do it.'

After a few rounds Geraldine's colleagues began to drift away, and she announced she was leaving as well.

'I'll walk you to your car,' Ian said.

It was a mild evening and they sauntered back towards the police station in silence for a few moments.

'Did you get to see Bev?' Geraldine asked as they approached the entrance to the car park.

'Yes.'

His response was so curt she regretted having asked the question.

'Sorry, I didn't mean to be intrusive. I'm just concerned about you. I mean, not in the sense of being worried about you. I know you're perfectly capable of running your own life. But I care about you, that's all. As a friend, I mean.'

Too late she stopped talking, aware that her words sounded crass. Somehow Ian had the ability to make her feel like an awkward teenager whenever they were alone together.

'She's fallen out with her new boyfriend,' he said.

'Is that a bad thing?'

'Geraldine, she's having his baby!'

He paused. Glancing sideways, she could see his expression tauten. After a few seconds he spoke again, his teeth clenched.

'She's a difficult woman. I'm not surprised he sent her packing. But did she really think I'd take her back? Why would I?' He gave an angry snort. 'She as good as accused me of failing in my responsibilities as a husband, abandoning her now she's pregnant. I really think she just assumed I'd be willing to go back to how we were before she left. But it's not my child she's carrying.'

He sounded so angry, Geraldine had to restrain herself from reaching out and putting her hand on his arm, the urge to comfort him was so strong. Instead, she resorted to the clumsy contrivance of words.

'Ian, you're under absolutely no obligation to take her back, or to support her. *She* left *you*, remember? Besides which, her baby has a father. It's *his* responsibility, not yours. Unless you want her back. Along with another man's baby,' she added, with a slight tremor in her voice.

'I know her baby's no more my responsibility than she is.' He frowned. 'A better man than me would take her back, and bring her child up as his own. But I can't. I just can't.'

'That's perfectly reasonable. And I don't believe most men would want her back after she cheated on you like that. I know I wouldn't if I was a man.'

Ian laughed. 'If you were a man. What do you know about it?' He shook his head. 'I think the hardest part of it is that after so many years, I have to acknowledge that I can never have really loved her at all. How could I have loved her, when I'm prepared to give up on her like this?'

'She was the one who gave up on your relationship, not you.'

He nodded. 'Yes, she did. She lied and cheated, and… Well, after her betrayal, we can never go back to how we were. But the curious thing is, when I saw her, I felt nothing.' He stopped and turned to stare at her, his eyes troubled. 'Is it possible to stop loving someone?'

Remembering Eddy's hysterical devotion to his wife, Geraldine shrugged. 'I don't know.'

'We were very young when we met,' he went on, talking more to himself than to her. 'Perhaps what I felt was never really love at all, but just an immature infatuation that carried on far longer than it should have done after we left school.' He took a deep breath and shook his head. 'Anyway, enough about me. What about you? How's your sister and her new baby? And your crazy twin?'

'She's not crazy. Actually she's doing pretty well. I'm hoping she's going to be OK. She's talking about getting a dog. That shows she's ready to take on some responsibility, doesn't it?'

'I hope it's not a Pitweiler.'

She turned to him, ready with a sharp retort, but Ian was smiling at her and she couldn't help smiling back.